THE CITY in the LAKE

THE CITY in the LAKE

RACHEL NEUMEIER

Alfred A. Knopf
NEW YORK

Visit us on the Web! www.randomhouse.com/teens

Educators and librarians, for a variety of teaching tools, visit us at www.randomhouse.com/teachers

Library of Congress Cataloging-in-Publication Data
Neumeier, Rachel.
The city in the lake / by Rachel Neumeier. — 1st ed.
p. cm.
Summary: A teenage girl who is learning to be a mage must save her mysterious, magical homeland, The Kingdom, from a powerful force that is trying to control it.
ISBN 978-0-375-84704-2 (trade) — ISBN 978-0-375-94704-9 (lib. bdg.)
[1. Magic—Fiction. 2. Fantasy.] I. Title.
PZ7.N4448Ci 2008
[Fic]—dc22
2008008941

The text of this book is set in 10.5-point Village.

Printed in the United States of America
July 2008
10 9 8 7 6 5 4 3 2 1

First Edition

To my twin brother and first reader, Craig—
I knew I'd learned how
when you said it was good.

Chapter 1

The City is beautiful at sunset, almost as beautiful as the Lake itself. The waters of the Lake run with crimson and flame-orange and deep lavender as the sun sinks beyond its farther shore, colors pouring across the water all the way to Tiger Bridge. At that moment the exotic lilies carved into the Bridge, crumbling with age, look whole and alive in the moving light and cerulean shadows.

But after darkness falls, it will be the tigers of the Bridge that look real and alive. They shake themselves out of stone and come down from their pedestals, the lambent fires of sunset in their eyes, to stalk on great velvet paws through the night—so it is said.

At the moment between sunset and dark, the wind off the Lake sometimes dies and the air becomes utterly still. If that pause lasts long enough, it is said, the water becomes a mirror in which a man may see his true face reflected, as well as the reflection of the eternal City. Few would linger at Tiger Bridge to look into the still Lake at that moment, both because truth can be a dangerous thing and because of the tigers that wake out of stone in the night. But that is the story that people in the City tell.

That, at least, is a true story. The Bastard, who did not fear velvet-footed hunters, came to Tiger Bridge sometimes to watch the sun set and look into the glass-still Lake. The face he saw in the water was indeed not the face the simple mirror in his Palace apartments reflected. The Bastard could not have explained even to himself where, precisely, the difference lay. But it was to try to find out that he came to Tiger Bridge.

The Bastard had a name: Neill. He had a place in the court as elder brother to Prince Cassiel and son of Drustan, who was King. But he was not the son of Ellis, the Queen. The Bastard's mother had been a woman who had wandered into the City and the King's bed from some far country beyond the shores of the Lake, beyond the farthest borders of the Kingdom. She had given her son her fine ivory skin, her ash-pale hair, and her dark secretive eyes. And she had given him a heritage that ran outside the bounds of the Kingdom, a mixed blessing at best.

The woman had lived in the City for a season, for a year—long enough to carry and bear the King's son. Then she had walked out of the City. *Though I go, this child will keep my presence always near you,* she had said to the King, laying the baby in his hands—so the tale went. *May he flourish in this Kingdom.*

Possibly the King did not appreciate reminders of his dalliance, especially once he married his Queen. It was well known he did not favor his illegitimate first-born son. Still, if he did not love Neill, he acknowledged him and kept him close to power.

Kings have no need to be ashamed of the evidence of their indiscretions as other men may, and more than one royal bastard has grown up to rule when all the children born on the right side of the blanket have been sickly, or girls. From childhood, then, the court had called the boy *Lord Neill* to his face with careful deference, and, behind his back, sometimes with no less respect, *Lord Bastard.*

When the Bastard was twelve years old, the true Prince was born, merry and bold even as a baby and beloved by all the City. By that time, folk in both the Palace and the City had learned well the habit of respect toward his elder half brother. The Bastard, even as a child, had a way of keeping his own secrets while finding out the secrets of others, and although he spoke softly, he never forgot a slight. So people said in the court. And that story, too, was true.

The Bastard watched the sun sink below the Lake, sending fire across the water, and waited for the wind to die. But the quiet on this night did not last long enough for the waves to grow still, and so the Lake did not turn into a mirror. The Bastard was, however, philosophical about small disappointments. He turned away from the Bridge, pausing for a brief moment to study the stone tigers before walking away. They were still stone under his gaze. After he turned his head . . . who knew what they might become? The Bastard walked back across the City to the Palace. Once he might have heard the soft pad of a great cat, but though he stopped in the street to look patiently into the dark for one shadow softer-footed and more dangerous than others to separate itself from the night, he saw nothing.

ぷぷぷ

The Palace was the heart of the City. Its walls were of cream-colored stone and its wide gates of silver, with brass-bound hinges. Silver tigers lay along the gates, gazing into the City out of emerald eyes. Beyond the gates were the stables and mews, with the graceful lawns and gardens beyond those, where the ladies of the court could stroll in pleasant weather. Early spring flowers dotted the lawns, invisible in the dark but casting their fragrance prodigiously into the night. A couple passed the Bastard. Their heads were bent together, and they did not see him. He knew them slightly and watched them pass, amused. They were young and thought that the love that had woken for them in this spring was the first love the Kingdom had ever seen.

The Palace had been built of the same creamy stone as its walls. Windows of the purest glass poured warm golden light out into the dark. Carved roses climbed along with living ones up its parapets and towers. A spiral stair wove its way up the nearest tower, which existed, so far as the Bastard knew, solely to draw lovers to its heights to admire the stars. The couple he had seen had probably been heading in that direction.

The main doors of the Palace were made of a creamy wood, carved with intricate shapes that teased the eye with the suggestion of forms that could not quite be made out. The doors were standing open. This was ordinary. But the shouting that came from within was not.

The Bastard hesitated, and then approached. A small crowd had gathered there already: guardsmen and servants, a multitude of young men of the court, and a scattering of ladies, all rather pale and alarmed. And the King, voice raised in a roar. That was not, in itself, unusual. But there was a note to it this time that the Bastard might almost have called fear. That was very unusual. The Bastard put himself quietly at the edge of the gathering and listened.

"Well?" roared the King at some of the young men, who looked thoroughly cowed. The King was a big man, with shoulders like a bull and wide, strong hands. His voice, too, could be like the bellow of a bull. He had cowed better men than the crowd of daring young courtiers that were the Prince's companions. "Well? What are you doing here, then? Why did you come back to this house without finding him?"

One of the young men, Jesse, among the Prince's close friends—a bony narrow-faced man of twenty or so, who was usually sharp-humored but seemed rather desperate at the moment—started to answer.

The King cut him off, jabbing a thick finger in his direction. "People don't simply vanish! Princes don't simply vanish! *My son* doesn't just vanish! Not in some ordinary little wood along some ordinary little stream! You get your horse and you get your gear and you go out there and you find him, you hear me?"

"But—" said the young man unhappily.

The King spun with unerring accuracy to focus on the Bastard, who came forward imperturbably under his furious stare. "Your Majesty?"

"Where have *you* been?" the King demanded hotly.

The Bastard bent his head slightly. "Walking in the City."

The King dismissed any possible interest he might have had in his older son's evening. His voice rose again to a shout: "Cassiel has disappeared! Something has happened to Cassiel! Go find him!"

"Yes, Your Majesty," said the Bastard quietly, and looked past the King at the young man who had spoken. He caught his eye and jerked his head. "Jesse."

The young man, with relief, started toward him.

"Thunder and ice! *I'm* not done with him!" bellowed the King.

"I beg your pardon," said the Bastard, with perfect composure. "I shall wait." He assumed a posture of patience.

"I told you to go find your brother!"

"Of course, Your Majesty. I await my chance to obey your command."

"Oh—" said the King furiously, "—take him, then!"

"Yes, Your Majesty," said the Bastard. He took the young man firmly by the arm, extracted him from the crowd, and swept them both down a wide hall lined with bright tapestries and shining lanterns toward his own apartments in the westernmost tower.

Before they had gone a hundred feet, the young man drew breath and started to speak. "Hush," said the Bastard. He turned a corner into a deserted hall that was sometimes used for receptions, ducked through one of the servants' passages, and brought them both to the western tower without passing more than a handful of people or needing to pause for any question.

Once in his own sitting room, the Bastard installed the young man in a cream-colored chair with turquoise cushions and carved legs, gave him a cup of hot spiced wine from a pot a servant had left at the edge of his hearth, and took a place of his own on a second chair. He said, "Tell me everything that happened."

The young man looked now rather as if he did not quite know which he least wanted to face: the furious King or the composed Bastard. He was clad in riding clothing of russet and blue, somewhat the worse for wear; his shoulder-length hair was tangled. His long face looked even longer, drawn with nerves and exhaustion. He picked up his cup of wine, put it down again untasted on a little table at his elbow, and protested in a tone that was a little too loud, "I don't know what happened!"

The Bastard looked at him for a moment. Then he leaned back, propped a foot on a stool, laced his fingers around his knee, and said mildly, "Then start at the beginning, and go on until you come to the end that brought you into the King's presence, with him shouting at you. You went riding with the Prince this morning?"

"Yes!"

"Jesse."

The young man stared at him. Then he closed his eyes, took a breath, and opened them again. He started to pick up his cup, but his hand was shaking and he put it down again quickly, before it could spill. But his voice was calmer when he spoke. "Yes. Yes, we went riding. Just as on any day. We went around the

Lake's shore, to the west, where the country is empty. I tell you, Neill, everything was ordinary!"

"You didn't go to the great forest," the Bastard suggested. "You might have made it there and back in one day, perhaps, if the road was in a particularly cooperative mood. Or you didn't ride out across country and find the forest unexpectedly there before you. I know Cassiel would have been the first to say, 'Let's all ride in just a little way.' . . ."

"No!" said the young man, shocked.

"Jesse?"

"No! I tell you, we didn't see the forest!"

"Pity." The Bastard tapped his fingertips gently against his knee. "It would have been such a simple explanation. All right, then, Jesse, tell me what did happen."

The young man took a breath. "We rode across the bridge—"

"Tiger Bridge?"

"The Bridge of Glass. We crossed at dawn and rode west, into the hills. Cassiel said he wanted to hunt, but really he just wanted to ride. We had hawks, some of us, but we didn't even fly them." Jesse grew calmer as he spoke. He picked up his cup again and this time drank before he put it back down. "We met a stream and turned along it. We rode upstream. We didn't meet anybody. There was a wood, but it was just a wood, Neill, I swear."

"Yes. Go on."

"Cassiel said he wanted to ride uphill and find the source of the stream. So we did. He wanted to ride alone, really, so the rest of us fell back a little, you know. . . ."

"Yes."

"At one place the woods opened up. Somebody started a hare and Ponns let his hawk go after it. Then we had to wait for him to get his hawk back. Cassiel was out of sight, but we didn't think anything of it! Why should we?"

"It seems there was no reason," agreed the Bastard quietly. "Then?"

"Well, then we went on. Ponns was complaining that his hawk had a broken feather and Sebes was saying if a hare could tear up his hawk it wasn't much of a bird, and we were all listening to the two of them. Nobody was worrying about the Prince. We came out of the wood finally and found the head of the stream: there was a cliff, and a spring came out under the cliff and made a pool. Cassiel's horse was there by the pool, but Cassiel wasn't with it." The young man stopped.

"Tracks? Broken branches? Signs of a struggle, of anyone else there?"

"No." Jesse looked at him earnestly. "Really. Nothing like that. The horse wasn't hurt or alarmed, and you could see the place by the pool where Cassiel had knelt to drink."

"Mm."

"So we searched. We really did. All the rest of the day. We only rode back because we knew we'd never find him in the dark. . . ."

"Perhaps," the Bastard suggested, "the Prince drank from the pool and became a white stag and ran into the woods, or a golden lizard with rubies for eyes that hid from you for fear of what you would do if you saw its eyes shine in the sun."

"We looked for tracks," Jesse said tersely. "Man or stag or fox or any creature. And do you think that we would be so stupid as to pluck the ruby eyes out of a golden lizard by the pool where the Prince disappeared? Do you think Cassiel would think that of us?"

"It does seem unlikely."

"I drank from the pool, and nothing happened to me. So we thought maybe a crowd keeps the magic quiet. So everyone went back into the wood and Ponns drank from it, but he was still there when we went back. So then we searched outward in a circle from the pool. I swear we covered every inch of ground and looked at every tree and rock and lizard—none of them were made of gold—for miles around that place, but we found nothing. Nothing!"

"All right," the Bastard said quietly. He made a little calm-down gesture and sipped his own wine. Then he picked up a bell by his chair and rang it.

"What will you do?"

The Bastard did not answer. When a servant came to the sitting room, he told the man, "Send for Trevennen. Or has the King already sent for him?"

The servant ducked his head. "Trevennen is with the King, Lord Neill."

"Ah. Then, do you know, did Marcos come with Trevennen?"

Servants always knew everything that happened in the Palace. The man said, "Yes, Lord Neill."

"Then, if it would not disturb the King, perhaps you would ask Marcos to come to me?"

"Yes, my lord," the servant murmured, and disappeared as quietly as he had come.

"At least Trevennen may be able to calm him," Jesse suggested hopefully. The King was famed for his temper in the best of times, which this night would assuredly not be, and when the King was in a rage, the whole Palace knew it.

Marcos was a round-bodied man, a man who loved soft living and good food. His face was also round, his eyes as long-lashed as a girl's. He wore rings on every finger and loose robes of cerulean blue, like the waters of the Lake at dusk. He was not old, though older than the Bastard by a year or so. He looked lighthearted and lazy, which he was, and also a little doltish, which he certainly was not. He was a mage: one of three who lived in the City.

The Bastard rose. "Marcos."

"Lord Neill," the mage said warmly. "And have you been getting the true account?"

"I think I have part of it." The Bastard gestured the newcomer toward a low couch, more suitable for his bulk than the narrow-legged chairs. "Sit, please. May I offer you wine?"

"Yes, yes," agreed Marcos fervently. "The King is in a fine temper, more likely to offer a man a blow than a cup. I'm grateful you summoned me." His eye fell on Jesse, who perched on the edge of his chair as though he might at any moment take flight. "Well, then, Jesse?"

The young man went through the tale again while the Bastard listened carefully and the mage nodded and rubbed his chin.

"Well," Marcos said at the end. "Well. Hmm."

"You are baffled," the Bastard diagnosed wryly.

"Frequently, yes. In this case . . . well, yes. Hmmm. Jesse, was the water clear? Could you see the bottom of it? Was it sand or pebbles or mud?"

The young man looked surprised, and then thoughtful. "Well . . . ," he said, and frowned. "I don't . . . I don't quite . . . It was all sand around the edges, you know, but . . ." He frowned some more, looking inward at memory. At last he said, "I suppose it was sand, but though the water was clear, I don't think you could see the bottom, you know. All you could see when you looked in was your reflection."

"Hmm," said the mage.

"Hmm?" inquired the Bastard.

"A clear pool can be more than water," observed the mage. "Perhaps the Prince drank a mouthful and turned into a shower of light, or a snow-white bird with a cry that could pierce your heart like a golden arrow. If that's the case, then we can expect to get him back, eventually."

"Or . . . ," the Bastard invited him to continue while Jesse leaned forward anxiously with his eyes on the mage's round face.

"Or perhaps the pool was a mirror. They sometimes are, you know," said the mage mildly. "But in that case, what did the

Prince see? And why, in that case, did he disappear? Did he flee from what he saw?"

"*How* did he disappear, even if he fled?" said Jesse. "We *searched*."

"Well, but a mirror can also be a door," said Marcos. "But a door leading where?" He rubbed his chin again.

"Or to what?" said the Bastard.

"Or to whom?" added the mage. "Well, well . . . we shall have to ride out to this pool tomorrow, Jesse, at dawn, I suppose"—he looked mildly sorry for himself—"and take another look about. Never you mind," he added when Jesse shook his head disconsolately. "We'll find him. It's the way things are: Princes get lost and are found. Cassiel will be fine, be sure of that. In the meantime"—he glanced at the Bastard—"the King is going to be a little upset."

The Bastard shrugged. "It's the way things are."

Jesse said, "You're not afraid of him at all, are you? How can you not be?"

The Bastard paused. He said after a moment, "I know how to move through the tempest." He eyed the younger man. "So would you, if you paid attention to anything but your friends and your gambling and your games. That's why the King disturbs you: he reminds you of your father and you feel he disapproves of you."

"He does disapprove of me," Jesse muttered. He got to his feet and lifted his chin arrogantly. "I'm going," he stated, but waited despite himself for leave from the Bastard.

The Bastard gave it with a slight tilt of his head. "At dawn, be at the Bridge of Glass."

The young man produced a jerky nod and was gone.

"He's afraid of you," Marcos commented. Rising with a low grunt of effort, he poured himself another cup of wine.

"Is he?"

The mage gave him a look both penetrating and, in an odd way, amused.

The Bastard shrugged minutely. "Should I speak to Trevennen?"

"I shall."

"And Russe?"

"—will, I am certain, search in her own way. Don't disturb her."

The Bastard half smiled. "I wouldn't dream of it. Have you any guesses yourself?"

The mage opened a thick hand, looking apologetic. "Not yet."

"Mmm. The City is the heart of the Kingdom, the King is the heart of the City . . . and my brother, Cassiel, is the King's heart." The Bastard spoke without bitterness: it was simply the truth. "If Cassiel turned into a bird with a cry that can pierce your heart, well, as you say, these things happen and we shall surely reclaim him in time. But if someone wished to strike at my father, then in this he has wielded a blade with a fine edge."

Marcos nodded. "And if someone wished to strike at the Kingdom, the same. I know."

"Well?"

"I don't think it likely. The Kingdom generally protects itself adequately. No, I think Cassiel has simply got himself into a bit of difficulty. And I think we can assume that Cassiel, of all people, wherever he may be and whatever may have happened to him, will land on his feet."

Cassiel, wherever he had gone, might have done. But though the Bastard and the King and the mages of the City and all the men of the Kingdom searched for him for many weeks, no one found him.

CHAPTER 2

Timou was a child of winter, which in the villages, where most children are born in the spring like lambs, was worthy of some slight notice. *A winter child:* in the villages the phrase might also mean a young one more solemn than most, just as an apple-blossom child is a merry, laughing child and a harvest child is practical and motherly. Timou was a winter child in both senses: serious and quiet even in her cradle, which was an exotic object carved of rosewood and inlaid with the paler woods of apple and thorn.

Her father had brought the cradle from the City with her already nestled in it, a tiny infant carried through the depths of winter. "Imagine carrying a baby all the way from the City in that weather!" said the villagers. "Over the Lake and through the great forest!" Who knew where Kapoen had gotten a baby, or why he had brought it out of the City to the distant village? Mages, everyone knew, had whims. Nobody minded. The people of the village were proud of their mage and trusted him, even when he came back from a journey with an inexplicable baby.

Every village has a midwife, of course, and usually the midwife is also a witch who can be relied upon for dependable charms to settle a colicky infant or cure milk sickness in a goat. If the village is fortunate, it may also have an apothecary, who, of course, is usually also a witch. Anyone can make willow-bark tea for a fever or elderberry syrup for a cough, but simply taking medicine from a jar marked with the apothecary seal makes it work better, as everyone knows. Timou's village was unusual, because in addition to a midwife and an apothecary, it had Kapoen.

The presence of a mage made the folk of the village feel secure and safe, even on the most violent storm-tossed summer nights when the blind Hunter loosed his hounds. Even on brisk autumn days, when the calm and generally prosaic woodlands surrounding the village might grow restless and begin to press against the pastures and fields. Even on winter dawns so cold and brittle that the very air might shatter from the light striking through it and let through glimpses of a sharper-edged and perilous brilliance. From all these mischances and dangers Kapoen protected the village, with a patient composure that itself lent an air of security to everything that he did.

Kapoen was dark himself: dark of hair and eye and skin as well as mood. So probably, the village folk estimated, it was the fair, pale winter that had made so fair and pale a child. "The cold bleaches the color right out of the womb," said the midwife wisely, helping Timou charm tangles and twigs out of her buttermilk-pale hair. Silky-fine, it was hard to keep in order.

"I'd rather have dark hair," Timou answered restlessly, her eyes on the gaggle of village children who were piling up great heaps of leaves and jumping in them, shrieking. Even her eyes were pale: a blue so light they were almost silver. *The color frozen out of them,* they said in the village. *And yet somehow there is something of her father in her eyes, ah? A thought or a mood hidden there, not quite in sight for the rest of us.* But the villagers did not mind. They were glad to have Kapoen in their village, and glad to have his daughter also, who with luck would become a mage like her father.

"They get twigs in their hair, too," the midwife pointed out. She charmed out the last twig and swept a brush through the resulting fall of clean hair.

"Not like I do," said Timou, which was true.

The midwife gathered up Timou's hair, twisted it into a knot, and bound it firmly with leather ties. "There," she said. "That should last a little. I wonder if your mother had such fine hair."

"I didn't have a mother," Timou said, startled. She had known all her life that she did not have a mother as other children did, and that this lack was cause for pity from those who did. Thus she had spent her whole young life watching other girls' mothers. She liked Taene's mother best: a small kind woman, quick to laugh and to draw laughter from others, who always took care to draw her daughter's friends into the closeness of her family. But it had never occurred to Timou that she might have once had a mother like that herself.

"And your father made you out of silvered grasses and hoarfrost, ah?" said the midwife. "Very likely. No, I expect there was a woman. Isn't there always, where there is a man and a mystery? A woman in the City, I expect, who captured your father's heart for a day and a night and another day, and gave you life, and then gave you to your father . . . for whatever reason a woman might do such a thing." If she guessed what that reason might be, she did not share her guess with Timou.

Timou went and sat at the foot of the tall flat-topped stone at the edge of the village to think about this startling idea.

Had a woman in the City caught her father's heart for a day and a night and another day? Why? How? Timou was not exactly clear on what it might mean to capture someone's heart, but she could not quite imagine anyone capturing her father's. She could not imagine her father marrying a woman, sharing his house with a wife, speaking her name as, say, Taene's father spoke the name of her mother.

Timou pictured a slender woman with white hair standing upon the arch of a shadowy bridge, holding out a baby in a rose-wood cradle to Kapoen and then standing alone to watch him ride away. Timou could not clearly see the woman's face, but somehow she thought the expression on it was calm: even when Timou tried, she could not quite picture any kind of extravagant grief. Was that how it had been: merely calm regret for the child given up? Why would a woman give up her child? What about a baby would make a mother give it away?

There were no answers she could find in her own thoughts. But that was the day Timou understood that there might be questions.

The girls found her then. Ness had realized she was not with the others and had sent Manet and Taene to find her. "Come on," Taene begged, sweet and beguiling. "There are chestnuts to roast, and Sime's mother is making butter candy."

Timou gazed at Taene. Sime's mother was a round cheerful woman who, in addition to butter candy, made fruit pies that melted in the mouth and toffee that stuck wonderfully in the teeth. Her kitchen was always warm and filled with light and good cheer, and it was Sime's mother who was the source of that warmth and bright cheer. Had Timou's own mother been like Sime's mother? Timou did not know. Her throat swelled suddenly with a startling sense of loss.

"And Ness wants you to help pick the right leaves for the King's Crown," Manet put in when Taene paused, clearly not noticing anything unusual in the quality of Timou's silence. Manet, the magistrate's daughter, was always trying to push past Ness and lead the other girls. She said in a commanding tone, "You know we need you to ask the tree for acorns for the Crown, Timou. Come on!" It was always the girls of the village who made the King's Crown in the autumn.

"Come on, Timou, please?" added Taene, catching Timou's hand.

The questions did not go away, but Manet's demanding tone and Taene's pleading made them seem less important. Timou jumped to her feet. But the questions settled to the back of her mind, along with the sense of loss she had learned suddenly to feel, and after that neither quite left her. In the slow quiet days of winter, when the snow came deep upon the village and people stayed mostly to themselves, the questions came back to trouble her.

Timou asked her father these questions one cold evening

when they both sat by the fire after supper. She did not mean to ask him. Timou sat on a rug on the floor—her favorite rug, with a maze of red leaves that wove into the center of the rug and out again, if you knew how to trace the pattern with your finger just the right way. She was leaning her elbow on the hearth and looking into the fire, but she was not seeing the coals or the burning wood. She was seeing a stone bridge and a woman with frost-pale hair holding out a rosewood cradle. And a tall somber man with her father's face, who reached out his hands to take it.

"Timou?" asked her father, watching her, wondering what was behind her silence, and when Timou looked at him, she forgot to veil her thoughts. He saw the questions in her eyes.

"Ah," he said softly.

Timou, since she was discovered anyway, asked him, "Is there always a woman, where there is a man and a mystery?"

Her father sighed and looked away from her, into the fire. "Likely so. And where there is a baby, there is likely a woman." He was not angry, but he had become serious. He added, speaking carefully and slowly, "Your mother was a beautiful woman, very fair, as you are, with winter-pale hair, as you have, but her eyes were dark as the winter sky."

It made Timou uncomfortable that her father should speak so carefully. She did not understand the shape of the secret she saw in his eyes. She asked tentatively, "Did she . . . did she die, then? Having me? Like Nod's mother?" She held her breath waiting for his answer: she was suddenly certain he would say, *Yes, your mother died as Nod's mother died.* No white-haired woman had given away her baby; there had only been the birthing struggle and then silence. That was why her father had brought her away from the City. . . .

Her father moved a hand restlessly. But he said after a pause, "No. She did not die."

"Oh." Timou was silent for a moment, reordering her thoughts once more. "Then . . . why did she give me away to you? Wasn't she sorry to watch you take me away?" She wanted to ask, but was not brave enough, *Were you glad to take me with you?*

The secrets in her father's eyes moved and shifted like fire- light, but did not take on any recognizable shape. His mouth thinned, not with anger, but with something even less familiar that Timou did not recognize. He said at last, "She could not keep you with her, and I . . . would not let her give you to any- one else."

Timou looked quickly into the fire so that the reflected light would hide the leap of her heart. When she thought she could keep her voice calm and the press of her questions secret in her eyes, she looked up and said, "Do you think she will ever— Do you think I will ever meet her?"

There was an infinitesimal pause. Then her father said only, "I don't know, Timou."

He spoke this time with a kind of restraint that made Timou wonder what he wasn't saying. She thought it was impor- tant. She looked into the fire again, wondering what kinds of se- crets might make her father sound that way. "Was she a mage, like you?"

"She was a mage, of sorts. But not like me," said her father, and stood up decisively to add another piece of wood to the fire. That was all he said, and Timou saw that he would not say any-thing else, so she did not ask. The questions, she understood, had not been answered, but they had been changed. But then her father began to ask her about the nature of fire, and Timou saw that she was expected to let the other questions wait.

One year was very like the next in the village. The children wan-dered without really noticing into the adult world. Ness some-times took the sheep out with her father and sometimes wove the wool into cloth with her mother. Manet, who had looked bored all through her childhood as her father tried to teach her the intricacies of law and justice, suddenly took an interest in the magistrate's business and learned to write a clean record of his adjudication. Jenne, the miller's daughter, kept the accounts at the mill. Taene spent her days helping her father, who was the apothecary, make decoctions and tinctures and herbal oils.

And Timou learned to follow the stars as they moved through their measured courses in the sky, and listen to the dark wild power that rolled behind the thunder of the spring storms. Once or twice she tried to tell Ness or Taene about these things, as they told her about their days. She found the other girls lis-tened with wide-eyed interest, but that they listened as though Timou were reciting poetry. The mention of storms frightened them. Not even Taene understood the beauty that Timou saw in the wild magic of the Kingdom.

So one spring progressed much like any that had gone before. One year, when Timou was sixteen, Tair, Taene's eldest brother, began to leave his work sometimes and go up beyond the hillside pastures. And sometimes Ness would leave her weaving to walk with him through the woods. Neither Tair's father nor Ness's mother seemed to mind; indeed, all the village watched the young couple with tolerant pleasure. Ness married Tair in the long slow days of full summer, first of them all to marry, as she had always been the first at everything. Her mother put Ness's hand into Tair's and then whispered something into her daughter's ear that made Ness blush and laugh out loud.

Ness's mother kissed Tair maternally on the forehead—she was a tiny woman, and had to drag him down quite far to do so—and he gave her the single brass coin that a bridegroom gives the bride's mother as a token to show that he can support her daughter. Whatever she said to him made him laugh as well and kiss her back, on the cheek as a son should.

Timou, standing with her father at the edge of the village commons, wondered what it would be like to stand out in front of everyone with a young man by her side. Would she be as happy as Ness looked? She felt her father's gaze fall on her and dropped her eyes. Then Manet caught Timou's hand and dragged her forward with the other unmarried girls to tease Ness, and the moment passed.

In the fall, when chestnuts ripened and the air occasionally tasted of the coming frost, Jenne left the mill accounts to her three brothers and married the dyer's son. The dyer built them a house next to his own. Dyes stained Jenne's fingers in different colors, but she moved smiling through her days and did not seem to mind. Nod and Sime married after Jenne, and Sime's mother, along with Nod's sisters, baked hundreds of tiny iced cakes to give away at their wedding, each with a single rose petal hidden in its heart.

Timou went to Jenne's wedding, and Sime's, and ate her share of the rose cakes. But she did not walk through the woods with any of the young men from the village. Sometimes a young man turned up again and then again in her way, finding chances to speak with her, assuring her that he saw only *her* face reflected in every drop of rain on leaf or flower. But Timou found that usually such young men did not really like to hear about the measures the stars traced in the heavens, or about the silence that lived at the heart of the fiercest storm. Even if a young man did not mind talk that turned toward mystery and magic, Kapoen's quiet impassive gaze falling on him usually chilled his interest. One young man and then another decided instead to court girls who knew how to talk about ordinary things, and whose fathers were not so intimidating.

Timou let them go with only the mildest regret. She learned instead to find the quiet air hiding behind the sharpest wind, to listen to the word whispered by each dying leaf as it fell, to send her mind through the rings of slow time that enclosed the heart of the old trees of the woodlands, to follow the brilliant flight of the falcon across the sky and the glitter of the minnows in the stream. She learned as well the limits of her own patience, and how to go beyond those limits so that she might come to the bright clean purity of knowledge and understanding.

She did not learn the limits of her father's patience. He would show Timou how to find the secret burgeoning heart of a dormant crocus, and how to wake it without harming the flower; and show her again when she found herself lost in the slow cold silence of the corm. And show her again after that, until she at last found the way to slide past the chill to the living kernel within. Then he would give her an approving little nod and move on to some other exercise of magecraft.

So Timou learned how to catch fire and the memory of fire in glass, how to contain the quick fire in a coal and how to let it loose again, how to find the fire that waited to spring eagerly forth from the heart of dry wood. And how to try again and again to find such fire when at first she could see nothing but wood, trusting that, because her father said it was there, eventually she would find the heart of it that wanted to burn.

Then she finally learned the way of it, and for a while she could hardly walk past a stack of dry firewood without flames bursting out of it. "Better than burning someone's house," Kapoen said, shaking his head, more disturbed at Timou's tears than at the inadvertent fire. He patiently taught her to smother fire as well as call it, and how to keep from calling it in the first place, and how to be calm.

"The heart of magecraft," her father told her, "is to be still and let the world unveil itself in its own time. There is no need to force it. It is very difficult to force anything against its own nature. But it will offer itself to you if you are patient. Clarity—and control, and precision, and good judgment—come to the calm mind and the still heart."

He meant that none of those qualities could be expected from a mind disturbed by shock at an unexpected fire. But he also meant, Timou knew, that they could not be expected from a mind cluttered with the thousand small daily thoughts of the village. She flushed.

Kapoen noticed, of course. He smiled his composed smile. "You are part of this village," he told her. "And so you must be. But the heart of magecraft is stillness. Learn to be silent. Learn to love solitude."

"But—" said Timou.

"Fire is part of the world," her father said. "But stillness is stronger."

He meant more than fire. And more than stillness. Timou wanted to ask him about mages and love. *Did my mother love me?* she wanted to ask, but she did not dare. She knew that this question might come too close to asking *Do you love me?* And how could she ask that? She rose instead, abruptly, to go settle her heart by walking in the woods alone.

The woods were not as solitary as Timou had expected, however, for when she came to the grove of nut trees above the village, she found Jonas there before her.

Jonas was a long-legged man who had drifted into the village several years past and who had as yet shown no signs of either really settling down or of moving on. By no means old, he seemed somehow older than the young men of the village who were actually about his age.

Jonas had a curious way of pausing in the midst of the most ordinary tasks and gazing, apparently bemused, at whatever he held in his broad competent hands, as though he had never seen anything more strange in his life than a hammer or hoe or hen's egg. Thoughts moved behind his eyes that were not the familiar thoughts of the village. Timou had wondered about him; about what life he might have left behind to come to this small village. Sometimes when he spoke, she thought she heard behind his speech an echo of words he did not say—but he had never gone out of his way to speak to her.

Jonas boarded with Raen, who was elderly and growing frail in these years. Raen's husband had died many years ago, so Jonas helped her with the tasks that took male strength. The widow said he was polite and thoughtful, as so few boys were in these days. She said this most pointedly to her own sons, who all lived on their own farms a day's walk or more from the village. They only laughed and invited Jonas to the inn for bitter ale when they came in from their farms.

Jonas also helped the apothecary blend his elixirs. He was careful and methodical, and he could read a little, so he did not have to depend on the scents of the herbs to know what he was mixing. The apothecary liked him, too, and wanted him to set-tle down and get married, preferably to his Taene. Timou hap-pened to know that Taene thought that every drop of dew reflected the face of Chais, who was the third son of a man who raised tall golden goats and black-faced sheep several miles from the village. Taene had not yet, however, mentioned Chais to the apothecary.

But what Jonas might think of Taene, or of any girl in the vil-lage, was hard to say. Timou had always found his habit of keep-ing his distance and his own counsel restful, particularly during this year, when she had so often felt restless and uneasy herself.

Jonas was whistling, swinging a widemouthed basket casually by its cord as he gathered nuts. But he saw at once that Timou did not want company and gave her a little nod of apology. "I'm sorry, Timou. I'll go. I can gather nuts another time."

Timou, embarrassed at his ready deference, flushed. "It doesn't matter," she said. "You needn't—you walked all the way up here, and you were here first—"

"An easy walk on a pretty day," said Jonas with a casual, dismissive wave of his hand. "And it will be just as pretty a day tomorrow, I'm sure. I don't mind." He hesitated a moment, and then added, "But if you feel more inclined for company this evening, and if Kapoen lets you loose to join the dancing, you might think of me."

Timou had never noticed that Jonas was especially eager to lead girls out at the village dances. Startled, she asked, "Do you dance?"

He smiled, a little tentatively. "Well, not often. But I do know how."

Timou thought Jonas would probably dance just as he hammered shingles on a roof or hoed in Raen's garden: with a kind of preoccupied, faintly bemused competence. As though he surprised himself by dancing, as he surprised himself by hoeing weeds out of the parsnip rows. She found herself smiling at the image she'd created.

Pleased, Jonas smiled more warmly himself. "I'll see you there, perhaps," he said offhandedly. He gave her another little nod and walked away, swinging the basket in a gentle arc at the end of its cord, whistling. It took a remarkably long time for

Timou to remember that the name of the song he whistled was "Meeting by the Lake," and that it was a love song.

"Do you like him?" Taene asked wistfully, later, when Timou told her about meeting Jonas in the woods. Taene's Chais did not get into the village very often in the evenings, even when there was dancing. Her father wanted her to dance with Jonas. "He's like a brother," Taene told Timou. "I like him—of course I do. But when he sees my face, it's not rain either of us thinks of. But how can I tell my father that?"

Timou nodded in sympathy. "I imagine he'll discover it for himself, in time."

"You're always so calm, Timou."

Timou looked at the other girl, surprised. If her father had been present, she knew he would not think she was especially calm. He would shake his head and ask her to make her heart still. She said after a moment, as her father had told her many times, "You live in the moment you have, Taene. The future will unfold as it will, and you have to be calm to watch it unfolding."

"Yes," said Taene doubtfully, and went back to the original question. "But do you like Jonas at all?"

Timou did not quite know. She thought he was *interesting*. Jonas was the only adult in the village who hadn't lived in it her whole life, the only person whose eyes sometimes held echoes of memories that had nothing to do with familiar places. But she did not know whether she liked him, exactly. And she did not know how to say anything of this to Taene.

But she went to the dancing that evening, and danced twice

with Jonas. Then she left early, walking back to her home
through the gathering dusk with a fat white candle to light her
way. Jonas had given her the candle, but he hadn't offered to
walk her back to Kapoen's house. He hadn't paid her any extravagant compliments either, but he *had* said, "I'm glad you came,
Timou," in a way that sounded like he meant it.

Timou was not certain she was glad she'd gone to the dancing. She felt unsettled, unmoored from the calm that her father
had tried to teach her. She tried to recapture it by spending the
rest of her night learning to hear the names of stars in the faint
music of their glittering dance. Kapoen lifted a resigned eyebrow
at the echoes of music and laughter, and the unsettled questions,
in her mind. If he saw Jonas's name behind her eyes, he did not
mention it. He merely taught her how to set her thoughts and
memories and questions aside so she could hear the voices of the
stars.

The stars' voices were clear and clean and remote. By dawn
Timou had become so entranced by them that she had forgotten
ordinary concerns; her father had to carry her to bed in the end
because she could not bring herself to turn from the slow measures of their crystalline music. She did not think of Jonas again,
or the ordinary life of the village, for days. When she did, it was
with a kind of distant shock: it seemed strange to her that the
music of the stars could exist alongside the music of the village
dances. And it seemed unlikely, and perhaps not really desirable,
that she should care for both.

Nevertheless, Timou met Jonas twice more that winter at village dances. Taene came to her house and pulled her bodily out

of doors once, laughing at Timou's halfhearted protests. "You'll wither away if you don't get some air," Taene told her. "It's a beautiful night. Come on! Your father won't mind if you leave your studies for one evening!"

Jonas wandered by the dancing a little while after Taene and Timou arrived. He danced with Taene once and Timou twice. He certainly did not put himself constantly in Timou's way, but Taene took a moment to whisper to Timou that somehow Jonas seldom appeared at a dance if she was not there. Timou did not know what she thought about this.

But Timou had a great deal to think about besides Jonas. That was the winter she learned how to ask a falcon or a fox for its true name, and how to catch and hold the light of the sun or the moon in a mirror, and how to lay a path before her feet that would take her unfailingly home if she'd lost her way. She learned to stand beside her father and send trees that had begun to walk back to their long slow sleep, and she learned to read the advance of the Hunter's imminent storms in the ragged move-ments of the clouds across the sky, and how to guide his storms safely around the village and its environs. And she learned that people were sometimes unwilling to ask a mage for what they truly desired, and so a mage had to uncover the meaning behind the words they spoke.

But though she listened carefully all that winter to what her father said and did not say, she did not learn the name of her mother, or the reason her mother had given her up.

In the depths of winter, on Timou's seventeenth birthday, her father took her by the hand and led her to the great stone marker at the edge of the village. Kapoen gave her name to the stone and laid a coiled strand of her hair at its foot. Then he released her hand, symbolically releasing her into the world. "You are become beautiful," he said softly. "May your beauty become light. May your light become joy. May your joy become wisdom. May your wisdom be beautiful."

He looked into Timou's face. "You have learned no trade nor art but mine, and need not, if you choose to follow my path. Is this what you wish, my daughter?"

"Yes," Timou agreed. She knew this was what her father expected her to say, and besides, it was true. She found, meeting her father's eyes, that she barely had to lift her head to do so. She had grown tall, and never noticed till now. The realization sent an odd feeling down the back of her neck. Time had passed, and she had not even thought to notice.

CHAPTER 3

Spring came slowly the year Timou turned seventeen, as though the winter was reluctant to loose its hold on the land. But it came at last. The crocuses put out their fat white and purple flowers at the edge of the woods, and witch hazels unfurled their thin yellow petals, casting their scent generously across the woodlands. Birds sang in the branches, building their nests of grass and twigs and bits of lost wool from the first spring shearing.

That spring Timou watched warmth creep into the heart of each crocus and wake it into bloom, watched the birds in the woods and fields, and spent hours turning the heavy pages of her father's books. She loved these books, which her father had made available to her after her birthday. She had not even known he possessed them until he had opened a door in their house she'd never before noticed and shown her the room that had been hidden behind it, cluttered with tall shelves filled with books. Now she found she loved their heft in the hand, which so contrasted with the brittle fragility of their pages. She loved the graceful or angled or tightly looping scripts that filled those pages. Deciphering the bits of old strange languages absorbed her attention on those days that the early spring rains shut out the world. Some of the books were illuminated and scrolled with fine metals, some plain and old and smelling of dust and somehow of magic. And some were impossible to open unless one breathed over them the proper words of release. Now seriously entering into the study of magecraft, Timou began to learn to open even these.

Occasionally her father gave Timou the word that would open one of his books, but more often he did not. She searched patiently for the words herself. Sometimes she discovered the key to one or another of the books when she found a word or a name or even an odd harsh syllable in an old story, or tucked into the middle of a bit of history, or hidden in her father's eyes. She always felt a blaze of delight and expectation when a book fell open for the first time in her hands, revealing to her at last its wonders and mysteries.

One evening, as the spring days lengthened and the crocuses and hyacinths gave way to the delicate grace of apple blossoms, she caught the whisper of an unfamiliar name in her father's eyes when he glanced at her. She had been sitting, legs drawn up, on her favorite spiral-patterned rug by the fire, with her father's oldest book in her lap, thinking of nothing in particular. It was a book she had not been able to open. Even though she could not open it, the book fascinated her because of its age and its whisper of power. She had not been able to find its key on this evening either and was sitting quietly, having given up the effort for the night. It might have been the quiet of her own mind that let her catch the glint of uncharacteristically unguarded memory when her father turned his head so that she, or the book, caught his eye.

Timou blinked and looked into the fire, and her father did not, perhaps, realize what she had seen. What she had seen was a word, a name, one that she knew he had not meant to give her. And a little while later, when her father went quietly up the stairs to his room, leaving her by the fire, Timou bent over the heavy book she held and whispered to it, "Lelienne." And the book opened in her hands, the pages falling gently to one side and the other, with firelight running across its creamy vellum and its glittering illuminations.

The illuminations surrounded an image, made with silver and powdered opal, of a man with harsh features and stark white hair. Startled and excited, Timou bent forward over the book, tracing the difficult slanted writing with the tip of her finger as she silently sounded out the unfamiliar words. The language was one she did not know. The script seemed harsh to her, the unknown words potent in themselves. She did not try to speak them aloud, but let them whisper to her if they would.

Deserisien. That was, she decided, probably the name of the mage pictured in these illuminations. She understood that he was, or had been, a mage. Or something like a mage. He had lived, she gathered, either long ago or far away, or perhaps both, in a brilliant, brutal, extraordinary Kingdom, a Kingdom where

Kings were sacrificed as lightly as leaves in the fall, where mages ruled and practiced a strange dark sorcery of making and unmaking—she did not understand clearly all that the pictures showed, or what the inscriptions said. But she understood that the sorcerer Deserisien had gathered about himself a group of men and women almost as powerful as he. And she discovered, with a thin shock that was in an odd way not a shock at all, that one of the sorcerers smiling out of the illuminated pages was a woman who shared her face. She puzzled over the words on that page a long time, finding in it few answers and many questions.

When Timou finally went up to her own bed, she took the book with her, laying it on a small table by her bedside. But in the morning the book was gone. Timou was startled by the quick resentment she felt; she tried to put it aside. But she did not know why her father had let the book come into her hand if he had not meant for her to open it. She looked for it in the days that followed, but she did not find it. The memory of the white-haired woman who had smiled from its pages troubled her. The smile, she thought, had been like that strange dark Kingdom itself: subtle and cruel and beautiful.

She did not ask her father about the book, or about the Kingdom it had described. But she wanted to. She wanted to ask him about the woman with a face that mirrored hers. She wanted to ask him whose name he had used to lock the book that held such power and strangeness within its pages. She wanted to shout, to demand answers to the questions she had always held, which had once more changed their shapes in her mind and her heart. It was hard to trust her father's wisdom and his teaching, though she had seldom doubted either in her life. When her father turned his searching gaze to her, Timou looked away, not allowing him to see the questions that gathered in her eyes. He must have guessed at them. But still she did not ask, nor did her father offer answers.

When she turned over in her mind the new-changed questions the book had raised, she did so uneasily. Without quite admitting that unease to herself, Timou ceased trying to open her father's remaining locked volumes and turned her attention back to the quickening life of the spring. She went to Taene's house and helped Taene grind powders for her father or roll out bread dough for her mother; she helped eat the sweet rolls, too. Taene's mother, an ample woman with a plain round face that was usually good-humored, welcomed Timou, pressed hot sweet tea on her, and showed the girls how to make a complicated pastry with honey and early mint and dozens of layers of thin dough.

Sometimes Chais was there, too, trading goat's milk and cheese for some of the apothecary's syrups and simples. One afternoon he gave a fine soft scarf of lamb's wool to Taene in exchange for a smile, carefully choosing a time when her father was out. Taene's mother suggested, with a sidelong look at Chais, that Taene might go for her to the miller's for flour, and perhaps Chais might go with her to carry it back, if he wasn't in too much of a hurry. "It's heavy to carry so far, and I'm afraid I can't spare the cart," she said with a wink for Timou, who had been helping her thin early peas and tie twine for them to climb up. "Timou can help me here, can't you, love?"

Timou was happy to help with the peas, but she did not know what she thought about Taene and Chais. She was happy for Taene, of course, but still she did not know what she thought. Or more, perhaps, how she *felt*. It seemed that everyone she knew, each of the girls with whom she'd grown up, was moving confidently into a new part of life from which Timou was somehow excluded. Ness and Jenne and Sime, and then Manet and now even Taene . . . Timou told herself she would rather follow the voices of trees and stars than that of any young man. Even though this was true, sometimes it rang a little hollow.

The next day, Taene seemed distracted, quieter than usual, with a tendency to smile at odd moments. Timou hardly knew how to talk to her.

Jonas also came that afternoon, to help the apothecary sort the powders left after the long winter and determine which would most urgently need to be replenished.

"Moisture got into this hyssop—look." The apothecary waved a box at Jonas. "It's a pity; everybody's got a cough in the spring. I could use twice as much as I have here, and now this is ruined."

Jonas took the box and gazed gravely into it. Then he dumped the powdered herb out onto a sheet of vellum and used the handle of one of the apothecary's brushes to gently sweep some of the powder aside. "I think mostly the top was ruined," he said. "Might this part still be good?"

Timou looked over his shoulder. He was right: some of the hyssop still seemed good. She said to the apothecary, "My father probably has some hyssop. If there's not enough, then I know he has some horehound."

"Thank you, dear, that's good to know," the apothecary said absently, leaning over from the other side of the table to stir the hyssop with one blunt-nailed finger. "You're right, Jonas, some of this is salvageable. I don't have another box—"

"I'll make you one tonight." In the meantime, Jonas swept the remaining hyssop into a small bowl and set a plate over it.

"Good," the apothecary said approvingly to this offer, glancing at Taene to see if she'd noticed this evidence of industry and good nature. She hadn't. She was across the kitchen at the other table, making Chais's favorite butter candy and smiling to herself.

"Fathers are sometimes blind," Jonas said to Timou later. He was walking her part of the way back to her house. The furniture maker's house, where he would collect some seasoned wood suitable for the apothecary's box, was on the way. He gave her a sidelong look. "Kapoen wouldn't for a moment miss the direction of his daughter's glance."

Timou said, "You're afraid of my father." She meant this as an observation, not an accusation, and Jonas took it that way.

He said equably, "He sees too much."

"It's the nature of magecraft, to see into a thing's heart. Or a man's."

Jonas gave a little nod. "I don't care for that in Kapoen. But somehow it doesn't trouble me in you, Timou."

Timou didn't know what to say to this.

"You probably know that I'm starting to see your face in the raindrops," said Jonas. He waved a hand at the sky, where a heavy overcast promised more spring rain on the way. "There've been enough chances for it lately." His tone was light, but the glance he turned her way was not.

Timou stopped in the road, turning to face him. "Jonas—"

"You needn't say anything. I'd rather you didn't."

"I will be a mage," Timou said as gently as she knew how.

"Yes," said Jonas, not understanding what she meant. "It seems a fine thing to be."

Timou just looked at him, not knowing how to explain the cool stillness that lay at the heart of a mage.

"Timou—"

"Jonas . . . I don't think I'll ever marry. I don't think mages do."

Jonas opened his mouth, probably to protest that this could not be true. But then he paused, doubtless thinking, as Timou was, of her father's untouchable calm. It was impossible to imagine Kapoen beset by passion or overwhelmed by longing. It was impossible to forget that he had not married Timou's mother.

Jonas bowed his head a little, his expression unreadable. He said after a moment, his tone still light, "Well. It seems a shame, if mages never marry. But you needn't, I suppose, if you don't care to." He made a little gesture toward the furniture maker's house. "I'll leave you here, then. Perhaps I'll see you tomorrow at the apothecary's house. I hope you won't let the prospect keep you away; I promise I won't trouble you."

It didn't occur to Timou until she was all but home that in fact she did not feel calm. That Jonas had promised a thing he could not, after all, give her. Because she *was* troubled.

⚇⚇⚇

Gradually, during these early spring days, the tension Timou thought had existed between herself and her father had eased away; she was not sure it had ever been there save in her own mind. She was certain Kapoen now saw the confusion Jonas had let into her heart, but if so, he did not speak of it directly. He only brought out a set of heavy leather-bound books that contained words written in gold ink in a narrow looping alphabet. He showed her how she could clear her mind and let the unfamiliar words speak to her. They told her tales out of the long reaches of history: tales of the young Kingdom and the first mages who found or created it and then wandered through it admiring its wonders and curiosities.

Some of the stories were familiar to Timou, for her father had told them to her—it seemed to her she must have heard them first while still in her cradle, for she felt she had been born knowing them. Others were new. The golden writing drew her into the tales until it seemed to her she lived them herself: as though she had stood with the mage Irinore when he first saw the City in the Lake and built in echo the City at the heart of the Kingdom.

These stories pulled her away from the daily life of the village and further into her own magecraft: she dreamed of forests and dragons and ruined towers hiding riddles at their hearts, and not of the village or of ordinary things. The bright brisk days lengthened and the oaks put out their first new leaves while Timou wandered among the ages of history. It almost began to seem to her that she might have imagined or dreamed the book that had shown her the mage Deserisien and the woman with Timou's face but her own dark smile. There was no mention of either in the books she read now. Sometimes she still went to Taene's house, and sometimes she encountered Jonas there. He gave no sign he thought more of her than of Taene; his smile at them each was the same, reserved and wry. Though Timou was glad of this, she found she was also somehow disappointed, as though she had wanted both—both the ordinary life he might have wanted to offer her and the life her father held out before her. Since she could not choose both and since this was hard to face, Timou found it easier to avoid Taene's house.

Then the first ewes dropped their lambs, and every one was born dead. And the goats their kids, the same. Even the sows, when they farrowed, which few did that year, produced small litters and weak piglets, and everyone knows that pigs are hard to touch with any spell or curse. By then Timou's mind was entirely occupied by the new urgency to understand this common trouble.

At first few people in the village understood that what afflicted their stock afflicted everyone's. Then they all understood, and began to be afraid. The midwife made charm after charm for the ewes and the goats, the apothecary made infusions of partridgeberry and milk thistle. But the animals continued to deliver stillborn young.

The village magistrate was the one who came finally to Timou's father. Timou let him in wordlessly and stepped around him to pull the door to when the magistrate left it a little ajar. She explained to the question in his gaze, "A door open is welcome, a door closed is denial, but a latch that does not quite catch is perilous," and saw another kind of question grow behind his earnest eyes.

Timou smiled and took the magistrate to the parlor and offered him tea, which he accepted a little warily, and went to fetch her father.

"Now, Kapoen—" said the magistrate nervously when Timou's father came into the parlor.

"I am aware," said Timou's father. "The lambing." He was frowning, an expression that made him look severe, although Timou knew he was only thoughtful.

"Yes," said the magistrate. "The lambing."

"It is not only the sheep," said Timou's father.

"I know. The goats, the pigs—"

"The eggs in the nest," Timou said softly. "The foxes in the den."

"Oh," said the magistrate faintly. He looked at Timou. "You are . . . you are growing up, aren't you, Timou?"

Kapoen gave his daughter a thoughtful smile, and the magistrate a thoughtful frown. "We are aware of the matter, Master Renn."

The magistrate twisted the tail of his coat between his fingers, quite unconsciously. "What are you . . . Are you doing something to make it . . . right, Kapoen? If there is . . . Is there something you can do to make it right?"

"We are waiting," said Timou's father softly. "We are watching to see the shape of this curse, if curse there is; we are looking for the pattern that lies behind what happens and does not happen."

The magistrate blinked. "What does not happen?"

"The trees have budded out," Timou explained, and the magistrate's eyes slid to her, surprised. She said, taking no notice of his surprise, "The spring breeze has warmed; the snow has melted; the flowers have come. But the squirrels in their nests have no blind young to nurse, and the owls hunt only for themselves and not for nestlings. The peas and radishes do not sprout. The early flowers set no seed."

"I see," said the magistrate. Timou was not certain he did, but her father said, tranquil and calm, "When there is something we know to do, you may be sure we will do it," and the magistrate seemed to find this reassuring. He finished his tea with evident relief and left quickly, not like a busy man, but like a man trying to look busy and not nervous. The magistrate had always been nervous of Timou's father, who was dark and quiet and rarely explained what he was thinking. Now, Timou saw, he was nervous of her, too.

Timou let him out and closed the door behind him, since he had not quite let the latch catch this time either. Then she went back to the parlor and looked with faint interest at the pattern the tea leaves had left in his cup. She said to her father, her eyes still on the leaves, "Ness is pregnant, you know."

"Yes," agreed her father.

"So you will put this right before she comes to her time?"

"Be calm," advised her father, and handed Timou a cup of

tea out of the air. She took it after a moment, wrapping her fingers around the delicate cup, and breathed in the fragrant steam. It was valerian and mint, meant to soothe.

"The disturbed mind perceives nothing," said her father, and produced a cup of tea for himself. "In serenity one finds the order that lies behind what appears random, the pattern that lies behind what appears to lack pattern."

"Yes," said Timou, and sipped the tea, tasting mint and honey.

The midwife hovered over Ness like a hen with one chick, as they say in the villages; the apothecary gave her teas and syrups and bitter decoctions, and shook his head when he met the midwife's eyes because they could both feel that nothing they did would help, that it was already too late—that nothing could be done to stop the gradual cooling of the life Ness carried.

Timou's father examined Ness only once, looking searchingly into her eyes and even more searchingly into her shadow. His dark patient eyes held regret. "There is nothing I can do," he said at last. "The child you carry gives up its life with every passing moment. I can do many things, Ness, but I cannot turn away this quiet death."

Ness tried to speak and could not. The breath she drew turned to a sob, which she turned her face away to try to hide. Timou, watching silently, found tears rising in her own throat and blinked hard.

Tair, standing behind Ness, put his hands protectively on her shoulders and asked helplessly, "Why is this happening?"

"I do not know. I will find out." Timou's father stood up. He looked at the apothecary and at the midwife and at Ness's mother, and last of all he looked at his daughter.

Timou looked back, her face smooth, trying to conceal her grief behind the enduring calm her father had taught her. She could not quite manage this, and she thought she saw a faint disappointment in his eyes: extravagant sorrow was perilous to the mage, as any strong emotion was always perilous. Timou knew that. She glanced down.

"I will find out," her father said, more to Ness and her mother than to Timou, and touched Ness's cheek with patient tenderness. "Many women have borne the pain you will bear. It is a hard journey, but you are not alone. Have courage in their company." He bowed his head and began to withdraw, and Timou obediently with him.

"Please," said Ness, not weeping, in too much grief for tears. "Please. Timou—will you stay with me?"

Her father turned his dark eyes to her, and so Timou did not weep. But she did go to Ness and take her cold hand in both of hers, and seat herself quietly on a stool by the woman's side.

So when her father left, and the midwife and the apothecary and Tair and even Ness's mother all left, Timou stayed. Sime came in, and a little later Jenne, with Manet and Taene—all the women who had been girls together so few years past. They were all married now, except for Timou and Taene, for Manet had married an earnestly self-important young man named Pol in earliest spring before the trouble had begun. But none of them had a child. In this, as in everything, Ness would have been first.

"Your mother told us we should come," Jenne said to Ness simply, "so we came."

"Yes," Ness said, and wept, suddenly and violently, covering her face with her hands. And they all wept with her. Even Timou. Whose heart was not calm or still at all.

Ness had her baby in her proper season, with little difficulty. But like the lambs and the calves, the child was born dead. On the day after the birth, after the infant had been laid in its tiny grave, Timou's father left the village.

"Stay," he bade Timou.

Timou bowed her head. "Where will you go?" she asked.

Her father regarded her from dark secret eyes. "To the City."

"Ah," Timou said.

"I see nothing clearly," he added after a moment. "This is . . ." He paused, uncharacteristically, but then continued, "I think it is with the heart of the Kingdom that this trouble lies. As the heart goes, so goes the Kingdom, and I think perhaps the heart has been . . ."

"Broken?" Timou hazarded in that lengthening pause.

"Lost," said her father gently. "And its future lost with it. Or . . ." Again, he did not complete the thought.

Listening carefully, Timou believed she heard what her father had left unspoken. After a moment she said, "Or taken?"

"Perhaps," said her father, lifting his dark brows in faint surprise. At the question? Or at her, that she had asked it?

Timou said slowly, "The heart of the King is the heart of the

Kingdom. How might the King lose his heart? Or who might take it? And for what?"

"All good questions, my daughter. But not the one question that is most important."

Timou thought them very important questions, but she tried obediently to think of another. "Where—" she said at last, "—where is the King's heart now, if it has been lost? Or stolen?"

"Yes. And how can it be regained?" said her father.

Timou did not answer. She knew that things lost—or taken—may not always be found.

"You are on no account to follow me, Timou."

Timou thought about this. She asked, testing the shape of a half-perceived pattern, "When should I look for you to come back?"

"Look for me by summer's end, my daughter; but if I do not return, more than ever you must not follow me." Her father paused and studied her. His face, usually serious, had become severe. He said, "You are young, my daughter. If I and the mages of the City cannot find what has been lost, do not try. Stay in the village and wait."

Timou listened carefully. "You believe there is danger," she said softly. It was not quite a question. "From what?" She saw that he would not answer, and asked, "Shall I be blind?"

"If you are, you will stay here, and wait for clear sight," said her father, a little sharply, he who was seldom sharp with her. "You will wait for the pattern to make itself plain to you. To act blindly or in haste is dangerous."

That he thought there was peril in the City, Timou under-stood. But there was something else in his eyes beyond that, which Timou still could not see. A name? A thought? A suspi-cion? The words he was not saying crowded behind his eyes. She asked him, "Deserisien?" and saw his surprise.

But he said only, "No. Not Deserisien."

Timou looked at him, into his face. Then she said reluctantly, "I will stay here. If I can."

For a moment she thought her father would speak more clearly, explain more plainly. But instead he only nodded and left her without speaking further. He went away down the road, walking quietly through the quiet warmth of the late spring. Be-hind him, Timou wandered consideringly into the kitchen to make tea and to think.

The season passed into summer, and then into autumn, and he did not return.

Timou watched the seasons' slow changing, and waited pa-tiently for her father's return, or for the breaking of the curse that held new life in check, or at least for the growth of her own un-derstanding. She waited in vain.

Sime had her child after Ness, as the season turned brisk and the days shortened. The baby would have been a harvest child, but she was born dead. Perfect and tiny and without a breath of life stirring in her. Sime touched the baby's face tenderly and gave her to Nod to take out and bury in the place they had pre-pared. She did not weep. Nod wept enough for them both. His brothers and friends went with him to stand over the grave in silent mourning. The women did what they could for Sime, except for Ness, who could not bear to attend so sad a birth. Timou gave Sime betony tea to stop the bleeding, though there was not much of that, and Manet rubbed her hands and stayed with her when the others at length left her to rest.

"Why?" said the midwife to Timou wearily. She had wrapped the tiny infant in a cloth for Nod. It hurt her, as it hurt them all, when there was a death instead of a birth. But she felt it more sharply because she was a midwife. "Why should this have happened to the Kingdom?"

"I do not know," said Timou.

"Where is your father?" asked the midwife.

"I do not know," said Timou.

The midwife sighed, washed her hands in a basin, and dried them on another cloth. "You," she said finally, "are going to have to go to the City."

"I know," said Timou. She left the midwife and walked away toward her father's house at the edge of the village, her head bowed and her steps slow.

Taene's mother caught up with her before she reached it, while she was still so lost in thought that she hardly noticed the woman's hurried approach, and Timou looked up in surprise when she heard her name called out.

"Timou—oh, Timou," said Taene's mother hastily, reaching out to catch her arm, "have you seen Taene this evening? Was she with Sime?" She looked anxious.

Jonas had come with Taene's mother, though Timou could not decide whether his frown also looked worried or merely mildly exasperated. She had seen him only occasionally through the long cheerless summer; she had spent most of her time with her father, trying to understand the curse that had fallen across the Kingdom, so they had not come together often. It had not been a summer for dancing. Now she found, with some distress, that he looked older, worn with the grief of the village. His eyes met hers and darkened with worry, as though he saw the same in her.

Taene had indeed not been with the rest of the young women at Sime's sad birth. Caught up in Sime's pain, Timou had not even wondered at her absence. She shook her head and looked inquiringly from Taene's mother to Jonas.

"She went out with Chais," Taene's mother said, all but wringing her hands in distress. "This morning—early. She hasn't come back yet." She clicked her tongue in worried annoyance. "Girls do lose track of passing time, at Taene's age. Look how long the shadows are. And listen! That isn't geese, that sound, is it? Do you think that is the calling of geese?"

When she listened carefully, Timou had to agree that the wild faraway cry did not sound precisely like the cry of flying geese.

"It sounds like geese to me," Jonas said, and shrugged when both women looked at him. "Well, it does."

"Maybe," Taene's mother said, but she did not sound like she thought so. "Do you hear thunder?"

"Not yet," said Timou. "She went out with Chais, did she?"

The older woman cast her eyes upward in fond exaspera-
tion. "Everyone knows it's Chais my daughter is fond of—except
her father, who will *not* see what's right in front of his two eyes!
That's all right—he'll come around, ah, and no harm to a father's
blindness, except what if that isn't geese? Look, Timou, love, it's
near dusk. Would you please, *please* go and find my foolish
daughter before the thunder breaks? If that is thunder?"

"Of course," Timou reassured her. "Though they will probably be back in the village before I am finished searching. Most
likely they are walking back right now."

Taene's mother gave a distracted nod.

"Do you know where they would have gone?"

The woman did not seem to, but Jonas thrust his hands into
his pockets and gave Timou a sidelong look. "The glade in the
wood behind the stone marker, I should guess. If I were guessing."

He did not sound as though he were guessing. Timou half
smiled, but converted it to a serious nod for the sake of Taene's
mother's nerves. "I'll look there first."

"Oh, *thank* you, love," said Taene's mother, patting her arm
again. "Jonas can go with you."

"If you don't mind, Timou," Jonas put in, giving her a look
that clearly said he had been dragged along by Taene's mother
and it wasn't his fault, but that he would like to accompany her
if she would not object.

Timou decided she did not mind. She said, "You can show
me your glade, then, and tell me what girl you last took there."

Jonas flushed a little, started to speak, and cut off whatever
he had been about to say. He had a long stride, and lengthened

it further now in annoyance, so that Timou had to stretch her own legs to keep up. He said over his shoulder, "I talk to Taene, that's all. And Chais, when I'm out that way. They only went there to talk, you know. Chais would rather roll through nettles than do anything to harm Taene, and Taene wouldn't hurt her father; and besides, it's not a quick tumble on a blanket under a tree that either of them has in mind."

Timou knew that. She took two running steps to catch up. "She thinks of you as a brother."

Oddly, Jonas flushed again, more darkly. "So she should," he said a little harshly, and lengthened his stride again.

"Please!" Timou protested.

Jonas glanced back at her in surprise and slowed abruptly. "Sorry."

Above them, something that might be only geese streamed away south, far aloft and far away, crying a wild cry. Both Jonas and Timou glanced up. "*Is* that thunder?" Jonas asked, listening for the storm that might follow that cry, if it was not made by geese after all.

Timou could not quite tell.

It was not geese, nor ordinary thunder. They learned that before they had quite reached the stone marker, never mind the woodland glade up on the hill behind it: they learned it when the storm broke suddenly across them, roaring through an evening that had been calm only moments before. The storm hounds, white and swift and fierce as hunting hawks, broke the quiet air into wild gusts with their passing and sent streamers of cloud skating in ragged shreds behind them as they raced the wind through the sky. Rain came behind the hounds, violent as autumn storms could ever be, but with a savage cold to it that was not normal for so early in the season. Thunder crashed, much too close, and it was suddenly dark, as though they had leapt straight across evening into the deepest chasm of the night.

Timou caught Jonas's hand and ran with him through the rain to the great stone, finding it by feel more than by sight. She tucked them both hard up against its leeward side. Raking wet hair from her forehead, she lifted her face to the storm. Her eyes were half shut against the dashing rain as she looked out into the sudden dark for the power that drove it. She saw nothing.

"What if Taene is out in this?" Jonas shouted in her ear, trying to get her to step back farther into the stone's protection.

Timou nodded, picturing that possibility with dread. She patted Jonas urgently on the shoulder, meaning *Stay still,* and stepped out from behind the stone into the full force of the storm, so that if it was seeking a target it would more likely find her and not anyone else foolish enough to be caught out in it.

Through the rain, through the storm, rode the dark Hunter on his white mare: lightning scattered from the mare's hooves and tangled in its wild mane; it tossed its head and settled back on its haunches, sliding down the wind to the road. Thunder rolled behind it, crashing as its hooves struck the ground, and the mare flung back its head, eyes crazed, muscles bunching to spring forward.

The Hunter checked it effortlessly, dark hand catching its white mane, and the mare reared instead, and came down again with a blaze of lightning and a bellow of thunder. Then it stood still, water from the storm streaming down its powerful neck and shoulders. The rain eased, and ceased: they were standing in the eye of the storm. All around them thunder rumbled. Somewhere far ahead and far above, the storm hounds gave tongue on the trail of some quarry. But the Hunter held his mare and did not follow them.

He seemed at once as vast as the storm and yet hardly taller than an ordinary man; he carried neither bow nor spear, nor needed either. Darkness cloaked him; it seemed he towered to the cloud-torn sky and yet Timou could see his face—or half see it, for it was masked by streamers of cloud and shadow. A crown of antlers or twisted branches rose in confusing patterns above his head. His eyes were wide and round and yellow, fierce and unhuman as the eyes of an owl, but blind. Yet he knew she was there, and turned his face toward her.

Do I not know you? demanded the Hunter. *Surrender your name to me.* His voice was dark and fierce and wild; thunder was in it and behind it, so that it seemed to echo measurelessly through the dark.

"Timou," Timou said, her voice shaking. "Lord, my name is Timou. Daughter of . . . daughter of Kapoen."

Behind her, Jonas eased out from the shelter of the great stone to stand at her back and put his hands on her shoulders. Timou was glad of his support; she felt her breath coming a little more easily, for all she might have wished him to stay out of the Hunter's way.

Daughter of Kapoen, said the Hunter. *Is that what you are? And yet I perceive you are very like your mother.*

Timou was stunned.

But do you have her power? demanded the Hunter. *I think not.*

"You . . . know my mother?" Timou came a half step forward, realized what she was doing, and drew back again. "Who was she? What happened to her?"

The Hunter gazed at her with his blind eyes. Timou thought his mouth curved in a smile that held cruelty and mockery and nothing of humor, but shadows lay across his face and she was not sure what she saw. *What happened to her? Nothing happened to her. She waits for you. As I have waited for her. And now I find you.* The Hunter moved a dark hand across the white neck of his mare, and the mare tossed its head and shifted its feet, muscles bunching with the desire to leap forward. He held it. Thunder muttered.

Timou stood still, with an effort; yet she did not know whether she wanted to run from him or press forward with questions and pleas. She asked quickly, "Do you know where my mother is, Lord?"

If you seek her, I think you will find her, said the Hunter. *Seek her.*

"I will," Timou whispered.

A terrible fierce satisfaction filled the Hunter's dark face, his blind yellow eyes. Lightning cracked around them in a sudden wild echo of that satisfaction; thunder crashed with brutal power all through the dark, and Timou flinched and tried not to cry out.

Jonas's hands tightened on her shoulders, and he gave her a little shake, as though to assure Timou that he was still with her. She leaned gratefully against his solid human warmth.

But the Hunter turned, shadows twisting above him and across his face. His mare settled reluctantly, tossing its head so that lightning flickered in its mane. Rain came through the dark—small hard drops, cold as slivers of ice. He said to Jonas, *And you, man? What are you, besides my quarry?*

Jonas did not answer. Perhaps he could not. He bowed his head over Timou's, and made no sound.

The Hunter laughed, a terrible wild sound with nothing human in it, and released his mare. It sprang forward, lightning tearing the air behind it, thunder crashing at the beat of its hooves, and the cold rain drove savagely in its wake.

Timou was trembling. Jonas put his arm around her shoulder. Neither of them spoke. Timou, at least, felt herself numbed beyond the ability to speak. There seemed no words that could encompass either the dark Hunter or the questions he had left behind him.

It was raining. The rain was cold. The road had gone to icy mud, though the terrible chill was slowly passing off the night with the Hunter's departure. They both could hear that the storm hounds had put up a quarry far away, so there was no need to be concerned for Taene or Chais or anyone from the village. So Timou walked, shivering, close against Jonas's side, and neither of them said a word.

Taene, it proved, was safe in her father's house, in her mother's kitchen. She was very glad to see them.

"I heard the storm break," she said, leaping to her feet to greet them. "And Mother said she'd sent you after me, Timou—I'm sorry to have worried you—"

Taene's mother pressed hot tea and little iced rolls on them both, and sent Taene's little sisters scattering to heat soup and find towels. "You're soaked through, Timou, love—I'm so sorry. Jonas, dear, I'm so sorry. Taene was already here when I got back, and there you were, out in all that weather. Wouldn't you know it?"

"It wasn't more than an ordinary storm, now, was it?" asked the apothecary, passing his wife a bottle of elderberry syrup for the tea, which she added generously. "Just a storm, ah? They come up fast in the autumn."

Jonas turned his head toward Timou. Their eyes met. He said after a moment, "Of course. Just a storm."

Timou did not contradict him. She accepted a cup of sweetened tea from Taene's mother and a warm towel from one of the little girls, and a place by the stove, and felt her shivering ease. She said, "I am . . . I will leave for the City tomorrow. Or the day after," she added more reasonably. "To find my . . . father."

The apothecary nodded soberly. "I was discussing this with Enith." Enith was the midwife. "After Sime, and no sign of Kapoen returning, I think you must, my dear."

"And I wasn't there for poor Sime," Taene said penitently, bringing Timou a steaming mug of soup. "I'm even sorrier for that than for sending you out in the rain. Poor Timou. Are you warmer now? Is Jonas going with you to the City?"

Timou turned her head sharply, and for the second time her eyes and Jonas's met.

The apothecary looked from one of them to the other,

looked finally at his wife, took in her knowing expression, raised
his brows, and sighed.

Jonas looked only at Timou. "Yes," he said.

"No," said Timou.

"We'll discuss it," said Jonas.

"As long as you discuss it in the morning," Taene's mother
said firmly, "in dry things, and after a good breakfast. You had
better stay the night here, Timou—just listen to that rain!—you
can have the girls' room, and the girls can go in with Taene. All
right, dear?"

Timou looked at her silently, and wanted to weep. She did
not even know why, except she thought that whatever she found
in the City, it would not be a kind, comfortable woman who
made tea and worried over one's getting soaked in a cold rain.

When setting forth on a journey, there are always some things
one should take and other things that one should leave behind.
Timou moved methodically through the next day, and the next,
sorting clothing and supplies, and thoughts and wishes and
hopes, into one category or the other.

"I should come with you," Jonas said. He had brought her
his own leather knapsack, saved from the days in which he had
journeyed. Timou had never asked him where he had journeyed
from, nor had he ever volunteered the tale. Now such a question
somehow did not seem appropriate, though she would have
liked to ask it.

Jonas added, "Anybody can get into difficulty on the road."

Timou did not answer. It had occurred to her with surprising

force that in fact she would like Jonas to come with her: that she
wanted his solidity at her side and his dark quiet presence across
her evening fire every night. She was immediately annoyed with
herself: was she a child, to need company in the dark? What
would her father think if he were here to see her, shaking with
nerves just because she was leaving the village? He would wonder if this was really his daughter after all.

"I know you said no," Jonas said. He was frowning. His
eyes met hers with concern, and something more: shared knowledge. "But it's a long way to the City, and the forest to cross before you get there. I know you're your father's daughter. But,
well . . ."

Timou said, "I don't think so," and did not say what she was
thinking, which was that nerves or no, it might indeed be hard
enough to guard herself on the way, never mind what she might
find at the end of her journey, and she would be foolish to put
herself in the position of having to watch after Jonas, too. Even
if she was silly enough to want to put herself in that position.

"I've been on the road once or twice. I can take care of myself," Jonas said, as if he had heard what she did not say. He
spoke as though choosing his words carefully. His tone was casual, but his eyebrows had drawn together a little. He wasn't annoyed or exasperated. He was worried.

"Jonas—" Timou said, "—I know you have. But I believe,
where I will be going, I will need to be able to think only about
one thing. If you are with me, I will also think about you."

His mouth relaxed with startlement, then crooked. "Well,
thank you."

Timou started to protest *I didn't mean it like that,* but then she closed her mouth again without saying anything.

"I don't like to think of you alone on this journey. Not after . . . well. You know."

She did. "Yes," Timou said. "But I need to think about—"

"Only one thing. Yes," said Jonas. "All right. And if you meet the Hunter on that road? Could you stand him off a second time?"

"I could never challenge the blind Hunter," Timou said seriously. She closed her hands together in her lap so that he would not see them trembling. "I didn't stand him off. He left us alone because he chose to. I don't know why. But I don't think he would stop me going to the City. Do you?"

Jonas frowned and moved a hand in an ambiguous gesture. "You had better come back, Timou. I don't think this village could take your disappearance, too. I wouldn't care for that very much myself."

"No," said Timou. "Yes. I will come back."

Jonas nodded and put the knapsack down on the floor, where Timou had been arranging things that she would take with her. "Then I'll see you later," he said—not *Goodbye.* "And I'll wish you luck in finding your . . . father." And he went out, closing the door carefully behind him.

Timou left the village quietly, without making any specific goodbyes of her own. She had been taking gradual leave of the whole village for weeks . . . for months, perhaps. It would have been hard to have people watching her walk away, so she did not call attention to her going.

She touched the stone at the edge of the village with her

fingertips as she passed it. The sun had not yet warmed it from the chill of the night. She looked for the prints of hooves before it where the Hunter's white mare had stood, but she saw nothing. Strangely, as she passed the stone, she found she left her nervousness behind; it was as though stepping past the marker was the one irrevocable step that let her commit herself to the road and the journey. She found she could look ahead now with a whole heart; that she could leave the village behind and simply trust it would still be there, unchanged, when she returned.

Autumn had come in quickly this year. Timou became aware of its beauty as she walked through country she had never seen before, so that she looked at everything with curiosity and attention. The road went through the woods for a long time. Many of the hickories were butter-yellow, and the occasional maple flame-orange. Crimson vines climbed trees, dangling from the branches like garlands.

Later the woods gave way to grasses, but the road went on under the suddenly widening sky. The road was broad and level, only a little rutted. There was a breeze in the daytime to cool the heat; the air was still at night, when it might otherwise have been chilly. It would have been a very pleasant journey, except that Timou always had in the back of her mind the knowledge that her father had gone this way and had not come back.

There were other villages and towns all through this country, but Timou knew that she was unlikely to pass any of them. From the moment she had set her foot on the road with the intention to go to the City, her journey had been her own.

And indeed, if there were other travelers, Timou encountered none of them. A hawk turning in lazy circles high overhead was company in the solitude. The crackle of a small fire at night was a reminder of the warmth of human company. Timou thought that if she met another traveler on the road, she might find she had forgotten how to speak to him. But she met no one.

And one afternoon, twelve days after she had left the village, she came over the top of a slight rise and found before her not the familiar vista of grass and sky, but the great forest.

CHAPTER 4

"Lord Neill," a servant said respectfully, holding a basin of water and kneeling by the Bastard's bedside. Pale early-morning light showed behind the fine curtains, which were of a creamy yellow, half a tone warmer than the light.

The servant's presence meant that the Bastard was expected to break his fast in the great hall with the King. And that meant that the morning would be difficult. The King's temper was uncertain—or rather, the King's temper had become all too certain. And the King's eldest son bore the brunt of it.

The Bastard did not permit himself to sigh. He sat up instead and set his feet on the cream-colored rug beside his bed. The air in the room was cool: the nights, though not yet cold, had lost the pressing warmth of midsummer. It was autumn, with winter to follow soon enough. But this year the coming winter held no promise of a burgeoning spring to follow.

The Bastard washed his face and hands with the water the man provided. The servant set the basin aside, proffered a warm towel, and went quietly to lay out appropriate clothing: black and violet, because the King, in his despair, expected all the court to dress in mourning colors. The clothing was simple, as austere as the Bastard could get away with in the court. Austerity suited him this morning. After dressing, he sat patiently in a chair while the servant braided his long ash-colored hair into its customary single braid. The servant did his work quietly, seldom glancing up, because the Bastard preferred quiet into the morning.

Properly attired and arranged, the Bastard had no reasonable excuse to linger in his room. He went into the corridor and turned toward the great hall. The morning light came in through high narrow windows.

The great hall was nearly on the other side of the palace. It had wide windows of its own, some of them set to bring in the morning sun and others set to catch the breeze that came off the Lake. It was a big room, brightened by tapestries in blue and gold and green. Lamps hooded with creamy parchment hung above the tables.

One long table took up a quarter of the hall: the King's own table. It had been made of a single great tree and had room for fifty places. At the moment only four places were laid. Only one was occupied, and it was not the King's place at the table's head. It was the Queen's, placed at the King's left hand. This was surprising. The King liked to be in his place first, so that he could watch others walk the whole length of the hall to come before his seat.

The Bastard walked the length of the hall. The captain of the guard was there, with half a dozen of his men, behind the Queen. This was also a surprise: normally the captain would have been attending upon the King, or else about duties elsewhere in the Palace. But this morning it seemed there would be nothing more important for him to do than watch the Queen at her breakfast. . . .

The Bastard looked at Ellis, the Queen. She sat quite still at her place, her hands resting quietly on the table, and watched him come. Servants hovered behind her. There were platters and bowls on the table already: bread with salted butter, fruit glazed with honey, little cakes made of ground walnuts and drizzled with syrup. The Queen looked at none of it. She looked only at the Bastard.

The Queen had been very beautiful when she had caught the King's eye, and very young. She was still beautiful, still far from old. If she had lost the rosy blush of youth, her skin remained very fine, and the delicate lines at the corners of her mouth and eyes only added character to her face. Her raven's-wing hair was hardly touched with silver. Her eyes, a remarkable shade of violet, picked up the lavenders and violets of her mourning dress, as though the Queen had been meant all her life to wear those grieving colors.

"Where is the King?" the Bastard asked her. He saw, now that he was close to her, that the Queen's stillness was not calm, but a brittle tight control overlying terrible tension. So he asked, out of mingled hope and dread, because he could imagine one reason above all that the King might be absent, "Has the Prince been found?" What he wanted to know, but did not ask aloud, was *Has the Prince been found, and is he dead?*

The Queen shut her eyes, which gave the Bastard a heartbeat to prepare himself before she opened them again and said, in a voice like a shout except it was quiet as a whisper, "What have you done with him?"

The Bastard gazed at her, wordless with surprise.

The Queen drew in her breath, rose to her feet, and, moving with sudden violence, seized the nearest plate of cakes and flung it at him. The Bastard barely got a hand up in time to deflect the plate. Syrup dripped down his shoulder and arm where a cake had struck him.

Servants scattered backward, and several of the guards twitched in startlement and dismay. But as there was no enemy for them to fight, they kept their places. Their captain stood a little straighter, but otherwise did not move.

"You killed him," said the Queen. Her voice was deathly, but she did not throw any more plates. She threw words instead, like knives. "You killed him and hid his body, as you did with my son! Murderer! Murderer! How dare you stand in the light of day?" She turned to the guard captain. "Arrest him!" she demanded. "Arrest him!"

The Bastard lowered his arm wordlessly. Syrup ran down his fingers. He, too, looked at the guard captain.

The captain met his eyes. None of his men had moved at the Queen's demands. They looked at their captain, and their captain looked only at the Bastard.

"The King is gone?" the Bastard asked, his voice quite calm.

"Yes, Lord Neill," said the captain. He was a meticulous man, but not without imagination. There was silvery grizzle shot through his pale-wheat hair, barely showing, but his eyes, light blue and holding all the chilly reserve of long experience, showed his age. He had served the King for thirty-six years and been captain of the guard for twenty-two. He knew everything that went on in the Palace and the City. He looked the Bastard in the face and spoke quietly. "He went to his rooms last night as always. His servants say he paced half the night. They were relieved to hear his steps cease. They thought he had gone to his bed at last, as perhaps he had. But he was not there this morning, though his bed had been slept in. No one went into that room past my men; no one came out."

"So it was not quite the same as with the Prince." The Prince had not vanished from a closed room. The Prince had merely gone out riding one fine spring morning and failed to return. Everyone had searched for him. There seemed nowhere, in this, to search for the King. "Have you sent for Trevennen, or Marcos?"

"No, my lord, not before your order."

"Then please do so. Direct the mages to go into the King's rooms and search there for any hint or echo or intimation that may suggest to them what happened there. Then have them attend upon me in the . . . in my father's study."

"Yes, Lord Neill. Yes, my lord."

The Bastard looked back at the Queen. She was silent. Her hands gripped the edge of the table. She looked at him bitterly and said nothing.

"You are distraught, madam," the Bastard stated, not unkindly. He said to the guard captain, "Have one of your men escort the Queen to her rooms, so that she may rest undisturbed."

"Yes, my lord," said the captain.

"Then come to me in my father's study. And," he added, a little drily, "have someone bring me a clean shirt."

The King had a surprisingly tidy mind, but he had organized his study according to some principle that escaped the Bastard. The King's servants clustered in a nervous knot on the far side of the suite while the Bastard went thoughtfully through the papers on his father's desk. Questioning had yielded nothing from the servants that he had not already known.

The captain, whose name was Galef, came into the King's study quietly, with a fresh shirt over his own arm. He met the Bastard's eyes with a wry expression.

The Bastard changed his shirt. He gave the soiled one to a waiting servant and washed his hands in a basin held by another servant. Then he dismissed all the servants with a jerk of his head. When they were gone, he seated himself in his father's chair and asked the guard captain, "How is the Queen?"

"She is furious. But she is not throwing plates. She is thinking instead. She is afraid of you," answered the captain directly. "Now she is also afraid of me."

The Bastard sighed, and leaned back in the chair. He asked after a moment, "And you? Are you afraid of me, Galef?"

"You rule now," said the captain without blinking. He had been a professional guardsman for too long to show anything in his face. "That is your right."

"And if I killed the King, as the Queen accuses, and hid his body? If I caused the disappearance of my brother, the Prince?"

"I have no evidence that leads to you, my lord."

Or I would act was clearly the unspoken message under that statement. "But," said the Bastard patiently, "do you think me guilty? In either case?"

The captain looked the Bastard in the face. He said after an infinitesimal pause, "If you arranged the disappearance of the King in order to gain power in the City, or simply peace in this house, I would understand. I might believe that of you, Lord Neill. There is no evidence of your hand in this, but you are a subtle man. But I do not think you acted against your brother, the Prince. I could believe that you are ambitious. I could believe that you have been jealous. I know you can be ruthless. But whoever stole the Prince stole the very heart of the Kingdom, and could hardly fail to know it after this past summer. I do not think you are so cruel a man as that—my lord. So I will serve you."

This was rather more direct than any answer the Bastard had looked to find offered to his face, from the captain or any man. It was clear to the Bastard that the captain had had that little speech waiting. He thought he understood: Galef wanted to set everything between them in order if he could, so that he might be free to serve—if not the Bastard, at least the Kingdom. The captain was not, himself, lacking in subtlety.

After a moment the Bastard let his mouth crook a little. He said in a level tone, "I will be glad to have your service. Where were your men last night, when the King disappeared from a room with only one door?"

The captain answered scrupulously, "My men were on guard

at that door, and they are good, responsible men. I oversaw them, and I questioned them. They are my men and I am sure of them." He hesitated a little. "Do you then doubt me? Or them?"

"I am sure we both doubt everyone," said the Bastard. "Why should you be excepted?"

The captain inclined his head with the sardonic air of a man well accustomed to the uncertainties of life. "I am loyal to the King. I swear you will have no cause to doubt my loyalty to you—if you did not yourself betray the trust of the Kingdom. As I think you did not. But if I find out such a truth, my lord, I will be your enemy. So," he added, "we know where we stand."

"I don't expect your trust," acknowledged the Bastard, not offended, "until my father is found. Or better, the Prince. Nevertheless, I do expect your loyalty. Don't move too quickly to make yourself my enemy, Galef. If you find yourself my enemy, I think you will find yourself overmatched."

The captain had to know this was true. He bowed his head a little.

"But it was not my hand. I did not act either against my father or against my brother. So we know where we stand." The Bastard touched a stack of his father's papers. "I'm glad you speak openly to me. I must hope you will bring anything you discover to me." He allowed only the slightest bite to his tone. "If the secret is here, I will find it, and I will share it with you. Some of these drawers are locked. Do you know where the keys are?"

"I know how to find them, my lord."

"Good. If you were going to steal a man from a closed and guarded room, Galef, how would you do it? Think on that, and come to me in my own rooms in three hours. Four." He looked at the clutter in his father's study and sighed. "Six. And find me the keys to this desk."

"Yes, my lord." The captain began to withdraw. "I will send a man of mine to assist you."

The Bastard looked up sharply. A small movement of his hand stopped the captain. He said plainly, as they had both been speaking plainly, "To assist me? You mean you will send a spy. If I tell you I will have no man of yours at my back in this room, what will you do?"

The guard captain answered after a moment, "What can I do, my lord, but hope that I may trust you?"

The Bastard inclined his head. "Indeed. So we must all hope that we may trust one another. And yet someone acts against us all. You may send a man of yours to me. So long as we are clear between ourselves, Galef, I shall be satisfied." He smiled, a smile that did not touch his eyes. "Tell your man to bring me something to eat, since I did not have breakfast."

It took the Bastard five days to go through all the King's papers, including the ones locked away in his desk. Some of those were interesting. None of them shed light on the King's disappearance, or that of the Prince.

The mage Trevennen came at the beginning, a distinguished and assured man of fifty, and an experienced and exceedingly subtle mage. He looked carefully at the King's rooms. "He was here, and then he was gone," said the mage, which the Bastard already knew. "It's hard to say how he went. Or where he might have gone. Hmmm."

This was not very useful. Nothing the mages had done in all this long year had been useful. The Bastard restrained himself, with difficulty, from saying so.

The Queen, on the Bastard's orders, kept to her rooms. She saw no one, also on his orders, except her women. He had made no effort to order the women to keep silent, knowing he might as well command the stars not to sparkle at night. There was considerable sentiment in the Palace favoring the Queen. Many in the Palace and the City agreed with Ellis that the Bastard had in some mysterious manner disposed of both his half brother and his father in order to seize power.

If he had, it had worked. Whatever whispers ran like mice along the walls, the Bastard ruled the Palace and the City. Half the courtiers were his men . . . no one quite knew which half. The young men who had followed his brother did not meet his eyes. They said *Lord Neill* when they spoke to him and *Lord Bastard* when they spoke to one another, and they walked warily around him. The guard was his, through the guard captain. The Bastard did not touch the circlet of interlocking golden leaves worn only by the King, nor sit in his chair in the great hall. But he gathered power into his hands and held it firmly.

But though he held power, he did not hold life. The heart of the City and of the Kingdom was still missing. That, the Bastard could not restore. He could not find whatever way had led the

Prince out of the Palace and the Kingdom. He could not find the way that had opened to take away the King.

On the sixth day, he went to see the Queen.

"Ellis," he said, since they were alone. Even the Queen's women had withdrawn into an adjoining room—with relief, because they did not know whether the Queen would shout and throw things, or if she did, at whom. And also because they were afraid of the Bastard, who was too quiet and too contained and whom the Queen did not trust.

The Queen looked at him steadily. She was clad in black and lavender, and wore a silver circlet set with amethysts in her black hair; the stones were almost exactly the color of her eyes. She occupied her heavy chair as though it were a throne.

The Bastard drew a lighter chair around and sat down in it, facing the Queen. He said, "Tell me of the King's last night. He visited you in these chambers, but did not stay. He went to his own rooms and vanished from there, after pacing half the night. But did he speak to you that evening? Of what did he speak?"

The Queen had raised her fine narrow brows in an expression of astonishment. "What is this pretense, Neill? No one is here but me."

"If you believe I am pretending, then humor my pretense," suggested the Bastard patiently.

The Queen studied him. The assumed astonishment had fallen from her face like a mask, leaving behind an expression harder and colder and more difficult to read.

"Deny it," she said. "Deny it to me."

The Bastard, meeting her eyes, said directly, "Ellis, you have
been mistaken. I do not censure you for thinking of me. But my
hand is nowhere in this. I am in no way responsible for the disappearance of your son. I am in no way accountable for the
disappearance of the King."

"You hated him."

The Bastard moved a hand slowly over the polished arm of
the chair, which was carved in the likeness of a swan in flight.
He traced the feathers of its wing, frowning, before he looked up
at last to meet the hard stare of the Queen. He said slowly, "Ellis,
you are mistaken again."

"I am not mistaken! He never cared for you: he loved my son
and not you, and you hated him—hated them both—and now
they are both gone and you have everything—"

"Ellis," the Bastard said. His quiet voice brought her to a halt.
He said, still quietly, "I did not hate my father. Or Cassiel. I
never knew until now that you hated me. It seems to me that
the only one who hates in this family, Ellis, is you."

The Queen did not answer. She stared at him, her eyes wide
and a little shocked.

"I am not now, nor have I ever been, your enemy. You are
unjust." The Bastard rose and took a step toward her, leaning
forward earnestly. "If it was not I, Ellis? What then?"

For a moment there was doubt in the Queen's wide violet
eyes. She was shaking, the Bastard saw. Then she moved, gripping the arms of her chair as though to rise, or as though to hold

herself back from rising. She said, furiously but not loudly, "I am not unjust. I am not wrong. Get out. Get out. How dare you come here and lie to me about your innocence?"

The Bastard straightened. He said with amazement, "You blame yourself. You rail against me to defend yourself. Ellis, what have you done?"

The Queen picked up a heavy silver pitcher on a low table nearby and threw it with considerable force at the Bastard, who fended it off with a raised hand and backed away as water arced across the room. "Get out!" she shouted at him. "Get out!"—and left him to retreat in the most undignified manner imaginable, because he could not raise a hand against her.

"How can the Queen be guilty?" he asked the guard captain later, still consumed by that sense of astonishment. "How can the *Queen* be guilty?"

The guard captain, leaning against the back of a heavy chair because he would not sit in the Bastard's presence, frowned. The mage Marcos settled comfortably in the depths of a huge soft-cushioned chair, answered instead. "I doubt she is guilty in quite that sense, Neill."

They were all gathered in the Bastard's personal apartments. The shutters of the sitting room were open, the late autumn sun lending the room a warmth and comfort that was at odds with the general mood, which was dark and rather grim.

Both the Bastard and the captain looked at Marcos. "How, then?" the captain asked.

The mage said obliquely, "A woman—or a man, for that matter—can feel guilt when no other would think to lay it at her feet."

"What?" said the captain blankly.

"Oh, come, Galef. Suppose you went to some man's house somewhere in the City, anyone's house, and knocked on his door, and told him when he opened it, *I know what you did.* What would he think, this man, a man, we shall say, who has done nothing in particular to warrant your attention? How would he feel?"

"He would feel guilty," acknowledged the captain. He looked thoughtful. "Hmmm."

"I did not think to accuse the Queen until I saw that she accused herself," argued the Bastard.

"Yes, and when you saw in her face that she accused herself, Neill, you with your discerning eyes, you frightened her. But I doubt that she accuses herself of direct guilt. No. Her son went out riding, and did not return. If she had kept him closer, would he not be safe? Her husband left her sitting alone in her private rooms and went to his, and vanished. Is she not at fault? If she had only loved them more, held them more tightly—"

The Bastard moved a hand. "Enough."

"You see," said Marcos comfortably.

"I see it could be true."

"When the Prince is found, she will forgive herself, and thus you."

"*If* he is found." The Bastard shifted restlessly in his chair. "Where is he?"

"I have looked into the eyes of every falcon and every wolf

and every stag from here to the very edges of the Kingdom," the mage said drily, "but I have never yet found the Prince looking back at me. Trevennen has looked through every mirror and every window and every fall of light, from the first gray glimmer of dawn to the last soft moments of dusk, but he has found nothing. Russe has looked—"

"I know all this."

"—through every dream and slow reverie of the great trees of the forest, and the little flickering half-felt dreams of the young trees of the hills, and she has found nothing."

"He is outside the Kingdom," Galef said abruptly.

Marcos looked at him in surprise. "Oh, I hardly think that is likely."

"If the Prince were within the Kingdom," said the captain doggedly, "then the heart of the Kingdom would not be lost. We would only not know where it was. *He* was. Is. If he were dead, the Kingdom would grieve, but it would recover and go on and find some other heart. So the Prince is not dead, but he is not within the Kingdom."

The mage steepled his thick fingers and regarded the captain over them, narrow-eyed. "Hmm."

The Bastard smiled slowly, and Marcos threw up his hands. "Well, all right, then. It's possible. The reasoning is sound."

"The City in the Lake," the Bastard suggested.

"No. The City in the Lake . . . is in some ways the heart of the Kingdom itself. If the Prince were there, he would not be lost, as Galef so cogently put it. Even if no one knew he was there."

"Then where?"

"I don't quite know," Marcos answered, and frowned. "It should not be possible to take the heart of the Kingdom out of the Kingdom."

The Bastard, regarding him, said nothing, but forcefully.

"I know," said the mage. "What *has* occurred is able to occur."

"What will you do now?" the Bastard asked.

"What would you have me do that I have not already done?"

"Talk to Ellis."

Marcos winced. "Have Trevennen talk to her. She doesn't care for me. You know that."

"Trevennen, then. You . . ." The Bastard paused, and finished gently, "Look somewhere you haven't looked before. Somewhere both within the Kingdom and outside it. Somewhere outside the fall of light and the dream of trees. Find such a place and look there for the Prince."

"All right," said the mage glumly.

"And I?" asked Galef.

"You . . . listen to the City, and tell me what you hear. Every dream and every thought and every word spoken, whether in public or in confidence . . . Will you?"

The guard captain, who had stood at the Bastard's back through the last few days and watched him gather into his hands all his father's power, said noncommittally, "I will listen. And you?"

"I will think," said the Bastard. "And wait for the pattern, whatever it may be, to reveal itself to me." He glanced at Marcos sidelong. "Is that not what the mages say?"

CHAPTER 5

T he forest was enchanted, of course. All great forests are, in one way or another. But this forest was special. Despite the season, there were no hints of autumn in its deep green. The shadows the ancient trees cast were darker and more secretive than ordinary shadows under ordinary trees. This forest had depths no one had ever seen, mysteries no mage had ever encompassed. To pass through it safely, a traveler must keep to the road. Even then the journey through the forest's dim reaches might take days or weeks, or even sometimes months, for the forest was not always the same size.

The road passed into the forest between two great trees that stood to either side of the road like gateposts. They were so large that it would have taken half a dozen men to wrap their arms about the trunk of either one; they had heavy knurled trunks and broad branches and dark green leaves that were silver underneath. They looked a thousand years old, and might have been older.

Timou made her evening fire by the side of the road just outside the entrance to the forest. She boiled water for tea and put sausages over the fire to cook. Then she sat cross-legged by the small homey light of her fire with her hands folded on her plain traveling skirt and gazed at the dim shade of the great forest. After a while she began to feel that there might be eyes looking back at her, although she saw nothing, even when she cleared her mind and let her own eyes go wide and dreaming.

Later, as the sun set, she sat on her folded blanket, sipping her tea and thinking of nothing in particular. When it seemed to her the right time to do so, she gathered a palmful of dust from the road and mixed it with a little water, forming it into a ball. This she set by the fire and left to harden. Then, taking her small mirror out of her pack, she angled it to catch the last molten rays of the sun and murmured over it the words of a charm so that it would remember light.

At last, spreading out her blanket, she lay down upon it and listened to the sounds the wind made: one sound as it whispered through the grasses in the open; another, more secretive, as it slipped through the leaves of the forest. It would be easy to hear voices in that sound: slow murmuring voices that spoke end-lessly of dim green places that never felt the sun. Timou finally fell asleep still listening to the voices of the wind.

In the morning, after a breakfast of bread and cheese and more tea, Timou carefully smothered her fire with a thought and slung her knapsack over her shoulder. Then, at last, she walked into the shade.

The road narrowed at once to a mere path. There would not have been room on it for a cart. Great roots crossed and re-crossed the path and great rocks lay tumbled and half buried everywhere among the roots, which made for uncomfortable footing. Timou wondered how wheeled traffic got through this forest. Perhaps if one came with carts or wagons, the road one found was wider and smoother? She thought she would some-day find a carter who came this way and ask.

At the moment she had enough to do to keep her eyes on her own path. Even the light was chancy, for the branches wove together far overhead and no sunlight reached down to dapple the surface of the path. There was always the feeling that there might be something—the tumbled ruin of a forgotten castle or a long graceful dragon coiled around a towering tree—hidden less than a stone's throw away, and one might walk past and never see it.

Timou found she loved it; loved the secretive shadows, the feeling of mysterious unbounded potential. There were surely strange dangers hidden in this forest, and yet she wanted to leave the path and weave her own way among the great trees. She lost her fears and her questions in the green shadows; she was cap-tivated by the language the wind seemed to speak as it passed through the leaves in the deep heart of the forest. She wanted to wander forever through the magic the forest held. It might be perilous, but she knew it would also be beautiful beyond mea-sure. Half a dozen times she paused, her hand caressing some great mossy bole, gazing into the green depths and wondering if perhaps she might go only a little way off the path. It took all the calm discipline she had learned from her father not to yield to this desire. She wished her father had brought her here him-self. She wished there were no need for haste, no urgency, no duty to compel her onward.

Timou had stepped into the green twilight of the forest at dawn, but without the sun to watch in its travel across the sky it was hard to know how long she had walked. She went quickly and eagerly, curious to see around every curve, to peer down every slope. She did not pause for more than a moment to drink from a stream that poured itself out of the forest on one side of the path and disappeared into the forest again on the other. The water tasted of earth and green shade, but it did not try to change Timou into a stone or a shower of light when she drank it. She almost regretted that it didn't; she would have liked to explore the spells of this forest.

When she became hungry, she took more of the hard bread out of her pack and ate it, walking. Perhaps it was noon, but the quality of light under the trees had not changed enough to judge. A wind she could not feel rustled the leaves so that she felt more strongly than ever that they spoke a language she might almost understand. There was no sign that any other traveler had ever walked this road; there was no hint that any ever would. It was as though Timou were the only traveler ever to step under the arch of the trees or dare the path through the forest. The only sound was the sigh of the leaves: there were no birds calling in the green heights, no squirrels, no deer that Timou saw. Not even midges humming in the shadows.

Quite abruptly, around a sharp turn, the path opened out into an unexpected glade in the forest. Ahead, light made its way through the forest canopy, as from a foreign country. The light lay warmly in the air, golden and heavy. There was a surprising glint of blue in that direction. Timou went forward readily, wondering what this could be.

The glade turned out to be smaller than Timou had thought: no farther across than she might have thrown a stone. It was carpeted with thick tufted grasses and blue star-shaped flowers that nodded on slender stems. The flowers echoed the blue of the sky, a blue tending toward soft dove-gray as the day was tending toward evening. Timou had not guessed it was so late.

There was a pool of water, small enough that Timou could nearly have leapt across it, in the center of the little meadow. The air was still, so quiet that the water was as flat and level as a sheet of glass. It cast back clear reflections of the sky overhead and of Timou's own face when she leaned over it. She met her reflection's eyes in its mirror, and it seemed to her for an instant that the reflection looked back at her with eyes that were not pale blue, but black as a moonless night.

Behind her, there was the sound of a soft step.

Timou turned quickly. Not ten steps away, a doe regarded her without apparent fear. It came another step closer, delicate and alert, huge ears turning to listen to sounds from the forest that Timou could not hear. It was the color of cream, of ivory— just a shade warmer than true white. Its eyes were blue. It walked past Timou, so closely she might have reached out a hand to touch it, and lowered its head to the pool to drink.

Then it flung its head up with every appearance of violent alarm and leapt away, disappearing into the forest with a thud of hooves and a swish of disturbed leaves.

Timou stared after it, troubled. She knew that the deer that had walked past her had had blue eyes. But she was almost certain that the deer that had leapt away from the pool had had eyes that were black.

In the pool rings spread slowly outward from where the deer had dipped its muzzle to the water. Timou backed away from the water. "What are you telling me?" she whispered, asking the forest. The forest seemed to listen, but it gave back no answer.

Timou had thought, coming into this meadow, that she might rest for the night under the open sky. But she found now that for the first time since entering the forest she was uneasy. The great trees crowding on either side of the path had seemed somehow companionable. But now the trees pressing close against the edges of this glade seemed strangely threatening. She did not after all want to linger in the late sun among the blue flowers. She walked across the meadow to its opposite side, where the path flowed once more between towering trees; she went into their shadows as though fleeing from a threatening storm into shelter.

She walked slowly after that, not thinking so much as waiting for thoughts to swim to the surface of her mind. She no longer knew whether she loved the forest or whether she was afraid of it—of what it might tell her, or show her. Perhaps both. When it was at last too dark to walk farther, Timou found a smooth place for her blanket and made a tiny fire so that she could have hot tea. She took her blanket out of the knapsack Jonas had given her and wrapped it slowly around herself, thinking of him for the first time since she had walked past the village marker and into solitude.

She had not missed him before; she had not missed anyone. But she wanted human company tonight, familiar voices to cushion her against the strangeness and silence of the great forest. She tried to remember why she'd refused Jonas's company; hadn't her reasons seemed good? Yes: she'd thought he would distract her, and she'd been afraid that there might be unseen, unknowable peril for a man lacking the training of a mage. At the moment neither reason seemed compelling. She felt now that she might be just as happy if she were never alone again, and that she would be glad of any distraction Jonas might have brought with him.

She missed her father, suddenly and intensely—more than she missed Jonas, more than she missed anyone. Kapoen would not be afraid or surprised by anything the forest had put in her way. He would understand everything. She imagined him sitting across from her, head bowed, firelight throwing shadows across his face. He would say something to her, something brief and wise that would make sense of the pool and the white deer and take away the lingering chill both had left with her.

But he was not with her. He had left her. He'd walked away without explaining anything. Timou blinked into the fire, holding back surprising tears that prickled suddenly at the backs of her eyes. Her father had not wanted her with him; he had left her behind—no doubt for very good reasons. Although, Timou thought now, a little more fiercely than was really comfortable, he might have explained to her what those *were*.

In flight from her own thoughts, Timou curled into her blanket, leaned her back against the great bole of a tree, and let her mind slip through its deep quiet existence until she could forget that she was small and human, and dream with the tree its slow circular dreams.

The morning came slowly in the forest, filtering past layer upon layer of green leaves. Timou's mouth felt dry and sticky. She was stiff from lying on the ground, and still half lost within the green memories of the tree. But she was much happier. She wanted tea, and she ardently desired a bath with hot water and soap, but the morning brought with it a welcome renewal of courage and curiosity. The desolation of the previous night seemed strange in the green light of the morning, like a feeling that had belonged to someone else, some other traveler lost in the forest, perhaps. Though she would still have welcomed company—though she still more than half wished she had let Jonas come with her—she could look forward again to continuing on her journey and seeing what it held. She laid a hand on the trunk of the tree that had dreamed with her, grateful for its solidity and calm.

She made tea, ate a mouthful of hard bread, and walked on into the forest.

That day was much like the one just past, except there was no clearing in the trees. Only silence and a wind that moved branches high above, and the continual feeling that strange and beautiful things lay just out of sight among the trees. Yet, though she saw no more deer, dappled or white, the strong urge to leave the path and walk away into the trees had gone. She kept willingly to the path, and although she still looked out into the depths of the forest, she was almost glad when she saw nothing there but more forest.

After that all the days seemed to blur into one, and all the nights the same. Solitude began to seem, not welcome as it had been at first, but at least natural. People did not belong in this forest; human voices would have echoed strangely among these ancient trees. Timou almost began to believe she would always be walking through this forest: that there was no farther side to the trees, and that this solitary journey was the natural condition of her life. Of a mage's life. There were echoes in this forest, she thought, of the stillness her father had taught her. Then she realized that, no, the silence her father had taught her was the echo; this great silence was surely its source. *The heart of magecraft is stillness.* Yes, she thought. *This* stillness. She understood that now in a way she had not in the village. She began again to be glad to be alone.

Once in those days Timou thought she glimpsed a ruined tower. She did not leave the path, though she was curious whether she might find a dragon coiled about the base of the tower if she went to look. Once, at twilight, she was certain she heard the music of a harp somewhere very close to where she lay gazing into the glimmering coals of her little fire. The music was sad, desolate. It drew her: she wanted to rise and go to the musician; lay down her heart to salve the sorrow she heard. She sat up and wrapped her arms around her knees and listened for a

long time to the harp, until finally it ceased. She dreamed that
night of leaves moving without wind and an endless harping that
wove through the rustle they made.

The next day, she found herself walking without paying
much attention to the path, listening to the green silence that
surrounded her. From time to time she thought she caught an
echo of slow thought, ponderous memory, speech in the sound
of leaves moving in the wind. . . . If she had not been listening
to the trees, perhaps she would not have been so surprised when
a voice spoke to her suddenly in human language.

"You look a fine, strong, young person," said the voice, husky
and sweet as clover honey. "Surely you will help me?"

Timou jerked around so quickly in her astonishment that she
caught her foot on a twisting tree root and fell abruptly to her
knees, gasping.

"Or perhaps not . . . ," said the voice doubtfully.

It was not a man speaking, nor a woman. It was a serpent,
coiled about the branch of a tree a little above the level of
Timou's head. It was jet-black above, with an intricate pattern of
gold worked into the scales of its throat and belly. Its head was
tapered and graceful, its eyes golden, slit-pupiled like the eyes of
a cat, utterly unreadable. Its tongue, when it spoke, was long and
black. Its delicate fangs were as long as Timou's thumb.

Timou got to her feet, rubbing her knee where it had struck
a rock. She knew, of course, that the serpent was a creature of
the forest. But she did not know what this creature intended, or
whether it was well- or ill-disposed to travelers. She said cautiously, "If I can, I might."

The serpent seemed to smile. Its black scales gleamed even in the dimness; its white fangs seemed almost to glow. It said, "There has been rain far away. A stream has risen and threatens my eggs. As I have no hands, I cannot move them. But you could move them for me, if you were kind."

Timou considered this. "Where are your eggs?"

The snake pointed with its long narrow head back into the forest. "That way. Not far."

But, obviously, off the path. Timou hesitated.

"If you do not help me, they will be ruined by the water," said the serpent piteously.

"But to help you, I must leave the road, and then I will be lost in the forest."

"I will guide you back to the road."

"Will you?" Timou dusted leaf mold off her knees—at least, as her traveling skirt was charmed against dirt, it did not stain— and swung her knapsack more comfortably over her shoulder. Then she looked back at the serpent, meeting its unhuman golden eyes.

"If you help me now, I will guide you when you most need guidance," promised the serpent.

This was not the sort of promise one disregarded. Timou smiled politely. "Then of course I will help you."

The creature flowed down out of the tree. It was larger than Timou had suspected: six feet, perhaps as long as eight feet, but slender and graceful. It led Timou into the forest with quick assurance, clearly knowing exactly where it was going. Timou could well believe it knew its way about the forest and never got lost. It moved quickly—as quickly as she could walk—gliding smoothly along the ground, slipping delicately around rocks and roots that presented a hazard to Timou's feet.

Not far, the serpent had said. Timou did not know what a serpent would consider far, but it seemed long enough before she heard the sound of a running brook. So there really was a brook, and indeed, when Timou paused on its bank, steep and thickly overhung with ferns, she could see it had been rising. The serpent wove its way up a tree near at hand and wrapped itself around a low branch a little higher than Timou's head. It turned its head from side to side, regarding the water anxiously.

"Where are your eggs?" asked Timou.

"In a hollow place in the bank," answered the snake swiftly. "Where that root twists out of the bank, just above the water—do you see?—there is a hollow above and behind that root. My eggs are there."

Timou could see the place the snake described. She could also see that to get to that place, she was going to have to step into the water. She sighed. She removed her boots and put her knapsack down beside them. She drew a circle in the soft soil around her things and whispered a word her father had taught her so they would not disappear and could not be stolen. Then she tucked her slit traveling skirt up through her belt, caught a handful of ferns to steady herself, and stepped gingerly into the stream.

The water was knee-high and cold—shockingly so. Timou set her teeth and waded cautiously along the bank, feeling sand and pebbles shift under her feet. The snake tilted its head to the side and watched intently. When she reached the protecting root, Timou peered into the dark hollow behind it. She could see nothing. Taking her little mirror out of her pocket, she angled it to throw light into the shadows. By that light she saw the eggs, just as the snake had described. They were small oval things, creamy white in the light the mirror cast. Nothing else was there. She thought she would be able to hold perhaps three of the eggs in her hand at one time.

The front of Timou's skirt already made a pouch. She made sure this was secure. Then she gathered the eggs into her skirt, using her right hand to pick them up and her left to hold the mirror. The eggs were cool, and soft to the touch, not like the eggs of a hen.

"Carefully!" said the snake. "Don't let them fall into the water!"

"I will be careful," Timou assured it. When she had all the eggs tucked into her skirt, she waded slowly back along the stream to the place she had entered the water, and paused. It was clearly going to be difficult to scramble out of the stream without risking her burden. Finally she turned, leaned against the bank, and hitched herself awkwardly back and up, like she was trying to jump up and sit on the top rail of a fence. It was not easy and for a moment she thought she would slide down and find herself sitting in the stream, but then she was far enough up to grab a solid rock ledge and heave herself the rest of the way to the bank.

She turned to the snake. "Where shall I put them?"

"Anywhere," said the serpent. "It does not matter. At the base of this tree, if you like." It uncoiled half its body and hung down from the branch as Timou made a little hollow in the leaves and soil and placed the eggs into it.

"Thank you," said the serpent. It lifted its graceful narrow head so that its eyes were level with Timou's. Then it opened its mouth, and opened it, wider and wider. Its fangs gleamed. The fine scales of its stretching throat flashed gold.

Timou stepped back, and back again, warily. The creature laughed and dipped its head, no longer narrow, but two hand-widths wide, at least. Catching up one of the eggs, it swallowed it whole. Timou, horrified, watched the smooth oval of the egg pass down its distending throat. "What are you doing?" she whispered.

The serpent looked up and met her eyes. It was no longer black, but white as frost. Its eyes were black. "They're best near hatching," it said in its sweet husky voice.

"Are they not yours?" Timou asked it, and found her voice was shaking.

"Oh, yes," said the serpent. "Only my own are worth con-suming." It swallowed another egg and added, a little indistinctly, "Would you like one?" In its sweet voice was a thread of amuse-ment and malice.

Timou put her boots back on with hands that trembled, picked up the knapsack, and walked away blindly.

"Wait!" called the snake behind her, the malice clearer still in its voice. "Wait only a little while, and I will guide you back to the road, as I promised!"

Timou did not wait. She was lost almost at once; enormous

trees rose all around her, the same in every direction. She went on thoughtlessly, in no particular direction, for a long time.

The forest's silence eventually brought her calm. Timou stopped at last and sat down at the base of a tree, where it spread its knobby roots out across a rocky ledge. Her breathing slowed. Green shade spread out around her. It was very quiet. Not even the leaves spoke in their continual breeze.

Timou found in her pocket the little ball of road dust she had made and kept with her. This she now warmed in her palm. She whispered to it, reminding it that it was part of the road, that it remembered the road, that it *was* the road, the one road that ran straight and clear from the farthest reaches of the Kingdom all the way to the shores of the Lake. Then she cast the little ball into the shadows, rose to her feet, and stepped after it. She found the path before her. Her foot was on it already. It wandered up a gentle hill to her left and spilled down a starker slope to her right, with trees crowding close on each side, but it was indisputably the right road. It felt right. It almost felt safe.

Timou made her fire high and bright that night, and even so did not fall asleep for a long time. She watched the shadows under the trees for the swaying head of a serpent with a sweet voice. When she might have slept, she thought she heard a voice crooning, *Only my own are worth consuming,* and woke again with a start. Only at dawn, with the light coming green and pearly through the trees, did she finally slip into a light doze.

She dreamed at once. She dreamed she was lost in the forest, and there was no road to guide her. She searched for it but could not find it; she realized she was searching, with mounting anxiety, for something else, but she did not know what it was and could not find that either. Light fell in sheer planes through the trees, which rose in smooth black columns around her and cast shadows that were chasms into darkness. A doe ran by, white as frost, pursued by a stag black as night, crowned with great antlers that brushed stars out of the sky; falling, the stars cried out in high sweet voices. The stag looked at her with the cold yellow eyes of an owl and leapt away.

Timou, trembling, backed away and ran, knowing that she must find . . . she must find . . . She did not know what she needed to find, but she knew it was important . . . but she could not *remember*, and there was no way out. . . .

Before her a black serpent reared up out of a shadow. It offered her an egg and said in a voice like smoke and honey, *Eat this and you will be able to find your way through any maze.*

No, said Timou, horrified.

Then I will, said the serpent, and, opening its mouth, lowered its head toward the egg.

No! cried Timou, and took the egg into her hands. It was much heavier than it looked, heavy as a stone. She could feel the life in it through its soft-walled shell. *When will it hatch?* she asked the serpent.

Very soon.

Even as the serpent spoke, the shell tore open and a tiny snake thrust out through the opening, twisting about so violently that Timou nearly dropped it and only just caught it back again, heart pounding. It was as long as her forearm, but not so big

around as her smallest finger; it was white, with an intricate fil-
igree of blue tracing down its throat; it looked at Timou with
pale blue cat-pupiled eyes. Then, coiling itself around her fingers,
it struck quickly, driving tiny delicate fangs deeply into the base
of her thumb.

The pain was immediate and intense. It woke Timou, who
sat up with a cry by the embers of her dying fire.

There was no black serpent, no tiny white baby snake. The
forest, though immense as always, was held back by the bound-
aries of the path: she was not lost, not searching through the forest for something whose name she could not remember . . . there
were no pinpricks of blood on her thumb where a baby snake
had struck her. But she thought there might be a faint ache echoing all the way up her arm to her elbow. . . . She rubbed her arm
slowly, wondering what besides the residue of dreams she might
carry out of this forest. Her initial delight in the forest seemed
inexplicable to her. She felt now she could not be out of it
quickly enough. Rising, she cast soil over the remnants of her fire
and turned her face again toward the end of this journey.

And it did end. Timou came out of the great forest at last on
the evening of that same day, having walked without rest until
the light had very nearly failed. She stopped now, with immense
trees at her back, and looked out on country that had nothing to
do with ancient forests and strange enchantments. The air at her
face seemed much colder than the green-infused air that breathed
out from the forest at her back, and she thought perhaps she had
left autumn behind in the village and walked through the forest

into winter, though the forest itself still lingered in a warm slow summer.

Gentle hills with copses of ordinary little trees stretched out before her; snow dusted the grasses. The sky seemed to stretch out forever. It was gray and heavy with the promise of more snow to come, but still held enough light that Timou could see how the road widened and turned off in a broad sweep to run into the distance. There was a village visible where the road turned, comfortable little houses with a gentle haze of wood smoke rising from their chimneys. It was almost a surprise to know that the Kingdom was inhabited by more than haunts and shadows and the folk Timou had left behind on the other side of the great forest. She went forward slowly, glad to leave the forest behind, and yet in the end finding herself somehow reluctant to pass again wholly into the human realm.

Timou walked past fields that held tall sheaves of gathered hay, past a pasture that held a dozen heavy-bodied cows the color of new butter. One lifted its head to look at her incuriously. Above her, the first stars came out into the sky.

This village was larger than Timou's home; almost a town. There were dozens of neat little houses, of wood or a pale gray stone. Folk were inside, mostly, by this hour, although one man strode by on the other side of the road. Timou smiled at him and began to ask where she might find the village inn, but he only gave her an unfriendly stare when she spoke to him and did not even slow his step. She turned away, startled and a little dismayed by his rudeness.

The inn turned out to be at the northeast edge of the village square; it was fortunately not difficult to find. It was a large stone building, with its door set firmly open to show that anyone was welcome. The warmth and light spilling profligately out from within brought an unexpected lump to Timou's throat. She went slowly across the square and, after only the briefest hesitation, into the light.

Conversation quieted. The inn was crowded with folk at their dinners, but they were, Timou supposed, all people from this village, and so of course a stranger was interesting. She did not know what they saw. She felt weary to her bones and wished they would all go back to their own talk so she could be private in the spaces between their words.

The innkeeper came up while she stood there, before anyone could lose interest. After a swift summing look, he said kindly, "You'll be wanting dinner, then? A private room for the night? We've several free."

"Yes," Timou said faintly, relieved that he was kind. "Please."

The innkeeper guided her to a small table, occupied at the moment only by a pair of motherly older women. "We have duck tonight, brought in fresh this morning, and pigeon pie, and beef stew with parsnips."

Timou, feeling that she could do with all of that, hesitated.

"The duck is good," one of the women put in unexpectedly. Her face was broad and kindly; hair the color of wheat was bound firmly at the back of her head, but escaped wisps riffled out of the knot. Her wrists were thick, her hands broad; she looked strong, like a woman who had spent a competent lifetime lifting bales of hay or thumping bread dough down on a board. Empty bowls and plates in front of her and her friend testified to their enthusiasm for the food. "With plums and walnuts, my dear. Not but that all the food is good here. Tinnis has a fair hand with meat and pastry, but she's best with game."

The other woman did not speak at once, but leaned back in her chair, laced her fingers across her stomach, and smiled in a friendly way. There was a similarity in the women's bones and the shape of their hands, and in the way they moved; Timou thought they might be sisters.

"The duck, then," she decided.

"Surely, surely," agreed the innkeeper. "It comes with bread and sugared squash."

"Thank you."

The innkeeper lingered. "Out of the forest, are you, then?"

Timou looked at him in surprise. "How could you tell?"

"You have the look of it in your eyes," said the innkeeper, and bustled away to bring her food.

"Sort of green and shadowy," commented the woman. "On your way to the City, then, ah?"

"Yes," answered Timou, a little uncertainly. She had all but forgotten the City while walking through the forest. And she doubted suddenly whether she would find her father there; perhaps he had gone somewhere else. Again, more intensely even than during that lonely night in the forest, she wished she had let Jonas come with her: he would know how to speak to strangers, even to the people of the City. She felt obscurely that her present doubts would not have seemed so smothering if she only had familiar company to sit beside her instead of these strangers, no matter how friendly they might be.

Her stomach growled, unmindful of her doubts. The woman said cheerfully, "Oh, sit, sit, and tell us where you are from, my dear. It's a hard journey you've had—though that's always a hard journey, so they say."

Timou put her knapsack on the floor by her feet and sat down, sighing. "How far is the City from here?" she asked after a moment.

"Oh, four or five days, mostly, if you're on foot," answered the woman, just as cheerfully as before. "Sometimes farther, occasionally nearer. You know how it is. Now, I'm Anith, and this is my cousin Ereth. I bake—better than the bread here, though Tinnis does well enough, I suppose. Ereth helps her husband with their farm."

Timou gave her own name in return. It seemed strange and not entirely comfortable to have to do so. To speak to women she had not known all her life, to be unknown, so that no one looked at her and thought, *Ah, Kapoen's daughter.*

"Did you come through the forest all by yourself, then?" asked Ereth. She leaned forward confidingly. "I went into the forest once, just a step in. I barely went out of sight of the edge, and I stayed on the road. But when I turned around to come back out, it still took almost till dark."

"It can be like that," agreed Timou, and turned gratefully to help the innkeeper unload his tray on the table. There was, besides the duck and mashed golden squash and soft dark bread, a fresh little berry tart, still bubbling around the edges.

"It'll still be hot for you when you're ready for it, and this way you're assured one," explained the innkeeper. "They go quick on a chilly night like this."

"Thank you," Timou said, warmed by the man's thoughtfulness. She tried the duck. It was excellent.

"I shouldn't care to go through the forest alone," Ereth said chattily. "Not all the way through. Did you stay on the road, then?"

Timou agreed that she had, mostly.

"I wouldn't go off it for a moment," Ereth said. "Weren't you frightened?"

"Not . . . really," Timou said slowly, thinking about it. "I liked it at first. Some of it at the end . . . I wasn't frightened, exactly, but it was . . . disturbing."

"I have no doubt," Anith replied sympathetically. She said to her cousin, slyly, "*You* wouldn't like it, I'm sure."

"No, I wouldn't," Ereth said comfortably. "Who knows what might happen? I have my heart's desire right here, ah, and no need to go haring off into the forest after it."

"I thought I might go, once. But, well, I never did." Anith lifted a mug of the cider the two women had plainly been lingering over and cocked her head at Timou. "And did you find *your* heart's desire, dear?"

Timou thought involuntarily of the serpent and tried not to flinch visibly. "I don't think that was what I was looking for."

"Ah, well, they say sometimes the forest will show you your heart when all you wanted was a handful of herbs for the soup. And they say sometimes you don't recognize your heart when the forest shows it to you." The woman sounded wistful, as though she would have liked to test these tales for herself. "Well," she added in a stronger, more matter-of-fact tone, "but I suppose I found my life was good enough right here. Until this spring."

"A grandchild?" Timou guessed.

"Should have been, should have been. Big and bonny, a boy it would have been, but, well, this spring . . ."

"I know. I'm sorry."

"Ah, so were we all, and so are we all," said Anith: "They say the Prince went riding in just an ordinary little wood, not this great uncanny forest we have here, mind, but something got him and he's lost."

"Do they say what took him?"

"Ah, that they don't, or at least everybody's got her own story about it, you know. King's men went through the country-side, even into the forest . . . mages searched in other ways."

"But no one found him," Timou finished softly.

Both women shook their heads. . . . There had apparently been a great frenzy of searching early, but this had tapered off as everyone lost hope. No one now, it seemed, really expected to find the lost Prince. At least not by searching.

Timou finished her food, said her farewells, and went up to the room the innkeeper showed her. There was a basin of warm water for a bath, not really adequate but far better than a cold stream in a forest. The bed had a good mattress and soft linen sheets. But even so, it took a long time for Timou to sleep. Her hand ached where the hatchling snake had bitten her. It did no good to look again at the unmarked skin and assure herself that the bite had only been a dream. She feared what she might dream, even now that she was out of the forest. But if she dreamed again that night, she did not know it.

In the morning Timou paid the innkeeper three pennies for the dinner and the room, and another for food to take with her on this last stage of her journey. A farmer gave her a seat on his wagon, refusing her offer of payment. "Though I'm not going all the way to the City, mind," he warned her. "Only to town and back again. But you're welcome to join me."

So all that day Timou watched the countryside draw slowly past at the pace of the farmer's pair of mules. It was not as fast as walking on her own legs would have been, but the wagon made a pleasant change. She let the farmer talk to her about the past year and all he had done and seen during it, for he was a garrulous man who welcomed a passenger who would ask the occasional question and otherwise listen to stories that had, Timou thought, probably been told and retold a hundred times.

There were many travelers on the road. There were pastures with cut hay standing in long stooks, and farms every mile or so, with cattle or goats or sheep. Barking dogs ran out into the road when they passed one farm or another, where the mules eyed them. The dogs stayed wisely out of reach of the mules' hooves. One woman offered fresh milk and a loaf of bread for three of the parsnips the farmer was carrying, and the farmer gave her four with a wink because she was pretty.

The farmer slept under his wagon, and, it seemed, expected Timou to join him. Nor was he as kindly as she had thought him when she refused; she finally overcame her shock enough to draw fire out of the bed of his wagon. After that he believed her refusal. Timou smothered the fire again at once, but he was angry along with his alarm, for all he did not quite dare curse at her.

After that she was glad enough to walk on down the road until she eventually found a bed in a pile of hay in a field near the road. She thought she might dream of serpents, but she dreamed instead of the farmer, angry and fearful and wanting to know why she had accepted a seat in his wagon, ah, if she hadn't wanted to pay for it? In its way this was just as disturbing, and she woke, cold and stiff, before dawn.

The town, when she finally reached it toward evening, was much bigger than the village had been. The streets were cobbled against mud, and many folk were abroad despite the lateness of the hour. They all moved purposefully, as though they knew precisely where they were going and for what. Timou looked at them with a new wariness, wondering which might hide unpleasant motives behind apparent kindness. None of them looked back at her with more than passing curiosity. Shops, some still open, offered a variety of goods for sale that startled the eye of a young woman who had never before found herself in a town: cloth and clothing; apothecary supplies and candles; glassware and porcelain; jars of jams and smoked meats.

Timou found an inn on the near side of the town. She hoped the farmer would not put up at this same inn, or that she would not see him if he did. She ate white-bean soup, which she was almost too tired to taste, and listened to the conversations of the men and women around her. The talk was mostly light and quick and animated. But underneath the lightness, Timou thought she could hear an undertone that was very different, of worry and grief that, for whatever reason, the folk here did not want to put into words.

She caught snatches, exchanges in low tones, not furtive so much as simply private, as though no one wanted to share their worries indiscriminately with the room . . . brief references to the missing Prince, and to the bastard—that would be the Prince's elder half brother—the bastard who ruled now—*The bastard who ruled now?* Timou leaned back in her chair and folded her hands in her lap, listening both to the half-heard conversations and to the undercurrents of the things that were not said. If it was the bastard elder son who ruled, where was the King?

The King, she gathered eventually, was, like the Prince, missing . . . missing for a few days now. Opinions seemed divided: He had gone somewhere, perhaps even out of the Kingdom entirely, to search for the Prince. He was not really missing, but had shut himself up in the highest tower of the Palace and would see no one. The bastard had done away with both the Prince and his father. No, Lord Bastard had grown weary of the intransigence of his father and shut him up in the highest tower, but he had never moved against his brother; why, the two of them were friends, everyone knew that. No, no; it was the Queen whom the Bastard—by now Timou could hear the capital letter, the way the word was used like a name or a title—it was the Queen whom the Bastard had shut up in a tower, and the King was truly gone. . . .

Timou went slowly up to the private room the inn offered, wishing she knew more of the people who moved like old tales through these guesses. More of what the King was like, of what the Bastard was like. . . . She felt provincial and ignorant, and very tired. Too tired to think.

The hot soup had been welcome; the bath the inn offered was even more so, with abundant soft soap that came in a copper bowl and water so hot one could hardly step into it. Timou washed her hair three times, then braided it back neatly to keep it out of her face. For an extra penny, the inn offered laundry services. No charm against dirt could compete with a really good laundry: Timou gladly paid her penny and fell asleep before her clothing was returned, finding it neatly folded on a shelf just inside the door in the morning.

And finally, late in the afternoon of the next day—Timou had purchased a place in a coach, which had hard seats and jounced worse than the farmer's wagon, but was much faster—she saw, for the first time, the City that rested at the heart of the Kingdom.

The City occupied, as she had known, an island that lay in the center of the Lake. Though she tried, Timou could not see the farther shore. All she could see was the City, gleaming golden cream in the late sun. A bridge carried the road forward over the Lake, dropping a pillar from time to time into the water for support. It looked improbably slender to span all the distance from this shore to the City.

Everyone leaned out the windows to look. "This is Tiger Bridge," one woman said to Timou wisely. "Best be across well before dusk."

"Oh?"

"They say the tigers come to life at night," the woman explained.

"Oh." Timou remembered that story. She asked curiously, "Do they?"

"Probably," said a dark young man with unexpectedly pale hazel eyes. He smiled at Timou, rather experimentally, but she thought of the farmer and did not smile back. His tone grew more uncertain, but he went on, "In the City, many stories are true. But I believe myself that the tigers walk only in the other City."

"You mean the City in the Lake?"

Encouraged by her question, the young man smiled at her again. "Yes—the one in the Lake. Watch for it when we are closer."

Timou took his advice and, as they drew closer to the City, looked carefully both at the City that rose before them and into the Lake. It was different to see the City and its reflection herself than to listen to stories, and Timou stared, enthralled. Looking at both together, she saw that there was a greater contrast between the two Cities than she had expected.

The real City was old—battered and worn by time. It was all stone, butter-yellow and cream. She could see as they drew closer that the stones of the Bridge and the walls had once been intricately carved with leaves and flowers, blurred now with age.

In the Lake, the City was new and sharp-edged, bright as though it lay in a warmer light than the light that fell on the City above. Looking at the reflected City, Timou saw the carvings with all their delicacy intact, untouched by time. Looking up, she could see the echoes of the original forms, half hidden now by age and by encroaching mosses. "How strange," Timou breathed. "How beautiful."

"See the tigers?" said the young man.

Timou looked up at the great stone tigers frozen on their plinths, and then down quickly at the tigers in the Lake. The water moved, running up against the shore in little waves, seeming to suggest with its movement a possibility of echoing movement in the reflected tigers. Then the carriage was past, and slowing at last to a halt.

"This is your first time in the City, isn't it?" said the young man, flinging open the carriage door and jumping down without waiting for the step to be placed. He held up a hand to Timou. "Tell me where you're going, if you like, and I'll escort you."

Timou took the offered hand after a moment of hesitation, not wanting to appear rude, and stepped down from the carriage to the cobbles of the street, standing at last within the City at the heart of the Kingdom. She reclaimed her hand and looked off into the City. "I think . . . ," she said, "I think I am going to the Palace."

CHAPTER 6

For several days after Timou left the village, Jonas went about his life there with a kind of absentminded thoughtfulness. He thought of Timou, but wistfully. He would have gone with her if she had let him. But, well, she *was* Kapoen's daughter. Probably she would find herself more suited to walk on strange roads through this land and into the City at its heart than he would have been himself. She would go to the City and find her father, and all would be well. Then she would come back. He mixed potions for the apothecary and repaired a gap in Raen's fence and had a mug of bitter ale with Pol and Tair at noon. He did not let himself remember that Kapoen himself had not come back from the City.

Jonas had come to this village four years before from a town six days' walk to the south—a town of nearly a thousand families, much larger than Timou's village. But that had not been his home: Jonas had been born far away. He had come into this Kingdom entirely by accident from the lands beyond. This Kingdom was like a dream to a man from beyond its borders: warm and peaceful and quiet. He had been walking, exhausted and half blind with memory and grief, down a road like any other road.

Jonas remembered that, from time to time, although he tried not to. He remembered the broken walls of Kanha at his back, and the black smoke rising up behind him into the ash-gray sky. He remembered the distant cries, the defeated and victorious indistinguishable at that distance. He remembered the refugees on the road, their shocked empty faces. They had kept out of his way.

He had not known he would walk away from his army, and his life, and ruined Kanha. He had not clearly known he *had* walked away until the sounds died behind him, until the black smoke faded from view in the dimming light. Then he had known. And then he wanted nothing but to walk away forever and never go back. He had walked through the night, and somehow, when the sun rose—which it did from an odd direction—he had been alone on the road, and it was not the same road.

Jonas had traded his second-best knife for a loaf of bread, three hard-cooked eggs, and a seat on a farmer's wagon when the farmer took his beets and lettuces to town. In town—a town without walls, a town where no one had heard of Kanha or knew there was war—Jonas had sold his short heavy sword and had bought a bath, clothing such as people in the Kingdom wore, and a decent meal at a clean inn. Then he had started walking again. He had walked until he came to a small village, set amid pretty wooded hills and green pastures filled with peaceful sheep. He had found a room at a widow's house to stay in, and work that had nothing to do with soldiering.

And he had drifted quietly through his days in this village, Jonas reflected, with hardly more thought in his head than a sheep might have had, until one day he had happened to notice that every drop of morning dew and every falling drop of rain, as they said in this country, reflected Timou's face. . . .

He had been patient. It was abundantly clear that Timou would always back away from a man who coaxed and importuned and followed her about the countryside begging for her glance. No. Still very young, Timou was not yet certain she cared for the interest of men. What she wanted was to learn the arts of the mages . . . of which Jonas had only the vaguest idea, except magecraft in this country bore little resemblance to the violent sorcery of the land he had left behind.

Certainly Kapoen was nothing like the sorcerers of that land. When Jonas had first come to this village, Kapoen had given him one thoughtful, summing look that seemed to pierce him through. Then the mage had said, in his deep voice, "Time is the best cure for deep wounds. Go speak to the apothecary. I believe he could find work for a careful man."

This easy knowledge had shaken Jonas, who had thought he had learned to keep his private thoughts private. He had avoided the mage after that, as best he could in a small village. But Kapoen, a private man himself, had not seemed inclined to intrude; Jonas had eventually learned to trust that he would not.

Jonas could not guess whether the mage had known when he had begun to see Timou's face reflected in the rain. He had avoided Kapoen even more assiduously, and the mage had not seemed inclined to seek him out. So Jonas had waited, saying as little as he could manage. And Timou went quietly on through her days, apparently oblivious, learning magecraft from her father and that men were fools from the one or two who thought they ought to catch her eye. Jonas had hoped he might persuade her otherwise. He'd been willing to face Kapoen for that chance: Timou's father might have a cool way about him, but Jonas knew Kapoen loved his daughter, and thought the mage might eventually learn to approve of a man who did the same.

And then the spring failed, a spring Jonas had looked to with hope. Kapoen left the village, and then Timou after him. It had hurt her when Kapoen left her, Jonas suspected. She was not as cool of heart as she thought herself. He'd seen the way she was with other girls' mothers, with Taene's mother. He suspected that the absence of her own mother, accepted so matter-of-factly by the villagers who'd known her all her life, had been harder on Timou than anyone understood—than Timou understood herself. And then Kapoen had left her behind as well. . . . No wonder Timou had followed her father. And no wonder she had refused all his offers of companionship, no matter how carefully offered: of course she was afraid to let herself grow close to anyone who might leave her. Jonas regretted now that he'd let her go away on her own, that he hadn't insisted on accompanying her, or followed her.

On the sixth night after Timou's departure, Jonas dreamed of a savage wind that came down from the heights and whipped massive dark clouds into froth that streamed past the moon. Great trees as old as the world broke and crashed around him. High above, something that was not the wind wailed, urgent and predatory.

Timou ran past him, down a path that twisted through the forest. She was all in white and her white hair flew behind her:

in the wind-torn dark she seemed to shine with a light of her own. There were spots of blood in the tracks her bare feet left. Jonas, stunned, reached his hands out to her, but she was past before he could catch hold of her. She did not see him. He tried to go after her, but in his dream he could not move. She ran past and was gone.

After Timou came the wild hounds of the storm. Lean white hounds, each the size of a pony, they coursed Timou like a hare: their eyes were the wild yellow eyes of birds of prey, and as they ran they gave tongue with the high cries of hunting eagles. Behind the hounds rode the Hunter on his white horse. He seemed to fill the whole world. A tangle of black antlers crossed the sky far above him, or perhaps he wore the branches of a great spreading oak as a crown. His horse shone like the moon. It was shod with lightning; thunder crashed when its hooves touched the ground.

Jonas tried to cry out, but he was voiceless and made no sound. The Hunter turned his great antlered head and met Jonas's eyes with his own: frosted golden eyes, expressionless and terrible, eyes that saw him clearly, though everyone knew the Hunter was blind when he rode through the land outside his own dark Kingdom. Then he was past, rain lashing down in his wake, piercingly cold, like arrows out of the night, and Jonas knew that he drove Timou to a dark destination, but he could not imagine what that might be.

He woke shaking.

That day was hard. Jonas went on with small tasks about Raen's house, loading the loft in her barn with hay and repairing a hole in her poultry shed before a fox worried it big enough to get in. But through these tasks he several times found himself standing for minutes at a time looking at nothing, the hammer forgotten in his hands, listening for the high wild cry of hounds running before the storm.

He went, out of habit, to the inn for his noon meal, but when he got there, he found he did not want to go inside. He stood for a moment listening to the voices within—cheerful, ordinary, everyday voices, with an undertone of worry that no one wanted to acknowledge openly—and felt suddenly that he could not bear to pretend to be one of them when he was not. To pretend to be well when he was not well, when nothing was well—when he felt nothing might ever be well again. He went back to Raen's house and took bread and cold meat out to the fields to eat under a tree. The tree was butter-yellow with autumn. It made him feel the pressure of time at his back, as though this was the first year he had ever watched move toward its end. When a long line of geese went by overhead, Jonas flinched at their voices.

That night he dreamed the same dream, and woke with tears cold as rain on his face. It was raining when he got up and went to the window. There was thunder in the distance. Jonas listened to the thunder with foreboding, as though it were an omen. He had never thought of omens before in his life.

He went through the whole of that day as though he were still half asleep, which might have been true, since he had spent half the night staring out the window and listening to the distant thunder. After he drove the hammer down on his thumb twice,

Jonas put his tools away and went instead for a long walk through the fields. He took his small rabbit-bow so he could pretend to be hunting. He did not even string the bow. It was too easy to imagine the feelings of the rabbit. He thought he might never go hunting again. He came back at dusk, walking with long strides to beat the night to Raen's door. He had never feared the night before. He feared it now.

He lay awake for a long time. Then he got up and paced. Weariness drove him to lie down again near dawn. The first pale hints of coming light were in the window before he felt safe enough to close his eyes. He should not have felt safe: it seemed he had no more shut his eyes than the dream had him. For the third time, the storm hounds ran before the Hunter, pursuing Timou through his dreams. This time, when he woke, he was muffling a scream behind his hands, as though he was afraid even to make a sound.   .

"What is it?" the widow asked gently when Jonas sat at her table that morning stirring the breakfast porridge without tasting it. He had been late to the table, but Raen had said nothing. He had thought she had not noticed his trouble. He had not meant her to notice. When he only looked at her wordlessly, she said, "I don't mean to intrude. But I bore five children, and raised them through all the troubles and joys and heartbreaks of their youths. If some difficulty has found you, my dear, you might do worse than tell me."

Jonas told her his dream.

The widow leaned her chin in her hand and listened quietly

while he told her, her eyes, wise with her years, on his face. Then she said, "Well, Jonas, you are going to have to go after her, aren't you?"

"Do you think I should?" Jonas stood up restlessly and went to the window. The day was dawning fair and cloudless. There was not a hint of stormy weather anywhere about, and yet he thought he might feel thunder in the earth, right through the floor of the widow's small neat house. "She didn't want me to go with her."

"Do you think you will be able to stay here, waiting and blind?"

Once the question was asked, the answer was obvious. "No," Jonas admitted.

"Then you'll have to go. Once you find her, I think she will manage to cope somehow with your presence."

"If I find her," said Jonas.

"Oh," said the widow calmly, "I think you'll find her. I've known young men in love before, once or twice. I think you'll find her."

Jonas had given Timou his leather knapsack. He was not sorry he had given it to her, but he was sorry he did not have another. He borrowed a satchel from Raen.

"Nerril and his family will be sorry to see you go," Raen observed. Nerril was the apothecary.

"I know," said Jonas.

"He will fear for you."

Jonas shrugged. "Many people travel between the City and the outlying lands. Most of them arrive safely where they want to go."

"Not all."

"I've been on the road before."

"Not *that* road," said Raen. "I came that way, once. I walked that road once, from the City, where I was born. I came here and lived here and was happy. I never went back to the City, but I remember the road that lies between."

Jonas's hands had stilled on the table, where he had been sorting out the best candlelighter and candles from the assortment the old woman had dropped in front of him. He said, surprised, "You're from the City?"

"When you've lived somewhere sixty-two years, people forget you ever lived anywhere else. But I did once. Does it seem amazing to you that I should stay here, so far from the great City, where I lived as a child?"

Jonas made a little gesture of negation. Nothing seemed more likely or more reasonable. He thought about living in one tiny village for sixty-two years, never going more than a day's travel from its quiet and peace. He thought it sounded a really fine idea, if he could do it with Timou. He said, "What is it like? The great forest?"

"Haunted," the widow said tersely. "Hunted."

"Hunted. By what?"

"Who knows? The blind Hunter, I suppose, and his storm hounds. Or maybe by something else, something quieter." Raen was quiet for a moment. "You have to go, of course, my dear. You should go. But be careful. Never leave the road."

"I know that," Jonas protested mildly. He did. He had heard stories. He had always listened carefully, if a little skeptically; he had once been trained to be skeptical. But then he had met the Hunter and looked into his blind eyes. . . .

"Of course you do." Raen looked at him, frowning. "Never leave the road, or you'll wander in the forest far longer than you intended: there is no other way through that leads straight from the start of your journey to its end. Drink no water that does not flow across the road, eat nothing you did not bring with you, and be careful of anyone you meet under the great trees. You won't meet any other travelers once you pass into the forest. No one ever does. So anyone you do meet belongs to the forest. Be brave, and kind and courteous to everyone, but be sparing of trust. Tell no lies and make no promises. Don't tell anyone your name, especially if he asks."

"I will remember," Jonas promised soberly.

"Huh. So you had better. Don't cut living wood—you know that, I suppose. Don't pick the flowers, if you see any at this time of year—well, you know that, too. Be careful with any fires you make. Let me think." The widow gazed dreamily at her kitchen fire. Jonas waited patiently.

"Ah," she said after a while. "I remember one more thing. The man we traveled with, he went back to the City every year. I remember he told us, before he took us into the forest, that if you do get lost under the trees, you should not go into any

house or tower or castle you find; but if you do, you should expect to pay a price to get out."

"What price?" Jonas asked.

"I don't know," said Raen. "I never got lost under the trees.
But whatever price is demanded, you had better be prepared to
pay it honestly and willingly. Men—ah, and women, too—will go
into the forest to find their hearts' desires, but some that come
out have lost more than they would have dreamed of paying. It's
a chancy place, that forest. Stay on the road, that's my advice,
and stay out of enchanted towers."

"Believe me," said Jonas fervently, "that is all my intention."

Jonas went quickly, his long legs taking him through the woods
and out of the woods, under the sky. He did not think he was
at all likely to overtake Timou. But he nevertheless *felt* that he
might, if he could go quickly enough. He would have welcomed
the sight of her in the distance. He looked ahead eagerly, but he
saw no one on the road in front of him. The road was deserted.
This seemed strange to Jonas, who had traveled a great deal
through other lands in his youth. He knew that one never goes
for long on any road without encountering strangers, without
passing houses and whole villages built along the road, without
seeing granaries and pastures and somebody taking a wagonload
of something from one place to another. This road seemed like
it had been made for him alone. It made him walk all the more
quickly, trying to put it behind him, to come to some more comfortable place where men lived.

He never did. He walked alone and slept under the sky

alone—fair skies, always, with no hint of rain, but he feared each night and hated to watch the sun set. He found places off the road under trees at first, out of sight of the sky. When he came to the open country, it so horrified him that he could not rest, for all he told himself there was no reason for his dread. The road was clear enough, running like a broad silver stream under the passionless moon: Jonas walked by the moon's pale light and lay down only when the sun was back in the sky. He did not dream, or if he did, he did not remember his dreams.

Jonas came to the great forest nine days after he had left the widow's house. The forest, too, horrified him. He could feel its power and its age, like a pressure against his skin. When he visualized Timou walking, tiny and alone, between those great trees and into the green shadows, he could hardly bear it. It was impossible to know how he would have felt if he had come to this place with Timou, were he not haunted by dreams. He suspected he would have been awed. He hoped he would not have been appalled. Jonas made a fire there, at the entrance to the great forest, and rested beside it, but he could not sleep. He could hear the wind in the branches, though no breeze blew through the smoke of his fire. In the morning his eyes were gritty and his head felt stuffed with wool.

It was the memory of Timou's voice saying, *If you are with me, I will also think about you* that drew him finally past the ancient sentinels and into the waiting green dimness. He could hear her quiet voice as though she were in front of him, looking at him with her eyes the color of the sky at the exact moment the gray dawn became the clear pale blue of a winter morning.

Jonas walked fast for a while . . . he did not know how long, because the green light hid the passage of time. He walked with his head bowed and his attention on the road. Great roots twisted across the path, dangerous for an unwary foot, but he was careful and never stumbled. Sometimes streams dashed across the road. When there were stepping-stones available, Jonas crossed the water on the rocks. When there were no stepping-stones, he got his feet wet. He did not complain out loud, because he felt that his voice would echo too loudly in the great quiet under the trees. Though there was no one, it occurred to him eventually, to hear him. No one and nothing. No bird or squirrel, no whining insect. . . . Jonas walked even more quickly for a while, thinking about this, and about the way the forest itself seemed to watch him and press in on him. He always wanted to move more quickly when he was frightened. He was frightened now, and knew it, and set his teeth against it.

Well, he told himself, Timou was somewhere ahead, and he surely walked in her steps. The road did not branch, but ran straight on. A man must simply follow it, and it would lead him out of the forest as it had led him into it. . . .

After a while—Jonas did not know how long—he found he had grown weary. It was many days' walk through the great forest, but even so Jonas was reluctant to stop. Hard as the forest pressed around him during the day, he knew it would press much harder at night. So he tried not to notice the fading of the light. But it faded anyway. He would not be able to walk at night under the trees, where true darkness would come with the passing of the day. So when the green light had turned dusky gray, he finally stopped and sat wearily down where he was, in the middle of the road. He heard a breeze in the leaves above, although there was no breeze near the ground. It was not a pleasant sort of sound, though there was no reason it should have disturbed him. He sighed. He wanted to say, *I am going as fast as I can. I will trouble you as little as I can.* But he did not want to offer his voice to the listening trees. He did not want to draw attention to himself at all. He had a blanket in his satchel, and bread and cheese for his supper, and a handful of dried apples. He thought about the sweetness of dried apples. It was a comforting, normal kind of thought.

He was just opening his satchel when he heard a long high wailing cry far above and far away. The wind carried it, but the sound he heard was not the wind.

Although Jonas knew he should be safe on the road, his fingers nevertheless froze on the satchel's buckle. He sat very still, listening, wondering if Timou, somewhere in front of him, was hearing this same cry on the wind. It did not come again. But Jonas could not eat. He moved to the side of the road and put his back against a tree, because even a haunted tree for shelter from the sky was more appealing than no shelter at all, and stared into the growing dark, listening. He fell asleep like that, sitting up against the broad bole of a tree.

Sleeping, he dreamed he was asleep. He dreamed he woke to a wailing cry that pierced the air all around him. He dreamed he leapt to his feet and fled along the road, with that cry reverberating through the forest at his back. It was the kind of dream where you run and run and cannot bring yourself to look over your shoulder for fear of what you will see behind you.

He had lost the road, and ran through towering trees. At first branches slashed at him and he had to put his arms up to protect his face. Later the trees were tall and straight, with no branches near the ground. But it was darker in his dream, darker than night, darker than even a moonless night under the trees, and he ran into one great smooth bole after another, blundering and bruised, until he finally fell. Having once fallen, he could not get up and cowered, waiting for his pursuers to catch up with him and tear him apart. He waited in terror, and then the terror wore itself out and he found he was alone and it was perfectly quiet. And then he found he was awake.

All around him were great dark boles, rising straight and tall like pillars in some vast hall, not like trees at all. The moment he thought so, he saw that, indeed, he was surrounded by pillars and not by trees. He was not in a forest, but in some great hall or cavern. The ceiling, if there was a ceiling, was too far above to see. The floor was very smooth and flat, as the pillars were smooth and straight. It was very dark in this place, yet he found he could see a little, although it was not quite like sight. It was as though each pillar glimmered with its own darkness, a darkness like light, by which one could see. Or at least experience something like sight. The pillars cast shadows even darker than themselves that lay like chasms across the floor. There was no road or path anywhere. It was perfectly silent.

Jonas stood up stiffly. He did not know how much of his

terror and flight had taken place in dream and how much had really happened, but he was as sore and bruised as if it had all been real. His face was scratched as though he had been running through a forest; his arms were bruised from blundering into hidden obstacles. He was desperately tired. His satchel was nowhere in sight. He had no blanket, no food, no water, and no idea whatever of which way he should go.

On the floor before him a great shadow stretched out and out. The realization that it was there crept over him slowly, and with it a dawning horror. It was not his shadow. It was blacker than any shadow he might have cast in any world, darker than the shadows cast by the pillars. It was like the shadow of a man, but crowned with a tangle of branches, or antlers.

Jonas turned slowly.

Before him stood the Hunter. The Hunter was tall, taller than any mortal man, tall enough that his crown surely brushed the ceiling of this great hall. Yet Jonas found he could look into his pitiless unhuman eyes. They were round and golden, even stranger than he recalled: the eyes of an owl; hard, merciless, unmoved by the terror of its prey. Even in this dark place where there seemed no light to cast them, the Hunter's face was veiled by twisting shadows.

Jonas, said the Hunter. *You are come into my country and my Kingdom. Surrender your name to me.*

The Hunter's voice was dark, if darkness could have a voice. It was not loud, but it filled the world. Behind the words, Jonas thought he could hear, distantly, the wild cry of a bird of prey. He shut his eyes. Then he opened them again. "Lord," he said shakily, "Lord Hunter. You know my name already. You have spoken it." His own words sounded . . . dim, to his ears. As though his voice had less strength in this place than it should.

Not of your giving. I heard it in the wind. I heard it behind the rain. I heard it in the grinding crash of breaking stones when Kanha fell. Your name is mine. Surrender it to me, demanded the Hunter.

Jonas could not speak. He could not bring himself to refuse directly, yet he did not dare accede to the Hunter's demand. He was frozen, irresolute, unable to move or think. Yet he found, to his astonishment and horror, that a slow, unwise sense of out-rage was building somewhere behind his eyes. He set his teeth against it.

Jonas, said the Hunter. *Surrender to me your hopes and your fears. All this I claim.*

"You brought me here. You hunted me . . . you hunted me through my dreams, so that I would come here, to your empty Kingdom." Jonas knew this was the truth. Anger warred with the terror. "You . . . you pursued Timou. To drive her . . . to what? Her *mother?* Why? Why did you listen for my name? Or hers? What possible use is either of us to you?"

The Hunter tilted his head; far above, his vast crown of antlers or branches cast a multitude of shadows that twisted and bent in strange directions. He regarded Jonas out of passionless golden eyes. *I know her mother. So will she. She will go to the hand of her mother. You will come to mine. Jonas. Give me your name. Give me your eyes. Give me your tongue. Give me your hands. Give me your heart.*

"No," said Jonas. "No. I don't . . . I don't understand you. But I will give you nothing."

The unreadable owl's eyes did not blink. *Nothing is what you will find here,* said the Hunter. *You will find nothing here, until you find me again. If you understand me then, then you shall pay my price.*

And suddenly he was not there. He did not turn, or go. He was just gone. The darkness seemed thinner suddenly, as though relieved of the weight of the shadow the Hunter had cast.

Jonas got slowly to his feet. His hands were shaking. He was shivering all over. It was perfectly silent. There was no breath of air, of any living breeze. Around him a thousand featureless pillars gave no hint of any direction he should go.

CHAPTER 7

"The Palace?" The young man from the carriage was surprised. He turned to hail a cab, then turned back to examine Timou once more, a quick glance from head to toe that turned into a more serious scrutiny. She looked back a little warily.

"Well," the young man said. "Well . . . um. If . . . they . . . expect you at the Palace, you won't need my escort. Um . . . *does* he, that is, do they? Expect you? At the Palace?"

Timou's bewilderment must have shown in her face, because a flush suddenly rose in the young man's face and he said, "Never mind me. Look. Here's a cab for you. Good . . . um, good luck at the Palace."

"Thank you," said Timou, baffled. She didn't understand what she heard in the young man's voice. A kind of wicked amusement, perhaps, as though he thought Timou had invited him to share a joke at someone else's expense.

"I'm tempted to escort you for real." The man sounded half stifled. "But better not, I suppose. All right. Up you go! Good luck!"

Timou, utterly mystified, nevertheless accepted his hand and clambered up to the high seat. The driver glanced back at her in-curiously and lifted the reins. The horse started off with a jolt across the cobbles, and Timou braced herself on the hard seat and looked out the window.

At first she looked blindly, her thoughts turning curiously over the young man's odd comments. But then the City pulled her, despite herself, out of her thoughts entirely. She had never seen, never imagined, any place like it, not even when she'd watched it approach as the carriage had crossed the Bridge.

All the streets of the City seemed to be cobbled, the cobbles rounded smooth by time. There were a great many streets, much wider than even the streets of the town in which Timou had spent the previous night and crowded with the most startling people. As Timou watched, a pair of women in amazingly intri-cate yellow gowns passed in an open carriage, their seats so high they were in no danger whatsoever of being splashed with mud. A boy clinging to the back of another carriage flung a coin to a man selling cakes right off a cart on the street. The man tossed a cake back to the boy, who caught it in one hand, clinging—rather precariously, it seemed to Timou—to the carriage with his other. The boy raised the cake in salute to the man, grinning. A flock of younger children ran by, brightly clad and noisy as finches.

Houses—or perhaps they were shops?—crowded along the streets, separated from the traffic and from one another by deep gutters. To enter them one must cross to their doors over little bridges of stone or wood. Buildings and bridges alike were made of the same creamy stone that all this City seemed made of, a stone the afternoon light turned to gold. Sometimes she could catch tantalizing glimpses through doors set ajar to draw in passersby; others were closed and private.

As the cab went on, the streets became still broader, the buildings grander, and people fewer. The street turned, and turned again, climbing a hill in slow stages. Then it turned once more and Timou saw at last the gates that led to the Palace. The gates were silver; they stood open; tigers lay along their tops, gazing outward with green eyes. Timou stared back at them, wondering what they might see in the winter-pale girl who passed between them. Had they seen her father, perhaps, pass through these gates before her? Their jeweled eyes kept their own counsel.

The cab took Timou right through the gates without pause, past a wide courtyard where a dozen boys led horses in and out of a vast stable, and right up to the graceful, many-towered Palace itself. The driver jumped down, handed Timou out, accepted payment—Timou was not certain afterward how much she had paid him—and jumped back on his high seat to turn his cab and head back into the City. Timou did not watch him go. She was looking at the Palace.

Flowers and leaves of stone spilled down the Palace walls, worn but still recognizable; stone roses climbed its towers, disguised sometimes by real roses that bore white flowers even this late in the season. The Palace doors were twice Timou's height and delicately carved in shapes like the wind moving across water. They were guarded by two men in uniforms of gray and silver, with swords at their hips. The men looked at Timou with a stolid disinterest that made her hesitate, uncertain of how to proceed.

Then one moved forward a step. His eyes had narrowed. He said something to his fellow guardsman, too low for Timou to hear, and both men looked at her with a peculiarly intense speculation behind the professional neutrality of their eyes. "Yes?" the first man said, and added, ". . . my lady?"

Timou looked back at the guard, uneasy at the curiosity she saw behind his eyes. She said after a moment, "I would like to . . . to speak to the King's elder son. If I may."

"Would you?" said the guard. He looked at his fellow, his eyebrows raised.

The other guard shrugged, his mouth crooking, and said to Timou, "You, ah . . . My lady, we do not allow just any . . . person . . . to wander into the Palace and disturb, um, Lord Neill. Who is a busy man. But for you . . . Is he expecting you, then?" There was a peculiar emphasis to the way the guard asked this last question.

"I wouldn't think so," said Timou, her own brows rising.

"I'll get the captain," offered the second guard, with a sidelong look at the first. "And, ah, if you would care to follow me, my lady, I will show you to a room where you can wait more, um, comfortably."

"Thank you," said Timou, wondering, and followed the guard into the Palace. They passed only a handful of folk: a tall young man with a long lean face and fine clothing barely glanced at her, but a woman carrying a stack of towels looked curiously at Timou, then looked again. She bumped into the corner she was turning, and barely escaped scattering her towels down the hall. Timou stared after her.

"Here is the small parlor," said the guard. "If you would wait here, please. I do not think it will be long. Um."

"Thank you," Timou said again, baffled, and watched him walk away. He cast a glance back over his shoulder and all but walked into a wall himself.

The parlor did not seem very small to her. It had cream-colored walls and rich dark furniture, most of the chairs drawn up close to a wide fireplace. There was a single picture on one wall, wider than Timou was tall, of the Lake on a stormy day: waves rose against the wooded shore and light lanced past torn clouds; rain fell slantingly into the gray water. Across one corner of the painting, the crumbling stone lilies of Tiger Bridge were visible, but the Bridge cast no reflection in the storm-tossed waters of the Lake.

Timou walked across the room and stood for a moment looking at the painting, trying to decide whether she liked it. Something about it disturbed her. But before she could decide what, the door behind her opened and she turned.

It was another guard who stood there, along with the man who had let her in . . . but older than the first, Timou saw, with an experienced, weary face. He had a badge at his shoulder. His eyes, pale blue, rested on Timou's face with a strange expression. He said to the other guard, his tone wondering, "Does the Bastard, then, have a bastard?"

Timou's brows lifted. It was clear what inference the man

was making, but she could not fathom what made him think such a thing. She said courteously, "I beg your pardon?"

"Forgive me." The man inclined his head a little, but his eyes, Timou saw, did not drop. "I am captain of the Palace Guard. My name is Galef. I will serve you if I can. Your name, then . . . my lady? Your business with, ah, Lord Neill?"

Timou folded her hands before her and looked back at the captain steadily. "My name is Timou. I am looking for my father, the mage Kapoen."

"Your father?"

"So far as I know," Timou said with deliberate calm, and saw a faint flush rise into the captain's face.

"I will inform Lord Neill you are here, then. If you will wait. I think . . . I do not think it will be long." The man gave another slight nod of his head and withdrew, taking the other guard with him. Timou could hear their voices in the hall; the younger man speaking excitedly and the captain answering in a stern tone.

Timou moved slowly across the room and sat down in one of the chairs by the fireplace. Thoughts tried to coalesce in the surface of her mind. She dismissed them: all the half-formed guesses, all the whispers of speculation and curiosity. The heart of magecraft was to be still and let the world unveil itself in its own time. She stilled her mind and waited.

The door to the room had been left open. Steps went by: light and not pausing, soft-soled shoes and the rustle of stiff skirts—a lady of the court, Timou surmised. More steps, a moment later: quick and firm, heels ringing on the stone floor: a

man. The steps did not slow at her door. After that there was silence for a time. Finally there were more steps: more than one person this time. Timou rose to her feet and turned to face the door.

The first man through it came forward several paces and
stopped, looking at her. There were others at his back; Timou
barely saw them. All her attention was on the first.

He was tall. He wore black and violet: mourning dress.
Against those colors, the paleness of his skin was stark. The lines
of his face were harsh, his jaw angular: wolf-featured, they
would have said of him in the village. His hair, nearly as white
as hers, was drawn back into a single braid, the way she wore
her own. His eyes were different: dark as the Hunter's night,
opaque, ungiving.

Timou drew a slow breath. She said nothing.

Of course this was Lord Neill, the Bastard, elder son of
the King, and Timou felt now that she might easily believe
any manner of rumor concerning him. He moved suddenly,
crossing the room and putting a hand beneath her chin to lift
her face. She met his dark eyes with her own pale ones, and
wondered what he saw within them. Or what he might think
he saw.

"How old are you?" Lord Neill asked abruptly. His tone was
sharp, crisp; his voice was not deep, but neither was it light. It
held confidence: the expectation of command.

"Seventeen. Almost eighteen."

"Seventeen," repeated Lord Neill. He lowered his hand and
stepped back.

"Is it possible she is yours?" asked a man who had come in

at his back. His tone caught Timou's attention: academic, inquiring, as though he offered no judgment in either case but was merely interested. It was the tone in which a mage might ask such a question. He did not look like a mage to Timou: he was too heavy, too soft—too ready, judging by his face, to smile. But he was a mage. Timou did not know how she could tell, but she was certain. She saw him recognize this in her as well: his eyes widened suddenly.

Lord Neill had missed this moment of mutual recognition. He said absently, his eyes still on her face, "It would be barely possible."

"My father's name," said Timou, watching the mage as well as the bastard elder prince, "is Kapoen. Or so he told me."

"Kapoen." Lord Neill glanced at the mage he had brought with him.

"He came to the City this spring," Timou said.

The mage with Lord Neill pursed his lips and lifted wide shoulders. "If he did, child, he did not come openly. We did not see him here. We would have welcomed him if he had come to us."

"He told me he would come here. Perhaps he did not come to you, but he was here." She turned to Lord Neill. "He did not come to you or to your father?"

"What?" It was clear the lord had heard nothing they were saying. He said abruptly, "Did Kapoen ever tell you directly that he was your father?"

"Yes," Timou said patiently. "We are alike, but not, I suppose, quite so alike as that, my lord. It is only the hair."

The mage grinned, and the guard captain coughed.

"It's not only the hair," said Lord Neill, and took her suddenly by the arm. Timou let the man draw her with him. Everyone else, and there seemed something of a crowd, pressed aside
out of their way—his way—and followed in their wake.

He did not lead her far; only to a room down the hall, a
room cluttered with little tables and large armoires and intricately carved wardrobes. A huge mirror with a silver frame took
up all one wall, and of course it was this that was Lord Neill's
aim: he brought Timou to stand with him before the great mirror. She looked into it and was silent.

Lord Neill was harsh-featured: the bones of his face were
strong, too severe for beauty. In Timou they had been softened,
but she could not deny that the lines were the same. They had
the same mouth: thin-lipped but graceful. The same long slender
nose and high cheekbones, though his were strong and hers
gentle. The same pale winter-bleached skin. The same hair: frost
for Timou, ash for the son of the King. Only, his eyes were dark,
and hers light, all but colorless in this pale room. Drawn by some
impulse, Timou reached slowly forward, her reflection in the
mirror echoing her gesture, until they touched fingertips.

"So . . . ," began Lord Neill, but then did not complete what
he had been going to say. He had paused, startled; Timou
watched both their eyes widen in reflected startlement. In the
mirror, hers were as dark as his. Darker. Dark as the night captured at the heart of the world. In the mirror, she smiled. Timou
was not smiling. She tried to lift her hand away from the mirror,
but another hand caught hers in a strong grip. She sent her mind

into the mirror in swift defensive reflex, looking for glass that could be broken and for the world that should exist on its other side. But she found no fragile glass, only tilting sheets of light that gave way before her and closed again behind her and all around her, unbroken, unbreakable. There was no Lord Neill at her side, no crowd at her back, no mirror. There was only light, rising in angled sheets and planes all around her. Timou took a step and stopped. She stood still. She had no idea where she was.

Or rather, it was clear enough where she was. She was behind the mirror. Someone hidden in her reflection had come out, and Timou had taken this person's place behind the mirror. In whatever place this was.

Timou calmed herself. She made her mind as still and clear as a pool, so that she would be able to see clearly everything there was to see. It took a moment. It took longer than she would have liked. She had risen at dawn to find a place on a coach, endured the hard seat the coach offered all day, crossed the Lake and the City, found a man who was a mirror and a mirror that was a doorway. . . . It seemed unjust, to have to cope with this, too, now, when she was already tired and frustrated. Timou wished bitterly for her father. She tried very hard not to think about her mother. . . . She was ashamed to find tears prickling behind her eyes, rising in her throat, threatening the calm she had just worked to gain. She held her breath, rubbing her eyes hard with the heels of her hands, struggling to still her heart again. After a long moment she was able to lift her head and take a breath that did not tremble much at all, in a calm that was almost real. And, at last, she was able to take down her hands and examine the place to which she had come. Been brought. By her mother . . . She *would not* think of that. She turned instead in a slow complete circle, looking around herself.

It seemed that she stood at the narrow bottom of a sharp-edged valley made of flat planes of light rising and tilting outward, so that they spread out infinitely far to either side as they rose. Other sheets of light fell at sharp angles, intersecting the narrow valley in which she stood: other paths, she surmised. Each sheet of light seemed infinite, each path led away forever.

There were no shadows because light was everywhere, concentrated and hard to the touch, like glass. When Timou sent her mind experimentally into one sheet of light, she found nothing but more light that stretched out straight and clear forever: nothing that she could touch or hold or break. When she followed the lines of it with her mind, it seemed to run infinitely far in strange directions, oddly seductive in its geometric purity.

It was difficult to pull her mind out of the light . . . in fact, when she tried, she could not. She was being swept along into its infinite reaches; she had lost her body, her sense of herself; she would never get out. . . . She calmed herself again, with an effort, and tried to break sideways out of the light's streaming path. Nothing happened. Her awareness was concentrated within the light, trapped by it. Yes, she thought. It *was* a trap. A trap for mages, who might reach out into light and never again find a way back into themselves. . . . For the first time, panic brushed the edges of her mind.

Timou thought of her father, of his calm composure. The thought steadied her. She needed that steadiness. Was there, somewhere, an end to light? If she wondered that, she might begin to flail desperately about, and yet there was nothing in this that she could fight. Terror would not help her.

She let the light carry her, steadied her mind, and tried, rather than to break away from it, simply to halt her own rushing progress. This attempt, also, had no influence on her own motion, and she tried harder, and harder, and had again to fight against panic so that she might cease the effort and consider further. The light poured past her and around her, endless and formless. It did not speak to her as the forest had done; it was not aware of her at all. It was only light and motion.

So. Stillness again, fear put ruthlessly aside. There was, she knew, a way out. There was always a way out of any trap.

The great mage Irinore had once been trapped in the deep dark of the earth while he followed the roots the forest sent down to the heart of the world. Only with great difficulty had he found his way back into the light, which seemed, at the moment, ironic. He had done this in the end by folding himself into the water of the earth and letting the roots of the trees draw him back up along their intricate pathways until he was pulled at last into the light . . . a method that seemed to have limited application to her own situation.

Another famous mage, Simoure, had once found herself lost in something she had described as "the country of ice, the country where darkness becomes light and all directions are the same." Timou had not understood what Simoure meant, but she would not have said that darkness became light here in this place behind the mirror. This was true light.

Other stories passed through her mind. She searched within them for infinite planes of light. The powerful foreign sorcerer Deserisien . . . had he not once found a maze of glass? Yes, Timou thought, there had been a tale about that: Deserisien had come upon a crystalline maze that perfectly reflected the mind of the trapped mage so that its prisoner could not get outside it. But Deserisien had escaped, for he had made his mind reflect the maze and so discovered its exit. Later he had made it a prison of his own in which to trap others. Timou suspected uneasily that she had perhaps been trapped within the exact maze the great foreign sorcerer had discovered. But she did not know how to make her mind reflect the maze of light. The sorcery of Deserisien was nothing she knew: she doubted she could take his way out into the ordinary world. She must find a way of her own, a way of magecraft rather than Deserisien's sorcery.

Timou, carried by rushing light, thought of the dark. The dark at the heart of the earth, where Irinore had once ventured; the dark of the storm; the dark that lies at the turning of the year, when the longest night of winter stretches coldly out to press back dawn. She remembered darkness. She shaped it with her mind. She poured herself into it; she spun it out of her heart and wrapped it around her awareness. Its silence engulfed her. It was a kind of stillness, a kind of emptiness, she thought; a dark that was more than an absence of light. It was an ending to light. It had a shape and a presence of its own.

She did not know how long she waited, wrapped in the silent dark. It seemed a long time. Long enough to remember her own body, the heft of it, the feel of muscle and bone and rushing blood and human life. . . . The darkness faded at last, as even the longest night fades at the dawn. Timou found herself standing once more at the base of a valley of light. Planes of light cut through space all around her. She was shaking, terrified now that she could afford the luxury of terror. But she was herself. Still trapped. But no longer caught in the deeper layer of the trap.

That seemed, at the moment, enough to be grateful for.

She walked slowly along the path of angled light, more because she wanted to walk and move and feel her human body than because she hoped to find anything useful by simply walking about. Other narrow paths intersected hers from time to time, at odd angles, and she chose one or another to follow at random. They all seemed the same once she set her foot on them: narrow, straight, absolutely level, with walls that tilted oddly outward as they rose.

Though she seemed to walk for a long time, Timou did not grow hungry or thirsty. Nor did she become weary. It occurred to her she might walk forever on these paths and find nothing. . . . The thought did not daunt her; she was too newly glad to be trapped only in a maze behind a mirror and not in a bodiless rush of light. There would be a way out, and she would find it. Her hand ached, and she rubbed it absently, welcoming the slight, ordinary discomfort . . . and came to a halt between one step and the next. She sent her mind not outward into the sheets of light, but inward, into her hand, looking for . . . she was not quite sure what . . . traces of venom, a memory of a cool snake's egg and a hatchling snake. She opened her eyes.

Around her wrist was coiled the tiny white snake from the disturbing dream she'd had in the forest, slipping into solidity here in this place of angles and light. The little snake was soft as silk to the touch, delicate as fine ribbon. It lifted its narrow head, no larger than her smallest fingernail, and asked, in a sweet husky voice, "What do you seek?"

Timou thought of the long sleek black serpent saying to her, *If you help me now, I will guide you when you most need guidance.* And now this little one was here. Was it truly a different serpent, then, or the same one in a different guise? Either way, Timou did not trust the strange creature as a guide—but she surely needed guidance. She said cautiously, "I seek the way out of this maze."

"Oh, no. That isn't what you seek," said the hatchling. It uncoiled itself, slid to the floor at her feet, and flowed away, down shadowless pathways of light. Timou followed it hastily.

The little snake, at least, seemed to have no question where it was going, or how to get there. It chose paths without hesitation, and slowed, finally, coiling itself into a tight little spiral. Before it, along a deep, arrow-straight channel with banks made of light, so wide Timou could not have thrown a stone to the farther side, ran a river of blood.

In this place of colorless light such a thing was doubly shocking. Timou stood at the edge of the river and looked at it, her eyes wide. The liquid was clearly blood. It ran slowly past, sluggish, thicker than water, darker and clotting at the edges, warmer than the air. Steam rose from it. She could smell it: like the butchering of pigs, but more disturbing because in this place it lacked all context.

"You won't need a guide now. Simply follow this river until you come to its source," said the serpent. Its voice was still sweet, but edged, as in Timou's memory, with malice.

She was more and more certain that both the black serpent and the white were aspects of the same creature—more and more certain that she did not understand at all what they were. Or what it was. "What are you?" Timou asked it slowly, not quite sure that she wanted to know.

"Do you not know me?"

"I . . . No."

"You should," said the snake.

Timou gazed at it for a little while, but when the snake did not speak again, she finally walked forward, along the river of blood. It did not follow. It was still there when she glanced back, until she had gone so far it was lost in the distance.

There was not much room to walk on the bank along the channel of blood. Timou placed her feet carefully. Trying to look ahead, she saw nothing but blood and light, diminishing in the distance. She walked on. There was no guide before her, but as the little serpent had said, she scarcely needed one.

The river dwindled as she walked beside it. She noticed this gradually. When she did notice it, she stopped and looked more carefully. She thought that now, if she had a stone, she could throw it easily to the far side. She turned back to her journey, but this time she watched the river and knew that it was narrowing as she approached its source. The time came when she might have leapt across the channel, and after that, when she might have stepped across.

Nor did the flowing blood seem deep at all. In fact, there was barely a channel here for it to flow through, as though this strange place of light had created the channel only when it had needed something through which liquid might flow. The blood was a ribbon of red, creeping along the floor of the path . . . it was a thin trickle, no wider than a hatchling snake, but longer, longer—she looked ahead and saw at last its source. There was a man lying there, in a place where the path widened out to create a broad place. Sheets of light came down on all sides, leaning outward dizzyingly as they rose. Timou thought at once, *Of course, this is the Prince. So he is dead after all.* . . . She walked forward.

It was not the Prince. It was her father.

He was on his back, limbs straight and face composed as though he had merely lain down to rest. His eyes were open, but blind. A narrow silver knife stood out of his chest and a tiny thread of his heart's blood ran from the wound and away across the floor. There was no doubt that he was dead.

I seek the way out, Timou had told the little serpent. *No,* it had answered. *That isn't what you seek.* And it had been right. She understood that now. She had wanted to find the lost Prince, but more than that she had wanted to find her father. Beyond that, Timou realized, she had wanted him to be *glad* to be found; she'd wanted him to welcome her and—could she have been so young and foolish as to hope for such a thing?—to take her himself to meet her mother. She'd hoped her mother would be happy and proud to meet the daughter she'd given away. That Kapoen would be happy and proud to show her to her mother.

Well, she had found him. Only to discover he had left her again, this time with terrible finality. And she had met her mother—at least, all but met her. A certainty settled from somewhere into her heart: a certainty that it had been her mother's hand on the silver knife. This certainty seemed somehow even worse than her father's death. Timou wondered what he'd thought when he'd found her mother here: Had he understood at once that she would kill him? Had he fought her? Or had he stood in disbelief while she set that little silver knife in his heart and let out the river of his life's blood?

Had he regretted leaving Timou behind him in the village? Or regretted his failure to explain to her why she should stay there? Perhaps he had had no time to regret either decision.

Timou walked forward very slowly to her father's side. She took a breath, and let it out. She had come all this way, along all these strange roads, searching for her father, hoping to find her mother. And all her hopes had come to this. She wanted to cry, or scream, or even laugh: she could not tell whether what she felt was grief or rage or incredulity. She did not make a sound. She felt she had been pulled apart into the light and had not after all managed to find her body again. Had it only been this very morning that she had crossed Tiger Bridge into the City and peered with such pleased interest at its reflection in the Lake? She felt she was no longer the girl who had crossed the Bridge; she had become someone quite different.

All her past reordered itself in her memory. Nothing about her life was as she'd believed it to be: She'd believed that her father, stern as he might be, must have loved her mother as the fathers of her friends loved their mothers. She'd thought her mother must have been sorry to give her away. Now she understood that, whatever her mother's reason for bearing her, it had surely had nothing to do with love. It had been part of the betrayal leading to this place, to the knife standing in her father's heart.

Timou sat down cross-legged by her father's body. She sat like that for a long time. After a while she reached out listlessly, took hold of the silver knife, and drew it out of the wound. She had not expected her father to come back to life after it was withdrawn. Nor did he. The knife melted in her hands, turning into wisps of thin vapor and dissipating in the air. As though all her volition had gone with it, she folded her hands over her knees and sat still.

After a while she noticed that the blood had disappeared. Sometime after that, she noticed that her father's body had grown somehow less substantial. It faded slowly. She could not see how it went; it did not seem to grow more distant or to become smaller. Only to be less completely present. She watched, too numb to be horrified, as her father faded . . . and faded. . . . She could see the floor of light through his hands where they lay at his sides . . . she could see through all of him. . . . He did not become mist, as the knife had done, and disperse in the air. But he was gone, as though he had become shadow and so could not exist in this place of light.

Timou wondered, her thoughts moving sluggishly, as though for the first time in a very long while, whether this way out was a way she, too, might take.

"That is not a way that leads anywhere you would wish to go," said the snake, lifting its narrow head to gaze at Timou from eyes like flecks of sapphire. It had come as her father's body had vanished: with such subtlety she had missed the moment of its arrival. It was just there, coiled and unobtrusive. There was no teasing malice in its tone now, but neither did it speak gently. Its voice held a strange kind of coolness, as though it did not understand human grief and so could not pity it.

It was a coolness that roused both envy and outrage in Timou. She jumped to her feet. "How could you?" she cried at it. "How could you not tell me?" She wanted to throw something at it, break its passionless regard, *make* it care that her father was dead.

"Why do you blame me for your father's failings? Or for your mother's cold heart?" asked the serpent, unmoved.

"I . . . ," said Timou, unable to form a coherent protest. "You . . ."

"When you're ready, your way lies there." The snake pointed with its head down a path of light that was, to Timou's eyes, like any other.

On an impulse born of grief and of surprising rage, not caring whether this was a wise thing to do, not caring whether it was a dangerous thing to do, Timou sent her mind toward the snake itself. It seemed both present and not present, both powerful and powerless; it did not seek to avoid Timou's probing

mind, nor did it defend itself, nor attack her. It only slipped
through her awareness like smoke, impossible to encompass. She
could not find the shape of it with her inner eye.

When she opened merely human eyes again to look for it,
the serpent was still there, but it had grown huge: coils rolled
out of sight all around her, disappearing and reappearing through
sheets of light. Its head alone was larger than a man's torso, its
mouth large enough to swallow her whole. It had become the
color of gold, of light. Its eyes, red and gold, contained fire and
the memory of fire. Delicate horns, crimson as blood and long as
swords, curved back from its broad flat head; its fangs when it
smiled were made of crystal and light. Astonished, shocked out
of the storm of emotions that had beset her, Timou tipped her
head back to stare up at it. She swallowed, blinking, and the
snake was suddenly once more tiny and white, with blue eyes
and a blue tracery across its throat. Dazzled, her eyes stunned by
light, she needed a moment to find it again.

"What *are* you?" Timou asked it when she could speak. Her
voice shook. "Which is true?"

It said, as it had before, "Do you not know me?"

Timou took a breath and let it out, looking in lingering
amazement for the shadow of the great fiery serpent hidden in
the shadow of this little hatchling. She could see nothing. She
could not imagine what it was. "No," she whispered.

"You should," repeated the snake, and added in a tone like a
promise or a threat, "You will."

Timou was no longer angry. She felt drained, hollow, emptied out of herself by emotion and amazement. She stared at the little serpent with eyes that felt gritty when she blinked. She asked after a moment, in a voice rough with unshed tears, "What do I seek this time?"

The snake tilted its head a little to the side. "What you will find if you go that way is the Prince," it said, not quite answering her question.

Of course. The Prince. Everyone had been seeking the lost Prince. The stolen Prince. Of course he was here, behind the mirror, in this strange place of solidified light where no one had looked. Except, perhaps, her father. And what had Kapoen earned for his cleverness? "I don't care whether the Prince is ever found or not!" Timou said passionately.

"You will," said the little serpent.

Even through shock, Timou knew that this was probably true. She rubbed her eyelids with the tips of her fingers, trying to calm her heart. The mere attempt made her think of her father and she found it impossible. She made a small sound, which she tried to catch back but could not quite suppress, and put her hands over her eyes.

"If not now, when?" asked the snake, unmoved. It uncoiled itself and indicated a narrow angle of light that crossed in front of them perhaps a hundred feet away. "The Prince is that way."

After a moment Timou stood up wordlessly. She hesitated, looking at the place her father's body had lain for her to find it, but there was no sign it had ever been there. The blood was gone. Yet she was oddly reluctant to walk away, as though as long as she stayed in this one place, her father might suddenly reappear, might not really be dead. . . . She knew this was not true. She was alone.

The snake had not waited. It was not out of sight, but soon it would turn along a different angle of light and then it, too, would be gone. . . . Timou moved, stiffly, to follow it.

It seemed this time that she followed the little snake for only a little while. It turned swiftly and confidently from one flat plane of diamond-hard condensed light to another, from one path to another that always led in some strange and unpredictable direction.

At length the snake stopped, allowing Timou to come up to it. Ahead of them a path crossed theirs at a nearly perpendicular angle, slanting upward steeply. "The Prince is there," said the snake.

Timou was still not certain she cared. But she asked after a moment, "Is he alive?"

The snake let its mouth open a little, seeming to smile. Timou could see the milky crystal of its fangs. "Go and find out."

"Where will you be?"

"Everywhere," said the serpent. It watched her, its winter-blue eyes impossible to read.

Timou turned her back on it, cleared her mind of expectation—this was difficult, because the image of a silver knife and a trickle of blood kept wanting to appear before her mind's eye—and walked forward, turning the sharp-edged corner when she came to it, and finding herself on a level path, as always.

The Prince was there. He sat staring intently into a wall of opalescent light, cross-legged on the floor, his hands on his knees, his back to Timou. She wondered what visions or memories or wishes the Prince might see moving within that wall. All she saw in it when she followed his intent gaze was a faint blurred reflection of his face.

The Prince's hair, dark oak-brown and perfectly straight, fell down his back in a neat braid, bound off at the end with gold. He wore a russet shirt with gold showing through narrow russet ribbons at the puffed sleeves, brown leggings embroidered with russet and gold, and black boots with an intricate gold tracery around their cuffs. He looked like a Prince. A naked sword with a black hilt lay by his side. Timou could see the rise and fall of his shoulders as he sighed, so at least she was sure he was not dead.

She came a step forward, oddly reluctant to speak and thus break the privacy and silence that held the Prince. But he heard her step and turned his head.

At once he was on his feet, and at once, in an attack wholly unexpected, that sword was in his hands and driving at Timou with all the fury and desperation of long trapped months. The Prince was very fast. Timou could never have avoided that blow. Vivid terror shocked her back into the moment; she melted into the blade instead, became a line of light reflected along its deadly edge, rode it through the arc of its attack, and poured herself into the wall of light on the other side. The light tried to carry her with it along its infinite path; for a moment Timou almost went with it, letting herself dissolve into it forever. But even as that impulse formed, Timou knew it was childish; she was ashamed even to have felt it. She pulled herself back into her own form, shaping her body out of the fall of light and the memory of darkness and the movement of air. It was harder to do this time than it had been when she'd first found herself in this maze: she had less to return to now.

The Prince, with a sound of despair, flung down his sword. "What do you want?" he cried. "Just tell me what you want!"

"I think—" Timou said shakily, "I think, Your Highness—you are Prince Cassiel, of course?—I think you are mistaking me for someone else."

The Prince stared at her. Slowly his expression changed. He did not look much like his older half brother. His face was gentler, elegant rather than harsh. His eyes were not the night-dark eyes of his brother, but a warmer color: the color of the wood at the heart of an oak. They were wide now, with rage and desperation just giving way to dawning surprise. His mouth was tight. He said harshly, in a voice not meant, Timou judged, for harshness, "Who are you?"

"No one you know." Timou came forward a cautious step. "No one who is your enemy."

"You are a mage. How old are you?"

"How old do you think I am?"

"Ageless," the Prince said. His voice shook, then steadied. It occurred to Timou that he was not, in fact, much older than she. "I think you are as old as the world, and as cruel as the sky. If you would tell me what you want, at least I would know."

"I am seventeen. My name is Timou. My father—" Timou

stopped briefly, and then went on with difficulty, "My father, the mage Kapoen, was here. He died here. Blood ran from his heart in a great river."

"I saw him," the Prince said slowly. "I followed the river of blood out of curiosity and found the man at the end. He was already dead. I did not know him, but I tried to draw out the knife. It was like smoke in my hands; I could not grasp it. He was your father? I am sorry for your loss." He sounded perfectly sincere, as though even in this strange place and suspecting her of being his enemy, the Prince could still spare a moment of compassion for the loss of a father.

Timou did not want to think about that loss, and somehow the kindness of the Prince's voice hurt her as the chill indifference of the serpent had not. She wavered for a moment toward tears.

The Prince's voice, questioning, steadied her and drew her back to the present. "Do you know who killed him?"

Timou bowed her head. "I think . . . my mother."

The Prince moved a little, and stilled again. "Your mother."

"I think you have seen her. I looked in the mirror in your Palace and saw myself reflected, but I think . . . I think it was my mother looking out at me. From this place. This trap she had . . . she had prepared for me. I wanted to find her," Timou confessed, "but I know now why my . . . my father did not want me to." She shut her eyes for a moment, waiting to be beset by sorrow or anger. But there was, for the moment, nothing but a cold silence. "If only he had told me about her," she whispered. "Why didn't he ever tell me?"

"Perhaps he couldn't bear to," the Prince suggested gently. "Perhaps he loved her, or feared her. Perhaps he hoped you would never need to know about her." He came closer to Timou and stood gazing down at her. She brushed her hair away from her face impatiently with her hands, blinked away tears, and stared back at him.

"Your eyes are different," he said at last. "Your face is a little different. Rounder. Softer. Or maybe that, too, is your eyes. . . . You look younger. She looks . . . Her eyes look like they have seen all the ages of the world. Your voice is different. You sound . . . She mocked me. She told me . . . well. Your voice is not like hers. Timou. Is that your name?"

Timou nodded.

"She would not tell me hers. But I know it, or at least I know the one she gave my father. Lelienne. Was that your mother?"

Timou closed her eyes for a moment. She was remembering that the name had unlocked her father's most private book. "I think that it was. I think it must have been."

"You are not her. I see that now. She could . . . I am sure she could make herself look younger or older. But I don't think . . . I don't think she could change her eyes. Not to your eyes."

"It isn't hard to change the color of one's eyes."

"I was not referring to the color." The Prince moved restlessly. "You say this is a snare she meant for you?"

"Yes," Timou said reluctantly. "For me, and for . . ."

"For your father, yes." The Prince touched her hand in quick sympathy.

"And for you, perhaps."

"I have indeed been trapped here a long time, I think. This is a good cage, and not only for mages. I have not found a way out."

"There is always a way out."

The Prince said, his voice sharp with despair, "Did your father teach you that?"

"Yes," said Timou. It was true, she realized. Her father had not told her about this maze of light, about Deserisien and his sorcerers . . . about her mother. But he had taught her to trust that no puzzle was unsolvable. And she knew that was true. The things he had taught her had been true. She drew a slow breath and let it out, feeling her heart begin at last to settle with that realization. She closed her eyes and sat down where she was, on the floor, her back against a wall of light. She said, her eyes still closed, "My father taught me that riddles have answers. We will find the answer to this one."

The Prince did not respond.

Timou wrapped her arms around her knees and bowed her head, reaching after stillness, the quiet of mind and heart that would let her find the answer she sought. She held in her mind the shape of this place, the space the Prince occupied, the space the sword occupied. She knew when the Prince bent and picked up the sword, and knew when he sat down on the floor, cross-legged, as he had been when she had first seen him. She asked, "What were you looking for, earlier, in that wall?"

After a moment the Prince answered, "Sometimes there are shapes, and voices. Sometimes you see movement you can almost recognize as someone you know. This place is the one where they come through the most clearly. I stay here and watch them."

Timou opened her eyes and looked at him. He was not looking into the wall now. He was watching her, his oak-colored eyes crowded with questions. She said, "So you have given up searching for a way that leads out of this place?"

The Prince shrugged, a minute gesture. "I searched at first. For a long time. There is no— If there is a way out, I could not find it. I tried to break a wall once, but my sword shattered first." He followed Timou's glance to the sword lying in front of him, whole and undamaged. He said, "I found a place where the broken hilt reflected between walls like a whole sword. When I looked at it again, it was whole."

"How strange," murmured Timou. "How strange." She looked, narrow-eyed, into the shadowless distance, thinking. She was relieved to find that she could, that she had not after all been stunned senseless by . . . everything. That she had not altogether lost the stillness her father had taught her. "I think . . . I think this is not a place at all. I think it is a reflection of something more real than it is. A trap, yes, but not made to be a trap."

"What, then?" the Prince demanded in clear frustration, getting to his feet. "It is enough of a trap for me!"

"She means it to be. But I think . . . I think really it is a puzzle." Serpents rose up in her mind, long and black, or small and white, or huge and made of fire. . . . Their eyes, slit-pupiled and unreadable, stared back at her out of memory. She said slowly, "Sometimes things aren't what they seem. Or sometimes there are, I don't know, layers beyond what you first see. This place . . . I don't think this is part of the Kingdom at all. But I don't think it's really outside the Kingdom either. I think the Kingdom encompasses it."

The Prince dismissed all abstract considerations with a sharp wave of his hand and went straight to the point: "If you are a mage, can you find a way out of this place, wherever it is? Puzzle, maze, whatever it is?"

"Well," said Timou, holding out a hand for him to help her to her feet, "I know that there is always a way out. That is a beginning."

CHAPTER 8

The Bastard did not for one moment mistake the woman who came out of the mirror for the girl who had gone into it. The girl had been a mystery, a curiosity, a puzzle . . . but she had not struck the Bastard as dangerous.

The woman, it was immediately clear to him, was exceedingly dangerous.

Her eyes were dark, darker than his: black as the night at the heart of the world. They had seen everything, and forgotten nothing. The weight of that dark gaze pressed on him like a physical force when she met his eyes. And the woman was smiling. The Bastard could imagine a tiger smiling like that as it found its prey at bay, trapped in a corner before it.

"Well," she said, and looked slowly about the room before bringing that heavy gaze back to press against the Bastard. Her voice was light and pretty. Behind the prettiness was something else: a sleek satisfaction that was deeply disturbing. "My son. Have you no greeting for your mother?"

The Bastard did not doubt this claim. He almost thought he remembered her himself, though he had been only a baby when she had left the City. Her name, he knew, was Lelienne. Her white beauty was as the tales described, but no story recalled her ageless gaze or the sense of power that clung to her: these things she must have hidden from his father. Questions fell through his mind like the pieces to a puzzle, then locked into shape. He said, knowing it was true, "You took my brother."

"Young Cassiel." The woman's smile became a shade more brilliant. "Oh, yes."

"Why?" asked the Bastard. He had not moved. He did not move now.

The woman did. She took a step forward. "You are my son," she said. "My son, and son of the King. You can give me the Kingdom. Young Cassiel must first give it to you."

"I will give you nothing," the Bastard said flatly.

The woman's smile did not dim. "How unfilial. My son, is that how you speak to your mother?"

Her tone had been gentle, but the weight of her gaze now became terrible: it pressed on the Bastard until he could not endure it. Though he fought it, it pressed him down. He went to his knees at last with a low cry of anger and humiliation, shaking. He was aware, tangentially, of Galef moving to draw his sword, and then stopping, white and still, with the sword half drawn. He was aware of Marcos beginning to move, and also stopping, one thick hand reaching suddenly out, as though for something beyond his grasp.

The pressure eased once he had been forced to yield to it. On his knees, he looked up at his mother. The Bastard had spent his life wondering about his mother, and now he did not need to wonder: he felt his heart pause in its beating, in terror and dismay. Pride demanded that he try to rise. Sense and the memory of her power suggested otherwise. The Bastard had both pride and sense in abundance, but he had always known how to rule his pride. Sense won. He stayed on his knees, grimly. She smiled down at him. Her eyes did not smile. They were expressionless, blank, filled with age and secrets.

"You cannot fight me," she said gently. "You will try, of course, and fail." She glanced around at the little dressing room, by implication through its walls and out around the Palace. The Bastard would not have been surprised if she could look through walls: he even expected it. Perhaps her gaze pierced beyond the Palace, to the City. Perhaps she could see beyond the City, to the edges of the Kingdom. He would have believed it of that gaze. When she returned her attention to him, the power of it struck him like a blow, and he could not keep from flinching.

"My son," Lelienne said, still gently. "You may kiss my foot."

The Bastard saw that his mother understood his pride, and that she meant to break it at once. She meant him to refuse. She would punish that refusal in a way that would break the nerve and the pride of everyone in the Palace. He understood this, and yet he also knew that if he did not try to sustain his pride in the face of this woman, the memory of that failure of nerve would break his pride forever. And besides this, he judged it important to see what his mother would do. What she would choose to do, and what she had the power to do. He therefore did not move.

The woman, smiling again, glanced once more around the room. Marcos, looking pale and strained, met her eyes for an instant and then looked away, his mouth twitching. Galef had shoved his sword back into its scabbard and crossed his arms over his chest. He looked at the Bastard, then at Marcos. When he saw that Marcos was afraid of the woman, he did not look down himself, but stared into her eyes, pale and steady; the Bastard wanted to shout at him to look away. There were several other guardsmen present. Taking their cue from their captain, they stood stolidly, waiting. She looked back at last at Marcos.

The mage shut his eyes. He blurred suddenly, shredding into the air—his own power, and not hers; the woman's dark gaze pulled him back ruthlessly into his own shape, pinning him in place. She frowned slightly. Marcos made a low sound in his throat. The air between them rang with power like a bell. Marcos was fighting her, the Bastard knew, but Lelienne did not seem to feel his power. She stroked the long fall of her white hair back ˙with both hands, looking satisfied; a delicate blush rose under her fair skin.

Marcos's hands stiffened suddenly, his arms, his face. He was turning to stone before them. Stone closed across his mouth, stopping a sound he had tried to make: a word, a plea. The stone cracked around the mage's fingers as he fought it, and closed again, merciless. His robes fell around him in folds of marble and lime. His eyes remained human, trapped in a face of stone, and after a moment it was clear that Lelienne meant to leave him that way: trapped and aware behind stone.

The guardsmen had fallen back, their faces white and set. Galef threw a stricken look at the Bastard, asking how he could fight this.

The Bastard looked only at his mother. He said, "Undo it. I will do anything you ask."

"I will leave him like this, and you will still do anything I command, my son. I will crush one man after another in my hand, until all who fight me are destroyed and all who are left have fallen at my feet. I can do this. Do you wish me to begin?"

"The more you destroy, the less you have to rule. Do you wish to destroy what you came here to hold?"

"Do you think you know why I came here?" asked Lelienne, smiling again. "You will hand me this City, and this Kingdom. My son. My King-born son. And my mage-born daughter will yield to me all the strange old magic that it holds. You will have no choice. Nor will she. Will you fight me?"

"Yes," said the Bastard.

"No. Or I shall break every stone in this City into pieces. You cannot even stand without my leave. Stand."

He could not.

"Kiss my foot."

The Bastard bowed his head, struggling against the weight of her regard. "Undo what you did to Marcos, and I will."

His mother's strength, limitless, crushed the Bastard to the floor and stopped his breath. All his bones bent under that pressure. The stones of the floor ground into his palms, into his face. He would have cried out, but had no breath for a cry. She said softly, from infinitely far above, "Never bargain with me, my son. I never bargain. But yield to me, and perhaps I shall be gen-erous."

Slowly, bone by bone, fighting for every movement and every breath, he crossed the few feet that separated them. It took all his strength to turn his head enough to set his mouth against her white slipper.

At once the pressure disappeared. Shaking, the Bastard dragged himself back to his knees. He did not try to get to his feet. He did not trust his own strength to make it upright; he did not trust his mother's whim to allow it.

"Who rules here?"

"You," whispered the Bastard.

"Whose hand lies upon this City?"

"Yours."

"You will give me this Kingdom."

The Bastard shut his eyes, opened them. He said steadily, "You have taken it already."

"You may kiss my foot."

The Bastard at once placed one hand on the stone floor and touched his lips again to his mother's foot. He stayed there, bent low. She moved above him; when he looked up, he saw she was smiling. Her smile sent horror prickling down his spine, but he did not move.

"I can be generous," said Lelienne, and began to walk away, adding casually over her shoulder, "You may stand, my son."

The Bastard got to his feet. In the time it took him to do so, his mother had already restored Marcos. The mage was pale. His eyes were open, but blind. He swayed, and would have fallen except that Galef took a step forward and caught him. It was a brave act. Lelienne glanced at him and away, fortunately disinterested.

"This is my City," said Lelienne, speaking to the Bastard. "I claim it, and all within it, and all without, to the very edges of this Kingdom. You, my son, may present me to your court and to the City, at dusk. There will be a great feast. See to it." She spoke without evident triumph, but only with that same satisfaction that had been in her voice from the start; she had known from the beginning that he would surrender to her power, that the City would yield to her strength, and so there was no reason for triumph. When she walked away, it was with quiet steps and no fanfare. She did not need fanfare. She already ruled, more subtly and with an infinitely tighter grip than the Queen in her tower, or the missing King, or the Bastard, whom she had made to bring all their power to her.

"How can we fight her?" Galef asked the Bastard later, while the sun slid lower in the sky and shadows lengthened. He had helped bring Marcos to the Bastard's rooms, where the mage now lay, eyes closed, across the blankets of the bed. His breathing was still ragged.

The Bastard watched him with concern, but answered the captain's question briefly. "We cannot. Don't ask such questions."

"But—"

"Neill is right," whispered Marcos without opening his eyes. "She will hear you."

"What is she? A mage?" asked the Bastard.

Marcos turned his head a little toward the Bastard's voice. "She is an echo in an old story. A name in a history older than this Kingdom. She is not a mage. I have no clear idea what she is."

"Is she really your mother?" Galef asked the Bastard, and then bowed his head under the Bastard's icy stare. "Forgive me—" he breathed. "I am stupid with fear."

The Bastard touched his arm, forcing a smile. He had spent his childhood dreaming of the mother who had left him in the heart of the Kingdom and gone away . . . and now this was the face of all his dreams. He made himself speak gently. "No. I am sorry. We are all stupid with fear, I think. Her name is Lelienne. That is the name she gave my father. She is my mother. What else she is, I think none of us ever knew, least of all my father."

"Her heart is stone," whispered Marcos. "Or ice. I am still made of stone. . . ."

"Hush," said the Bastard gently, and helped him to sit, offering him a cup of hot spiced wine.

Marcos waved away the cup. "Inside," he said. He touched his own chest. "She has enclosed me in stone, though you cannot see it. I move, I breathe . . . but, Neill, I am not a mage. The memory of power is there, but I cannot touch it, nor reach out of myself. I cannot light so much as a candle for you. Neill, I'm sorry. . . ."

"For what?" said the Bastard harshly.

"I can't help you. I can't. Even if I find a way out of her spell. I am afraid of her. Don't trust me, Neill. I don't think I can fight her." The mage met his eyes.

The Bastard touched his shoulder absently, considering this

extraordinary statement. He said after a moment, "I don't think you can either. It's all right, my friend. I understand."

"Do you?" Marcos asked urgently. "Do you? I'm sorry. . . ."

"Hush. I promise you I understand." The Bastard pressed his shoulder again, and rose. He stood thoughtfully, looking out the window at the deepening shadows. "It will be dusk very soon. Stay here, Marcos, until you are able to go back to your own house. Then go there and stay there, if you think that best, out of her way. Galef—" He looked at the captain. "Can you come? I must go to the hall, but can you stand at my back? I expect there will be some danger."

The captain picked up his sword, slung it on—a matter of habit, since he could not have imagined it would be useful. "More to you than to me, I should think."

"Oh, no. I am not in danger." The Bastard moved restlessly. "Save my vanity, I suppose. But she has shown already she will strike at others to punish me. I will try, but I do not know whether I will be able to yield my pride to her quickly enough to protect you."

The captain shrugged. "I will stand at your back," he said.

The great hall had been lit with all its multitude of white parchment lamps. Word had gone out without the Bastard needing to give any specific order: all the court was in attendance, waiting behind their chairs for the appearance of this newest and most surprising power that had come into the City. Courtiers were interested; ladies curious; the young men who had been Prince Cassiel's close friends and confidants looked suspicious and angry. The mage Trevennen was present, high up along the

King's table. He stood behind his chair with his hands folded on its carved back, looking contained, attentive, and patient. The guardsmen in the hall cast uneasy glances at their captain, and Galef left the Bastard's side briefly to speak to one and another among them. Servants hurried here and there, fussing with the last-minute table arrangements. They, probably the best informed of all the court, looked terrified.

The Queen alone was already seated, at her place to the immediate left of the head of the King's table. Her face was as still and stiff as if she had been made of wax. Her gaze, when she met the Bastard's eyes, was unreadable. Her ladies fluttered around her nervously.

The Bastard's mother was not yet present. No doubt, the Bastard thought, she intended to make an entrance; he thought she would enjoy creating a spectacle. He walked quietly to claim his place, at the right hand of the King's place. Galef walked behind him and took up a place behind his chair.

To the Queen, the Bastard said, speaking in a low voice, "Ellis, if you must throw something tonight, throw it at me. Do not throw anything at my mother."

The Queen gave him a level look out of her striking violet eyes. "Your mother."

"She is a mage, or something very like. She is very dangerous."

"She has claimed you, I hear."

"Is that what you hear?" The Bastard paused, then said harshly, "If you have hated me, Ellis, I think you will be satisfied by whatever claim my mother makes of me tonight."

"Yes," said the Queen, calmly deliberate. "That, too, I heard."

Lelienne came into the hall at that moment. All white she was, save for her black eyes: white hair dressed with pearls, stiff white gown embroidered with ivory, skin pale as the most delicately blushed rose. She seemed in the soft light to be younger than the Bastard himself.

The Queen had stiffened when Lelienne entered. She stared down the length of the hall at the white lady, her back very straight, her hands folded flat on the table before her, her face closed and still. Her violet eyes glinted in her face, almost as pale at that moment as that of the other woman.

Lelienne strolled up the long, long hallway as though passing through a private garden. And yet, though she quite clearly meant to make a show, there was a touch of humor in her smile when she at last reached the head of the King's table and met, for a moment, the Bastard's eyes: it was as though she played an elaborate charade and invited the Bastard to share her amusement with it.

The hall had quieted the moment Lelienne had stepped into it. The quiet had deepened with every step she took from the tall entryway to the King's table. By the time she reached the King's chair and turned to stand behind it, the silence was absolute. Turning to the Bastard, she said, in her light, charming voice, "My son, introduce me."

The Bastard closed his hands carefully on the back of his chair. He said expressionlessly, looking out at the assembled court and speaking to be heard at the farthest reaches of the hall, "This is Lelienne, my mother, once loved by my father the King.

In his absence, she rules this Palace and this City and this Kingdom."

Smiling, Lelienne seated herself in the King's chair. With a
rustle of stiff cloth and of whispers, the court moved as one to
sit, but a small movement of his mother's hand stopped the Bastard when he would have followed this example. "My son," she
said, smiling. "You need not sit. Kneel here, beside me."

The Bastard lowered his eyes to hide rage and shame. He
asked in a low voice, "If I refuse, whom will you punish?"

Long white eyebrows lifted as his mother turned to gaze at
him with apparent surprise. "Perhaps I will let you choose."

He moved, stiffly, to do as she commanded, kneeling on the
hard stone at her right hand. Whispers exploded down the length
of the hall, with a sound like birds taking flight off the waters of
the Lake. The Bastard did not look up. Color had flooded into
his face.

"You will eat the bread I give you from my plate," said his
mother gently. "You will not refuse. When I wish wine, you may
rise to pour it. When I speak to you, you will answer, and you
will speak truthfully. Who is powerful in this court?"

"I was."

"Who else?"

The Bastard named half a dozen men, men who had been
friends and advisors of his father, and three or four men and one
woman who were competent and knew how to direct affairs
within the City so that everyday matters ran smoothly.

"Will they fight me?"

"Not," said the Bastard precisely, "when they see that you have brought me to your heel like a dog." He could feel the covert stares of all the court from where he knelt, and knew this was true.

His mother smiled. She knew it, too. She said pleasantly, "You have not named Ellis, the Queen."

Glancing up, the Bastard saw the Queen turn her head and give Lelienne a hard, narrow stare from her violet eyes. He said swiftly, "She had my father's ear. Without him, she has nothing."

"She has power. Men's eyes will go to her, out of habit if nothing else. She could be a nuisance to me, if not a danger. As she might have been a nuisance to you—if not a danger. You shut her up in her own rooms. What shall I do with her?"

"Why not the same?"

"Why not," suggested his mother, "something creative?"

The Queen, her mouth thin, her hands shaking with anger, had leaned back in her chair and now stared at Lelienne, eyes sparking with outrage. The Bastard caught her eyes with his and held her silent through a flashing effort of will that amazed them both. When he looked back at his mother's black eyes, she was clearly amused, and he knew she had missed nothing. He answered, "Because the court would resent it, and that would be a nuisance to you, if not a danger. Put her back in her rooms and leave her there, and you will arouse no such resentment."

"Not regarding what I may do to you?"

"I have enemies, and few friends. The City loves the Queen. When my father shouts, only Ellis dares shout back at him. And behind her temper she is kind. She has spoken for many men before the King. When you humble me, many men will be satisfied that you should. Do the same to the Queen, and they will feel differently."

Lelienne smiled, her black eyes contained and secretive. "So," she said, "my son has a feel for the rule of men." She turned to Ellis. "Does the Queen have a temper she has not shown me?"

Ellis, amazingly, looked away, though an angry flush rose in her face.

"So. When you go to your rooms later, you will stay there, and be quiet. Perhaps I will forget you are there, if you are wise," Lelienne said, and looked out thoughtfully along the hall, where all the court was watching with covert fascinated attention. "And you, my son. What shall I do with you?"

"You have taught me not to fight you."

"You have begun to learn that, perhaps. And, evidently, you have no temper of your own. Who taught you that?"

"I learned it of life."

"You learned it of power constrained, and as restraint is the beginning of wisdom, you have begun to be wise. Do you yield to me?"

"Yes," said the Bastard tightly.

His mother smiled. "No. You resist me with every breath you take, and every lowered glance you show me. You are experienced at waiting, my son. But capable, I take it, of action. Where is your father? I had anticipated our reunion."

The Bastard thought she was mocking him. He flushed. But

Lelienne repeated her question, adding, "I took the son, and hid him in the light behind the mirror, but I had not expected you to remove Drustan from his high place for me. In that, you did surprise me. In that, perhaps you are indeed my son. However, I shall need him. I know he is not dead. Where is the King?"

"I have no idea," the Bastard said blankly. He still expected elaborate deception, though he could not imagine the purpose of it. He was off balance from this unexpected line of questioning, and thought she had done this to him intentionally. He was waiting for that hidden purpose to emerge. While he waited, he said cautiously, "I thought you took him, as you took Cassiel."

His mother glanced at him. Her ageless eyes pressed down on the Bastard with a weight like the iron darkness at the heart of the world. His breath jerked under the pressure, and he set a hand against the floor for support. "Where is Drustan?" his mother asked again, dangerously quiet, and he understood at last that she was in earnest. "I will not ask again."

The Bastard bowed his head. He said carefully, "I hid him in the eternal City. I hid him in the Lake. He wanders there, blind to what you do here."

Lelienne leaned back in the King's chair. She was smiling. Though she had her eyes on him still, the pressure had gone from her gaze. "The reflected City. That is where you put him? And you not even a mage?"

"He wished to pass into the eternal City," the Bastard explained, still with the most exquisite care. "And he is, after all, the King. That City was only a breath away, for him. It took no spell to carry him there, but only the smallest nudge. Now he is lost in the Lake because he cannot find, even there, what he seeks."

The Queen sat back in her chair, a hand lifting to touch her mouth, but his mother was pleased. "My clever son. Cassiel I have secured where I can reclaim him at will, but I shall need Drustan as well. You shall bring him to me."

The Bastard set his teeth against any sound of protest.

"And Trevennen, too, shall help me, since your friend Marcos has become indisposed," added his mother. "Where is Marcos? I see he is not here."

The Bastard was still for a moment. Then he said, "I have sent him away from the Palace. He fears you. He will not return, I think."

"He will return, if I summon him. Or, I have no doubt, if you summon him. Later, perhaps. He could be useful to me. Indeed, I am certain he will be. However— Trevennen! Declare yourself."

From his place only half a dozen seats down the table, the mage stood as Lelienne lifted her voice in that summons. His expression was composed, his gaze level. The Bastard saw that he was not surprised or offended or afraid, and understood suddenly why his mother had hidden Cassiel in a fall of light behind a mirror, and yet the one mage of the Kingdom who had looked behind every mirror and every fall of light had not found him there. Rage rushed into his throat and choked him. He made no sound. He was not certain what might have shown in his face. But no one was looking at him. Trevennen was looking at his mother, and his mother was watching the court. Only Ellis, the

Queen, spared a quick glance for the Bastard, her own face showing remarkably little. Her hand had closed hard around the stem of her wineglass, and he was momentarily terrified she might fling the glass the length of the table. But she did not. He had not imagined her capable of such restraint, and learned otherwise in that moment.

"Lelienne. Madam," Trevennen said. He bowed slightly.

"Whom do you serve?"

The tall mage bowed again, more extravagantly, a hand over his heart. "Madam, I am your servant."

The court had been listening in frozen anticipation, and for the second time whispers exploded down its length, with a sound like the rising wind. Neither the mage nor the white lady paid any heed to the murmurs. "Approach me," Lelienne commanded, and the mage left his place to make his way to the head of the table, where he kissed the hand she offered him and then straightened attentively.

"You have been listening to our conversation," Lelienne said severely.

Trevennen bent his elegant head in an acknowledgment that seemed to the Bastard only faintly guarded, as though he believed he knew the limits of Lelienne's humor. Even fighting rage, the Bastard wondered whether he really did.

"You have heard what my son has said. Is this truth?"

"I was intrigued to hear it, madam. I believe it could be true. Your son is an interesting and subtle man, and ambitious. And born of the royal house, as of course you intended."

"And thus able to see into the eternal City."

"Likely so, madam. Everyone knows he goes to Tiger Bridge
at dusk, to look at the City in the Lake when the Lake becomes
a mirror of the eternal dream." The mage gave the Bastard a look
both assessing and curious. "Yes, I think that is quite likely. It
would explain a great deal. If you did not, ah, remove the King
yourself from this ephemeral City . . ."

"No." Lelienne sipped wine and glanced at the Bastard, who
set his teeth, got to his feet, refilled her goblet, and resumed,
without comment or expression, his place kneeling at her side.

"I shall need him," she said, not to the mage, but to the Bastard. "You will bring him back for me."

Had they been alone together, the Bastard might have risked
a refusal. Amid this assembly, he did not dare, and only bowed
his head against her dark, dangerously perceptive gaze.

It was extraordinary how quickly the City accustomed itself to
the rule of a woman it had not seen in thirty-four years, and
who had been at that time thought to be only a woman who had
caught the passing fancy of the King. The City, the Bastard reflected, sensed power, as though authority were a fragrance carried on the wind that blew off the Lake and through every street
and alley and byway.

Everyone knew the Bastard had been brought to heel by his
mother, though she made little show of it after that first banquet
before the court. Everyone knew the Queen was pinioned in her
tower, and everyone knew from her women that she was most

uncharacteristically quiet and meek in her new captivity. Everyone knew that the most powerful mage in the City had kissed
Lelienne's hand and bowed his head under her dark gaze, and
that the other mages hid from her in fear. No one dared offer defiance to Lelienne, and no one dared openly slight Trevennen.

The guard had been reordered, so that men stood at the
Queen's door, and the Bastard's, and throughout the court at the
door of this man and that, but not at the doors of the King's own
apartment, which Lelienne had appropriated for her own use.
The guardsmen reported the movements of those they guarded
to their captain. And their captain reported to Lelienne.

Galef had tried to resign his post. The white lady had turned
the hands of one of his lieutenants into the talons of a bird, and
his voice into the cry of an eagle. Then she had, more pro-
saically, taken the newest and youngest recruit the guardsmen
had among their ranks and hung the young man by his wrists
over a bed of white-hot coals made from burning glass. When
Galef had tried in desperation to draw his sword against her, it
had shattered into light and mist in his hands.

Lelienne had relented only when the guard captain knelt at
her feet and pleaded, in the most abject terms, for forgiveness.
She had left the man with the voice of an eagle, although she had
restored his hands and Galef's sword.

"You should have known better," the Bastard said when the
captain came to set men on his door and beg his pardon for it.
"You knew perfectly well she would punish your defiance with
the pain of those for whom you are responsible. You were there
when she did it to me. How is the boy?"

Galef, shadows of humiliation and rage hidden in his eyes, bowed his head. "Badly burned."

"Will he recover?"

"He will. Though likely he is ruined for a guardsman. Not for his feet," the captain added when the Bastard raised his brows. "But how can he trust those he serves, if they would command such a thing to be done to him? Or me, as his captain, if I cannot prevent it? He thought all he faced were the moods of the King and the high temper of the Queen, and he found this. All he will want now is to go back to his mother's house in the City, and who can blame him?— My lord, if I do not report to her as she commands, I think she will know it."

The Bastard moved restlessly to his window and looked out across the City. From above, and to an ignorant observer, the City would have looked peaceful. The air was cold and still. Crystalline. Fine threads of smoke led straight up in narrow lines from chimneys. There was no movement to the air, and little upon the frosted streets. To the Bastard, the City's quiet seemed . . . fraught.

"My lord . . . ," said the captain tentatively.

"Of course you must report to Lelienne," the Bastard said impatiently. "Of course she will know it if you do not. She hears everything. I think she sees a great deal. Don't defy her. Report to her as she demands. Obey every command she gives— especially those directed against me." He looked straight at the captain, held his gaze.

The captain took a slow breath. "My lord. Yes, my lord."

And whether he understood what the Bastard had not said

was hard to guess. The Bastard said a little more explicitly, "If she is not made angry, everyone will be safer. Far better she should hear nothing that will anger her. Least of all defiance from you. Now, is that quite clear?"

"Yes," breathed the captain.

"So don't try to protect me." The Bastard emphasized the last word with no stress in his voice, only with a sudden direct stare into the captain's eyes. "We want no more boys hung over fire. Do we, Galef?"

"No," said the captain with only the faintest downward flicker of his own eyes to suggest he had heard the Bastard's meaning. He said, with absolute sincerity, "I would eat a great deal of humiliation to prevent that. As you have done, Lord Neill. As you do. Very well. If I must be her man, so I will be. There will be men on your door. They will go where you go. I will ask that you do not try to prevent them."

"No," said the Bastard distantly, and turned back to the window, resting his hands on its narrow sill. "Has she commanded that you cease reporting to me? Or that you refuse my orders?"

"No, my lord."

"Has she ordered a guard set on Trevennen?"

"No, my lord."

"No?" The Bastard thought this was interesting. "Very well. I order it, then. As my mother does not seem concerned with Trevennen's movements and activities, perhaps you need not trouble her with this guard's reports. Although of course you must decide what risks you will take, Galef. In any case, unless you are prevented, you may bring such reports to me."

"Yes, my lord."

The Bastard turned back to the guard captain, crossing his arms and resting his hip on the sill of the window. "Very well, then. Thank you, Galef."

"My lord," acknowledged the captain, bowing, and withdrew.

Turning back to the view, the Bastard gazed out of his window with eyes that saw nothing of the City. What he could not understand was why his mother continued, over these quiet days in which she amused herself torturing his guardsmen, to wait. He had no doubt whatsoever that she intended some precise object in her presence here, in all that she had done. So why, then, did she hold her hand?

It was the mage Trevennen who gave him, at last, the answer to this question.

CHAPTER 9

Since there was nothing else to do, Jonas walked in no particular direction, among pillars that were all the same, over a floor that might be made of black ice. The darkness fell through space like light and struck the eye with its presence. The pillars glowed with it, while their shadows drank it in and swallowed it, creating a strange textured blackness.

When Jonas lifted his eyes and tried to look ahead, he found a kind of radiant darkness along what might have been a horizon, far in the distance. It was not like light or even the promise of light, but it was a less heavy kind of darkness. He hoped—since he must hope for something—to reach it eventually and see what it might be.

Although the pillars were abundant, save for their presence this place seemed to Jonas to be absolutely empty. Where he had heard at least wind in the branches when he walked in the forest, here he heard nothing at all. The air was very cold and still.

He walked until he was too weary to go farther, and then sat down and rested, with his back against a cold pillar for want of any other shelter. For warmth he had only his jacket, which was not meant to protect against real cold. It had been only autumn when he left the village, and he had expected to find himself in the City before the descent of winter. Now he longed for warmth even more than for water. Neither seemed likely to be found in this desolate place.

As a young man, Jonas had learned endurance. He had learned it marching down endless roads in summer dust and spring mud and winter cold, and also during battle, when one must go on and on and never stop, not for all the arrows that came down, not for any sorcerous traps that waited to turn a man's bones to fire at his next step. He had learned it during long brutal months when his army besieged some stubborn town or, usually worse, found itself suffering siege behind its own walls. He remembered those years now, surrounded on all sides by darkness and silence. Pulling his legs up, Jonas wrapped his arms around them and bent forward, leaning his face against his knees. He rested that way, tucked up against the cold, for some indeterminate period marked by neither dusk nor dawn. When cramps in his muscles tormented him, he lay down on the icy floor, stretched out at his full length. And when the cold drove him back to his feet, he walked again, endlessly.

It seemed to Jonas sometimes that he could feel his lungs freezing, and his blood. He shivered continually, sometimes enough to send him staggering a few steps sideways. His fingers were numb, his feet also. He walked with his hands tucked under his arms to warm his fingers, but there was not a great deal he could do for his feet. He only walked on, on feet that eventually he could not feel at all, that might have been lumps of wood attached to the ends of his legs.

Almost as terrible as the cold was his thirst. If the pillars were ice, still he had no way to break off pieces so that he might melt them. His lips cracked with cold and lack of water. There was nothing to be done, and so he did nothing, but only went on, and on.

It was impossible for Jonas to tell how long he walked. He grew thirstier, and more desperately weary, and the tips of his fingers as well as his lips cracked from the cold and the dry air. He might have measured the passage of time by the extent of his misery, except it seemed always on the edge of unendurable. Sometimes he stopped, lay down on the black ice, and waited for either sleep or death to claim him. But he did not die and could not sleep. After a while impatience and cold would drive him back to his feet, and he would go on.

At first Jonas had feared to find himself again face to face with the Hunter, and had listened in terror for the cry of the storm hounds. Then the fear wore out, so that in time he waited with indifference for the sound of the Hunter's bodiless voice and the sight of the twisting shadows of his crown. Eventually he came to long for this encounter. He remembered what the Hunter had demanded from him—*your name, your hands, your heart*—and thought he would give the Hunter all he demanded for one breath of warm air and one moment in the sun. Then in the next breath he was angry, so angry he could not think and could hardly breathe, and was sure that he would gladly die before he would surrender anything of his to the dark Hunter.

At last, when the encounter did not come, the anger itself wore out as well and he came to doubt that he had ever met the

Hunter or spoken with him; he even doubted that the dark
Hunter existed. Jonas thought perhaps he had dreamed the meeting. It even seemed possible to him that he had dreamed the
Kingdom and the years in the village, and even Timou. He saw
her in front of him sometimes, white hair falling down her back,
light sliding through her pale eyes like a hidden laugh, a faint
blush rising under her fair skin at something someone had said.
He knew she was not really there before him. It seemed possible
to him that she had never really existed.

Sometimes he looked over his shoulder, expecting to see
burning Kanha behind him. When he turned his head to look,
he tended to fall, and since the ruined city was never there,
eventually he stopped looking for it. In time he also stopped
seeing Timou before him. After that there was just the dark, and
the necessity—he no longer remembered why—of continuing to
walk forward.

He began to dream while walking. He dreamed he walked
through a field beside a river with the sun overhead, but when
he bent down to the water it was not there, and when he
stopped in the sunlight it faded and lost its warmth. He understood after a time that he was hallucinating. He thought that men
he had known from the past walked beside him. He dreamed
they all walked through a desert night, thousands of them, so
that those at the rear of the column swallowed the dust raised by
those in front. He dreamed that huge stones burning with cold
flame fell through the air all around them. The flames were dark,
and every one gave off its little measure of cold as the stones fell.
They shook the road as they struck the ground, and he fell, and

blinked, and found himself on his hands and knees, surrounded by textured darkness and pillars of ice that glowed blackly.

"Get up!" commanded his sergeant, stopping beside him, urgent and furious.

"Up, boy!" a different voice seconded—his father's voice, rougher, from much farther into the past: from a childhood that seemed infinitely distant and infinitely desirable. Jonas moved a little, murmuring, trying to get his feet under him and unable to find the strength to rise.

"You must get up," said a much quieter voice, much nearer at hand, and Jonas blinked through the darkness and found Timou's father standing beside him. In this place and in this extremity, this seemed perfectly reasonable.

"You must get up," Kapoen repeated. He was standing quietly, his hands at his sides, not two feet away. The darkness lay on him like light. "Jonas. You must get up."

It seemed a great deal to ask. "Help me," Jonas protested, but though he reached out his hand, Kapoen did not move to take it.

"I would if I could," said the mage. "You must do it on your own. You've come a long way. You can make it the whole way if you are stubborn enough. I know you are stubborn. Up. Stand up."

Jonas put his hands on the ice, shoved away from it with arms that seemed to lack all strength. But he made it to his feet, and stood, swaying. When he looked for Kapoen, the mage was not there. This did not surprise him. He took a step, and another.

So he went on. He fell more often now. There was nothing to trip over. He fell when his knees failed to hold him, or when he tried to put his weight on a foot he could not feel. Sometimes he rested where he fell. The cold seemed to bother him less. It entered his bones, until he seemed made of cold, all his bones made of ice. Sometimes it seemed to him that he lay in a meadow, and sometimes in a bed: his own bed, from his boyhood, with his mother singing in the other room.

Then Kapoen would come back and peel illusion ruthlessly away. When Jonas tried to ignore him, the mage's voice would become a whip in the dark, driving, demanding, punishing, until Jonas fought his way back to his feet. He walked blindly some of the time, eyes shut, letting the mage tell him when he wandered off his course, walking into one icy pillar after another with a bruising force that he thought might mean he was, at least, still alive.

"Where is Timou?" Jonas asked the mage once, thinking that if he was to be harried by hallucinations, he would rather it were she.

"In great danger," answered Kapoen.

Jonas laughed and said, "Of course. How else?" It seemed to him that this warning had been inevitable from the moment the mage had started to walk through his waking dreams. "I came here to save her, you know," he confided to Kapoen.

"Foolish and brave," said the mage, "like so many young men. But it was you the Hunter marked for his need. If you had stayed in your home and barred the door, he would have come there and harried you into the dark even so."

"He doesn't exist," Jonas said defiantly, and laughed again. When Kapoen made no answer, he looked for him, feeling suddenly bereft, and was sorry when there was no one there. It seemed cruel of Kapoen, to force him to keep on and on and on, and then just go away like that.

And then, in this place of silent darkness, Jonas found that the strange dark glow he had seen before him from the first, but very far away, grew suddenly stronger and stronger, as though at last he drew close to its source. He seemed to gain new strength just from the thought. He walked more quickly, even lifting his head and looking ahead as though he cared what he might find before him.

At last he came out from among the pillars and found himself standing on the shore of a vast frozen plain of black ice. It was from this that the strange dark glow emanated. It stretched off, unbroken, infinitely far to both sides. But in front of him, out in the midst of the plain, Jonas saw that there was something that loomed: a crag of ice or a broken pillar vaster than any behind him. Or a castle. *No. A tower.* When he thought of this, he knew at once it was indeed a tower, standing vast and solitary in the midst of all that ice. And he knew whom he would find within that tower, and knew that everything he remembered had really happened, and that the Hunter not only existed, but waited there for him to enter that house. He remembered what the widow Raen had said—*Do not enter any house or tower or castle you find, but if you do, there will be a price to pay before you get out*— something of that sort. He had asked what price, and the widow had not known. Now he knew. Rage and terror tried to rise up within him, fought briefly for life, and died, because in all the cold exhaustion within his heart there was nothing to sustain either.

Surrounded by cold and silence, Jonas put his foot on the ice.

It took a long time to cross the ice, but it did not seem so long, because always there was the tower before Jonas, growing slowly larger. Having a clear destination was so new and so welcome that Jonas found himself both more impatient to arrive and yet better able to endure the slow progress he made. He no longer fell, as though the ice itself sustained him as he crossed it, or as though he had gone at last beyond exhaustion to some other state where he might walk forever. Sometimes Jonas watched the tower as he walked, and sometimes he looked down into the black ice.

There seemed reflections within it, as though the frozen ice caught fleeting glimpses from someplace that was not empty and dark and showed them to Jonas as he walked. Even the strange insubstantial darkness the ice cast forth seemed to him a reflection of light, and he looked for light locked frozen into the ice. He looked and looked for light trapped below, realizing only gradually that he had stopped walking. A moment later he understood that he had somehow come to be on his hands and knees, his face inches from the ice as he stared into it. Shaken, he clambered slowly back onto his feet and looked around again for the tower. He found it unexpectedly rising before him, looming, immense, so near he could have taken one step and touched its black stones, though he had no memory of having come so close. His breath caught, and he staggered, falling again. Caught in the tower's shadow, he found the shadow alone weighed on him so he could not get his breath, could hardly get to his feet. There was a door before him, three times his height, standing open to show a vast arch out of which darkness, heavy and absolute, fell like a chasm into night.

Jonas had believed himself beyond fear, but found now that he was paralyzed with it. This did not last. It could not: exhaustion will always defeat terror. *You will find nothing here, until you find me again.* Jonas had found nothing in all his long walking through the dark, and had come at last to this place, where he knew he would find the Hunter. He shut his eyes for a moment, longing to open them and find himself in the green forest, or in his room in the widow's house in the village; longing to keep his eyes closed forever against the dark and never open them to see the black walls of the Hunter's tower or the heavy darkness falling out of its open doorway.

He opened his eyes. The tower was there, rising harsh and uncompromising out of lesser shadows. The doorway was there. The dark was there, within it, waiting.

At last he made his way across those last few steps that lay before him and into the great dark that waited. The dark had seemed like a chasm, and Jonas seemed to fall as he stepped into it—his breath stopped and he did not cry out aloud. He might have truly fallen or only seemed to fall, but he caught himself, staggering, within a great hall. Sharp-edged columns came down from a high-vaulted ceiling far above. The darkness within the hall was fine and delicate. He could see in this place, almost as though there were true light. The Hunter was present, on a massive throne at the far end of the hall. Twisting, branching shadows shifted and moved immeasurably far above, confusing the eye; Jonas tried not to look up at them. The Hunter seemed at first enormous, many times the size of a man, and then only man-sized; at first very far away, so far Jonas might have walked for-ever without coming before his throne, and then close by, so close that three steps would bring him to it. He was not a hallucina-tion or a dream, and could never have been mistaken for either.

Closing his eyes, Jonas took three steps; then, sinking to his knees, he opened his eyes and lifted his head.

The Hunter was there. His hands gripped the arms of his throne, like the hands of a man but made of deep shadows. Bending his head so that shadows whirled above, he looked down at Jonas out of pitiless yellow eyes that were definitely not blind. *Jonas,* he said.

"Lord." Jonas looked up into those predatory eyes and shaped the word without sound, from a throat and with a tongue too dry to produce sound.

The Hunter moved his hand as though he held something, and Jonas saw after a moment that he did: a cup, larger than any two ordinary cups, short-stemmed and with a broad base. The cup held liquid, clear as crystal, glimmering faintly within.

Drink, said the Hunter.

Jonas took the cup from the Hunter in both his hands, hands that shook with shock as well as an extremity of weariness, and gazed into it. Then he looked up mutely.

Drink, the Hunter bade him. *Drink.*

Shutting his eyes, Jonas lifted the cup to his lips.

It was water, but it was not like any water Jonas had ever tasted. It was like drinking rain on a fine summer's day, or dew from a spring flower, or water drawn from a deep well from within the earth. It tasted like waking from sleep on a clear winter morning when snow has just fallen, or like the moment that comes after the lightning and before the thunder, or like the realization of first love. It tasted like light, or the memory of light. It slaked thirst, but it also healed the heart and restored the soul.

Jonas gave the cup back to the Hunter with hands that trembled now with a different kind of shock. It seemed to him that, after he had had the extremity of fear ground out of him in the Hunter's dark Kingdom, this extremity had now been restored to him as well. Terror ran through him, bright and quick as fire.

The Hunter said, *Perilous to drink from any cup you are given in any Kingdom that is not your own.*

Jonas took a moment to gather his nerve, and answered in a voice that shook only a little, "Lord, I have no hope save your mercy, and I have been told that you are merciless."

The Hunter turned his head a little, studying his captive. Immeasurably far above, shadows twisted and writhed in answer to that movement. *Surrender to me your hopes and your fears,* he demanded.

Jonas shut his eyes, shuddering. "Lord," he said, "I have nothing that matters of hope, and all my fear is already yours."

It seemed to him that the Hunter might have smiled. *Jonas,* said the Hunter. *Surrender your name to me.*

Bowing his head, Jonas yielded his name to the Hunter.

Yes, said the Hunter. *Jonas. Give me your heart.*

"I can't," Jonas pleaded. He opened his eyes to meet the passionless unhuman gaze that looked down at him, and said helplessly, hopelessly, "Be merciful, Lord Hunter. You brought me here to your Kingdom. Why? I don't understand. To torment me? Why should you care about me one way or another? Am I a tool for you to use against Timou? I will not be used that way. But what is it you want?"

The Hunter moved restlessly. Shadows swung and twisted. He said, *I want you.*

"I will give you everything you demand, but I cannot give you my heart!" cried Jonas. "Ask for something else. For anything else."

Your eyes, said the Hunter. *Your tongue. Your hands. Your heart.*

Jonas bowed his head, his hands closing into fists, gripping nothing. "Why?" he whispered. "Why?"

It is what I need.

"It's not," Jonas breathed, "a price I can pay." He looked up, and up, at the dark Hunter. It seemed to him that the Hunter filled the hall, filled the castle, filled this entire dark Kingdom: it seemed to him that the round yellow eyes were as large as moons, standing infinitely far above; that the Hunter's twisting crown crossed all the sky. When the Hunter moved, the darkness all around moved with him, shadows sliding and crossing everywhere.

You must, said the Hunter. *Jonas. You will.*

"I can't." Jonas could not stop shaking. "Whatever you will do to me, Lord, I cannot pay that price."

You will. The Hunter moved, reaching out, and Jonas flinched, stifling a cry of helpless terror. But the Hunter's hand only took him by the shoulder. His grip was not cruel, but there seemed no limit to his strength. He rose, drawing Jonas also to his feet; he seemed now tall, but no taller than a very tall man.

Come, he said.

CHAPTER 10

Timou stood with Prince Cassiel and watched echoes of color move through the plane of light before them. Sometimes she thought a shifting glimmer of color and form might resolve into the shape of a person, although this resolution never actually happened. Sometimes she thought she heard, faintly, a sound that might have been voices.

"I think," she said slowly, "this is a reflection of the real Kingdom. That we glimpse it here, dimly. It is distracting. But I do not think it offers a way out."

"Well," demanded the Prince, "how, then?"

"There's a way. Be patient." Timou saw at once that the Prince was not in a mood for this particular advice, and added hastily, "Prince Cassiel, have you seen your father here?"

The young man stared at her, completely startled. "My father?"

"He is missing, too, evidently. For several days, I think. Not nearly so long as you have been missing. But is he here? Or is he somewhere else?"

The Prince said sharply, "If I am here and my father is missing, then who is ruling the Kingdom?"

"It seemed to me that it was your elder brother. Lord Neill."

"Neill." Cassiel moved a hand across the wall, vaguely. "All right," he whispered. "All right, then."

"You think he is working with . . . my mother?"

"I think . . . I think he could be working with his." Cassiel studied Timou. "You could be his sister. I think you are his sister. I think your mother was also his. She trapped me here. But I have not met my father here. Where is he? If it was not that woman who moved against him, then who was it?"

"You think it was Lord Neill."

"It could have been." Cassiel seemed to be struggling with the idea. "I don't want to think so," he said painfully. Doubts crowded into his eyes, and he looked away.

Timou said sympathetically, "Surely not. I would not have thought so. Did my mother tell you any such thing?"

It took Cassiel a moment to answer. When he did, he spoke quietly and not quite steadily, without turning back to meet Timou's eyes. "She told me very little. Other than to tell me that she would possess my Kingdom and all its power. That she would unravel all its strange and wonderful power, she said, so that she could possess it for herself. She did not care that she would destroy the Kingdom. I said I would stop her." He did meet Timou's eyes then, shame and anger and fear struggling in his. "She said I was a source of power, but had no power of my own. She was right. I cannot even break free of her cage!"

Timou winced at the despair in that cry. She said swiftly, "There is always a way out. We shall find it. Wait." Then she sent her mind outward, staying clear of the measureless planes of light, looking for an edgeless, ungraspable presence. She found nothing. The serpent was not there. She could not find it anywhere in all the avenues of infinite light that surrounded them. It was gone.

"And if it is gone," she said aloud, frowning, "then there is a way out. It is still leading the way."

"What is gone?"

"A serpent," Timou said absently, barely listening to him. "A creature that sometimes seems to be a serpent. Or serpents, but I think in the end really they are all the same." She paused as the Prince shifted impatiently and started to speak. The point was— "The point is," she said, lifting a hand to forestall his words, "it is not here. Whatever it is, it was here, it was here and now it is gone. I wonder how it went?"

"Yes. . . ."

"Prince Cassiel. My mother called you a source of power. What power?" Timou gave the Prince a searching look, a look that she sent probing suddenly into his mind, into his heart. When, catching a startled breath, he moved to evade her, she only followed patiently, so that he found her always before him whichever way he turned. "What power?"

"Stop it," whispered the Prince.

"Can you stop me?" Timou touched his mind, riffling through memories of his ash-haired elder brother. These memories were difficult and confused. At one moment Cassiel remembered a man he admired, an older brother he loved; but in the next, a severe, self-contained man with dark secretive eyes— a man he feared he did not know, might never have known. He

fled from confusion into other memories, earlier ones: of his father, very tall, shouting with laughter or fury, or both, at some
moment important to a younger Cassiel; of his mother, volatile
but tender, reaching out toward him. Curious, Timou pursued
that memory.

"Stop it," said Cassiel again, half plea and half command. He
stood with his hands over his eyes, as though that might shield
him. It did not. His breath came hard.

"Can you stop me?" Timou asked again, then answered her
own question, thoughtfully, "No. A source of power, but no
power of your own. . . ." She drew back, behind her own eyes
again.

The Prince dropped his hands to his sides. He took a hard
breath. "Don't . . . do that again."

That had been a command, from a young man remembering
another kind of power. Timou bent her head. "I am sorry. I was
curious. Am curious. What power do you have?"

"Does it matter, if I can't use it?"

"It might. It does. You did not try to stop me."

"I tried. I couldn't."

"Couldn't you?" She studied Cassiel. "Do you know what
you are?"

"What?" he said uneasily.

"You are the heart of the Kingdom." Bending, she gathered
up his sword—it was much heavier than she expected, and wavered in her grasp—and offered it to him, but when he reached
for it, she took his hand in hers with the hilt between their

palms. "You are the source of power, and your power is the Kingdom. If you step away, I'll stop. Don't step away."

Startled, the Prince nevertheless stopped himself from drawing back. He looked into her eyes. Whatever he saw there made him set his teeth and hold still.

Timou met his eyes and sent her mind forward again, looking this time not for Cassiel, but for the Kingdom itself.

Power unrolled before her eyes, vast and complicated and far beyond her ability to comprehend: magic rolled through the air like smoke and bubbled up like water. It was dark and formless as the great forest, brilliant and piercing as light. It seemed to Timou that she heard a single perfect harp note, swelling and falling, underlying everything. The sound pierced her heart. She had never heard it before, never imagined it, but somehow it was familiar. She fell away from its unbearable purity and found herself gasping, clinging to Cassiel's hand as though it were the single point of stability in the world.

Cassiel caught her by the arm when she swayed. "Are you all right?" he asked with sharp concern.

"What?" Timou stared at him. She said in amazement, "You may be the heart of the Kingdom, but I think I just saw its soul. Does she think to possess that? Either she is insane or she must have terrible power." Timou shut her eyes. "She has terrible power."

"Yes," said Cassiel. "But—"

"Oh," said Timou. She drew herself back a step, steadying herself with an effort, shaking her head. "Yes. So do you."

The Prince let her go, watching her carefully. "But I can't use what I have," he reminded her. "I think she can use her power. I think she can use it delicately as a cat steps or powerfully as the hammer of lightning strikes."

"Yes," said Timou. "But she can't keep you in this prison. She could not keep you in any prison. You yourself are the way out." She held out a hand to him.

After a moment he took it.

"Close your eyes," Timou whispered. She closed her own and drew him forward, stepping forward herself out of the maze of light and into the Kingdom, blindly, knowing that where her foot would come down would be . . . would be . . .

She opened her eyes.

They stood hand in hand on a broad street embraced by the golden light of a hot summer afternoon. The pavement beneath their feet was dusty gold; the buildings to either side, tall and pale, caught the light and echoed it. Towers with rounded cupolas made of glass and silver shared the street with longer, lower buildings roofed with creamy-pink tile. Trees, some of them as tall as the towers, cast a dancing lacy shade across the cobbles. The street ran upward in a slow lazy curve, inviting the eye to follow; looking along it, it was possible to see in the distance the graceful white walls of the Palace.

It was the City. But it was entirely empty and completely quiet; it was filled with the heat of a still summer day that owed nothing to the late season of the City Timou remembered. "This isn't right," said Timou, shaken.

"No," said Prince Cassiel, and smiled suddenly. He still held his sword. It had changed: it had turned to glass, or perhaps to light.

Its hilt was made of shadow. It looked now delicate and deadly and somehow more perfectly like a sword. Cassiel seemed to take the sword's transformation for granted, perhaps because he had no attention to spare for it in the midst of all else that had changed. He turned in a slow circle, head tilted back, eyes wide open. He breathed deeply, seeming to want to take in all the air in the City at once. "Don't you know it? This is the other City. The first one: the real one. The City Irinore and the first King, Castienes, saw when they built our City. This is the City in the Lake."

Timou and Prince Cassiel walked through the City in the Lake slowly, side by side. Timou found this City disturbing despite its beauty. Cassiel loved it, with a deep unspoken love that she could hear in his voice when he drew her attention now and then to a finely carved balustrade or a particularly lovely screen made of delicately filigreed wood and ivory. She could see it in his eyes, which lingered like the eyes of a lover on the curve of stone that formed the flank of a tower or on the broad flat flagstone stair that led in a spiral down from their street to another at a lower level.

Timou did not know which was more real and true: the busy City with its thousands of inhabitants, worn by time, or this one, new and fresh, held in a perfect eternal summer within the Lake. Cassiel had called this one the *real* City. Timou thought perhaps both were real: layers of reality lying across one another. But she knew she had liked the inhabited City far better.

They walked toward the Palace. "It is at the heart of the City," said Cassiel simply. Since she had no better ideas, Timou acceded to his desire and walked beside him up the winding street toward the Palace. When the street turned, they could see it before them, white and graceful, growing slowly nearer.

Its gates stood wide open and welcoming, so that even the walls were made to seem welcoming as well, as though they hid secrets behind their sheer faces, but pleasant secrets that one would enjoy discovering.

The Palace was set beyond the walls in the midst of green and growing gardens. Timou remembered only a little of what she had seen of the Palace in the ordinary living Kingdom, but this Palace was as fine and delicate as a spun-sugar confection. Its walls were carved in intricate relief, but here, unlike in the living City, the carvings were fresh and clean, untouched by time. Stone roses nodded heavily above the subtly carved doors; they seemed so real that Timou almost believed one might pluck them from their thorny stems. Living roses, pink and cream and palest gold, swept up a great expanse of wall to the left of the doors: they breathed a warm and heady perfume out upon the air.

Prince Cassiel, moving as though in a dream, walked forward and laid a hand on the doors. Though they were tall and heavy, they swung smoothly back at his touch.

Timou had never had a real chance to see the interior of the Palace in the living City. This Palace amazed her. It was rich, lavish, opulent, and entirely unpopulated. Hallways had vaulted ceilings twelve feet high and floors of polished marble; walls were hung with jewel-toned tapestries.

Cassiel told her about the tapestries as they passed them, a few words about one or another. "This is the first King, laying the first stone on the shore of the Lake. This is my great-great-great-grandfather Casien, building the Bridge of Glass." Timou nodded politely to each and wondered whether the Prince knew where he was going. He seemed to.

Then Cassiel stopped in the middle of a word, turning.

Timou turned as well, looking back the way they had come. "Someone is here," she said nervously.

She had not needed to say anything. Prince Cassiel, intent, shifted his weight. The sword he held, with its blade of light and its hilt of darkness, glimmered in his hand.

The step that approached was firm. Decisive. Arrogant. It was a man's step: boots rang on the stone. The man turned sharply into their hall and paused, head up, eyes hard with pride and anger. He was a big man, but that was not what gave the impression of sheer power that he brought with him: mere size was not enough to yield that sense of power. That radiated from him like heat. His face was broad, with rugged bones and a generous mouth. His hair, grizzled with silver, was cut very short, adding to the impression of uncompromising harshness. His eyes, the color of dark rich earth, passed over Timou as though she did not exist and fixed on Cassiel. Timou recognized him from a memory she had taken from Prince Cassiel.

Cassiel, dropping his sword unheeded to the marble floor—when it struck the stone, it rang once like a bell and then was silent—took a single step toward his father, and halted.

The King strode forward, gripped his son by both shoulders, and shook him, not very gently. "Where have you been?" he demanded in a gravelly voice that rose almost at once to a shout.

"Where have you been?" He shook Cassiel a second time, harder, pulled him into a brief embrace, held him out again at arm's length, and suddenly drew back one powerful arm and struck him across the face with the back of his fist. His voice rose again, beyond a shout, to a roar. "Thunder and ice, boy, how could you do that to me?"

To Timou, this violent reunion was alarming. Yet Cassiel did not seem cowed or in any way tentative. Indeed, he was laughing, although there was blood on his mouth and a bruise rising already on his cheek. Seizing his father by both arms, he embraced him, and the King, blinking hard, returned the embrace with spine-cracking force of his own. Timou looked away, jealous of their joy despite herself.

"Boy . . . ," the King said, not shouting now. His voice, even in lower tones, growled. "Boy . . ." He pushed Cassiel back again and examined him anxiously. "You fool. You young fool. Are you all right?"

"Yes, sir," said the Prince, struggling, clearly, to keep his own voice from shaking. "Yes. Ah . . . you?"

"Storms and cracking *ice*, you young cub, I wasn't the one who rode off in the bright day and disappeared from all men's sight. . . . Everyone searched. *I* searched. You were hidden even from *me*. You were nowhere. I searched for you in my *dreams*, boy, until I walked out of the ordinary Kingdom and into this eternal dream behind it to find you, and even here you were nowhere to be found. . . . Where were you?"

"Trapped," said the Prince simply, and looked at Timou. "Behind the mirror. Until I was found."

Once she was in the King's eye, he gave her all his attention, overwhelmingly. Timou felt that, indeed, the weight of all the Kingdom was contained in that intense stare. She felt her own eyes go wide and still in response, ready, if the force of it grew to be more than she could bear, to flow away like water before that power.

"Lelienne!" said the King, and then looked more closely, eyes narrowing. "No. Who?" And then, with sudden certainty, "Her daughter. Are you?"

"I think I am," agreed Timou. She found herself becoming quiet and tranquil, an involuntary response to the King's violence and power.

The King looked from her to his son and back again. Deep lines came into being on his face, beside his mouth. He looked older suddenly, and bitter. He said to Cassiel, harshly, "*Lelienne* trapped you. Did she?"

"Yes," the Prince said gently.

"Yes." The King took in what seemed gallons of air in one slow breath, and let it out as slowly. "And you?" he said to Timou. "You are a friend of my son's? As well as a daughter of Lelienne's?"

"She found the way out," said Cassiel.

"A way out," corrected Timou. "This aspect of the Kingdom is not what I meant to find. But it is what the Prince found. . . ."

"This is the truest Kingdom," the King said with a satisfied little nod, as though it pleased him that Cassiel had come here and not to the living City. Then his attention descended on Timou again, like a hammer. "Who was your father?"

Timou stared at him, for the moment wordless.

"You are frightening her," said Cassiel mildly. "Her father was a mage. Kapoen. Lelienne killed him."

The King continued to stare at Timou. "Kapoen," he rumbled. "A King and then a mage. That woman sets her sights high."

Timou swallowed, and managed to speak even under the weight of his regard. "I think I'm only beginning to understand what she wants. . . ."

"Oh, I know what she wants," the King said harshly. Turning on his heel, he made an impatient gesture for them to follow and strode away, moving with long decisive strides.

CHAPTER 11

The Bastard, some few days after the appearance of his mother, had gone to the heights of the tallest tower of the Palace to look out over the City. It spread down the island on all sides, with the Lake spreading out beyond it as far as he could see. A haze was over the Lake today, so that there was only the faintest hint of the farther shore.

The Bastard had gone to the tower to think. Its solitude allowed an illusion of privacy. He leaned his arms on the marble balustrade and stared down. The City sparkled below. It all looked, from this distance, very peaceful.

Trevennen found him there, after some measureless interval of cold and silence. "Lord Neill," said the mage courteously.

The Bastard set his face in an expression of detachment and inclined his head in return. "Trevennen. Did you seek me?"

"Yes," said the mage. He leaned on the balustrade near the Bastard and looked out, as the Bastard was doing. "You must despise me."

The Bastard turned his head to meet the mage's eyes. He replied, in a perfectly civil tone, "Yes, I'm afraid so."

The mage sighed and looked down over the City. He said

after a little while, "Lelienne is very powerful, and very wise. She gave you a heritage of great power."

"I had rather been the son of a laundry maid. I should prefer that heritage."

Trevennen smiled faintly, still gazing outward rather than at the Bastard. "I would not have thought you would be so quick to reject power. Whatever its source. You know as well as I that power exists to be used. Lelienne believes she can encompass the Kingdom entire, absorbing all its mystery and power for herself. She will find she is mistaken, in the end, but in the meantime, she brings with her into this Kingdom a great deal of power and knowledge we have never known."

"For your delectation, if not mine," commented the Bastard.

The mage shrugged. "In the end, the Kingdom will not be encompassed by any one woman, however powerful, and Lelienne will learn that and go, doing no permanent harm. While she is here, her power flows into the very air we breathe and enriches us all."

The Bastard did not comment on the mage's confidence, which seemed to him badly misplaced. He said instead, "You speak very freely."

Trevennen turned and leaned back against the balustrade, elbows on the railing. "She cannot hear me at the moment. Nor you, my lord. Did you really cast your father into the City reflected in the Lake?"

"I said so, did I not?"

"So you did."

"What use does she mean to make of him? And of me? And of Cassiel?"

The mage moved his shoulders slightly. He seemed to be thinking of other things, and answered in a somewhat abstracted tone, "Ask her."

The Bastard gave a short laugh. He wanted very badly to throw the mage from this high balustrade, except that, of course, doing so would not harm the mage, and might bring punishment, from his mother or possibly from Trevennen himself.

"You will have the opportunity," said the mage mildly. "She sent me to find you. She wishes you to attend her in her rooms."

"My father's rooms," corrected the Bastard. "Why now? For what purpose? Do you know? Or does she trouble to confide in you?"

The mage knew. The Bastard saw it in his eyes, in his face, in the uncomfortable tilt of his head as he glanced away. His own eyes widened. He moved a step closer to Trevennen. "What does she intend?"

"Her power waxes with the acknowledgment of the court and the City," the mage said obliquely. "As men learn to fear her strength, she becomes stronger. It's a very interesting phenomenon—"

"She has become more and more powerful while we waited," the Bastard said huskily. "She has been gaining the strength it will take to do whatever it is she intends to do. And you said nothing. You let this happen."

"You couldn't have fought her even at the beginning," the

mage said in a surprisingly gentle tone. "She is a sorceress. She is very old and very powerful. She was one of Deserisien's own acolytes, and she has his power. You could never have fought her."

"Could you?"

"Fighting her is not precisely what I have in mind."

The Bastard considered this. He said softly, "I do not know anything of sorcery or magecraft or this Deserisien of whom you speak. But, Trevennen, I am beginning to think you know less than I."

The mage only shrugged. "I suggest you not keep her waiting, Neill."

The Bastard stood still for a moment, looking at him. Then he went, without a word, back into the tower and to the long spiral stairs that would lead down into the Palace proper.

Lelienne was not surrounded by ladies and attendants, as Ellis would have been. She stood quite alone by the fire burning in the broad fireplace. The fire was of the black wood that grows in forests where the sun never reaches the earth. That wood made a fragrant smoke that left a bitter aftertaste in the back of the throat.

The Bastard offered a respectful bow and waited.

"Neill," she said briskly, and dropped into a large chair drawn close to the fire. "Come here, by me."

Without a word he obeyed, standing by the hearth some few feet from her chair.

"I need your father," she said directly. "Time runs through

my hands like sand. . . . Soon. Tonight. You will have to bring him back here for me."

The Bastard drew a breath, and let it out. He looked up, meeting her eyes, so like his own. "What is it you intend for him?" he asked her. It was a risk, he thought, to ask; she might be offended if she took his question as defiance. But he also thought she might answer; whether she would tell him the truth he could not guess, but perhaps he might learn something of her intentions from whatever answer she made.

She did not smile, and for an instant he took that as a sign that she was not offended. Then she said, "My son, I want a coal of black wood from that fire. Get one for me. You will not need to use the tongs. Your hand will do."

The Bastard caught his breath. He said, "I do not mean to defy you. I will obey you. I would only like to know what you mean to do with him. And with me. And even with Cassiel. Whatever you intend, I know I cannot prevent you. I would only like to know. Is that so much to ask?"

"My son," said Lelienne, "you must learn not to question me."

He stood still. The fire drew his eyes. It was burning very nicely. The black wood made coals that were a darker, more sullen color than the brighter coals that would have been made by, say, burning apple wood or cedar. It was very easy to imagine what it would be like to thrust a hand into that fire, to take one of those glowering coals into his fingers; the Bastard found that sweat had sprung out on his face at the thought.

He came a step forward, sinking to his knees at his mother's

feet, so close to the fire that he might reach out even from this
spot to touch the coals. "Please," he said, bowing his head. "No.
I will not question you again. Trevennen advised me that I
should ask you. I see now he mocked me."

"Trevennen," said his mother. She leaned back in her chair,
cupping her chin in one graceful hand and looking down at him.
"Did he so advise you? Look at me, my son."

Lifting his head, he met her eyes. It took no effort at all to
put fear in his face, in his mind. He tried very hard to put
Trevennen there as well, although in fact he believed, on the
strength of considerable recent evidence, that his mother could
hear only what words were spoken aloud, and not those that existed in the privacy of a man's thoughts.

"Well," she said, considering. "Very well, my son. Bring your
father to me, here, now, and we shall say no more about your
impudence."

The Bastard said carefully, "Please do not be angry. I would
obey you if I could. I do not know what I did to set my father
in that other Kingdom. I desired it and it came to pass, but I am
not a mage and I do not know what I did or how to undo it. I
would not know how even if you forced me to take every coal
out of that fire with my bare hands. Please do not punish me for
a failure I cannot help. I believe you know that I speak the
truth."

What he believed was that if his mother could distinguish
truth from deceit, she would make him take every coal out of the
fire with his bare hands. He held quite still, and waited.

Lelienne frowned, but she did not instantly declare him false.

She said instead, "Take a coal from the fire, and hold it in your hand."

The Bastard hesitated for one long, involuntary moment. Then, setting his teeth, he moved his hand toward the fire burning on the hearth. The heat of it, promising pain beyond measure, stopped him.

Without expression, Lelienne lifted a small bell that rested on a table by her left hand and rang it. A servant came in at once in answer to that summons: an elderly man who had served in the Palace all the Bastard's life and who had somehow been chosen to serve this new and most terrifying lady. Perhaps he had even volunteered: many men would show surprising courage in sudden adversity, even, unexpectedly, old men and servants. The man dared a quick covert glance at the Bastard where he knelt by the hearth, and then looked with wide eyes at Lelienne. She said, "Come here."

"No," said the Bastard, pressed beyond fear of his own pain. "No." Reaching down to the fire, he took a coal from the edge and held it in his hand. It was certainly not the largest nor the hottest coal in the fire. Nevertheless, the pain was immediate, astounding. Tears of agony sprang instantly to his eyes, and he set his teeth hard against a shaming cry, which in the end he could not entirely prevent. His hand shook with the effort it took not to let the thing fall.

"Go," said Lelienne to the servant, and to the Bastard, "Tell me about the night your father disappeared. What happened that night? How did it come about that you opened a way for him into this other City? How did he go there? Was this possible because he is King? Is it a distinct Kingdom, or another face of the same one? Do not," she added coolly, "drop what you hold."

It was impossible to think past the pain. But the Bastard understood the nature of the City reflected in the Lake. He could speak of this without endangering his private thoughts. He answered Lelienne in a low gasping tone, which was all he could manage, "It is— We say it is a reflection of our City, we think of ours as the true City. But that is not so. The Lake holds—it holds—it holds the eternal City, which the mage Irinore and the first King, Castienes, used to build our—our City. Ours is the reflection. The true City lies in a different layer of truth and dreams. But it is an aspect of eternal truth. It is—it is more real than this ordinary City can be. Sometimes we—sometimes we dream of it—of the truth that lies beyond our own City. The King can always dream of it. If he is a true King, then he is King in that City as well as in this. His dreams—his dreams show him truth, so he can—can rule righteously."

All the time he spoke, the coal burned in his hand so that the flesh charred and the bones cracked.

Lelienne rested her chin in her palm and listened thoughtfully. "So that, and not this, is the true Kingdom?"

"They are both—both real. Each in its own way. Please—"

"And from what you say, that one is the original, and the basis of this one's magic. So I shall in the end have to encompass both in order to take for myself the magic of either," Lelienne said, sounding more intrigued than concerned at the prospect. "Well, that is an aspect of this Kingdom that I had not anticipated, but I believe I will be able to contrive." Then she asked him, ignoring his plea, "And that night? What did you do with Drustan?"

The Bastard did not know how long he had held the coal in his hand. But he had discovered, with a sense of distant amazement, that the pain was not without limit. It had a certain depth and breadth, and was not infinite; though it was unendurable, yet the Bastard found that, as he had no choice but to bear it, it could after all be endured. If his mother had forced him to lie in the first moments, he thought he would have been unable to do so. But he had learned, now, the limits of this pain. He was able, now, to lie coherently, and set himself to do so.

"My father was desperate to find Cassiel. Of course he was. I only suggested that Cassiel might—might have fallen somehow into the City in the Lake." His voice shook, and faded out at odd moments. He did not try to steady it. "And I put—I put dried aconite to burn in his fire, to help him dream—"

"Aconite is a poison," Lelienne observed.

"Yes. Yes, but it is also—the travelers' herb. We say its smoke carries a traveler in dreams to where he would go—"

"I see." Lelienne leaned back in her chair, looking thoughtful.

"The King—the King stands always close to the City in the Lake. He must, if he is a true King. For him, that other City is only a step away. I know I helped a path open between them, but it was—it was his choice to take that step. I don't—I don't know how to bring him back."

"I see," Lelienne said again. She stroked her chin with the tip of one graceful finger. "I do not imagine you wished to bring him back."

"No," agreed the Bastard. "No. I did not want him to come back. Why would I want him to come back? I—did not try to open that path a second time." He had leaned forward, supporting himself with his good hand against the floor. He still held the coal in his burning hand, resting now on his knee because he did not have the strength to hold it up as he had done at first.

"How would you suggest I open such a path?" his mother asked him. She was unmoved by his agony, neither pleased nor regretful, as she never seemed moved by the pain or fear she caused. Her tone remained merely thoughtful.

"I don't know."

"Would Trevennen know?"

The Bastard tried to think what would be most useful for his mother to believe, but could think only of how badly he wanted her to turn her cold, inquiring attention toward the mage and away from himself. "Yes," he said, voice husky, failing at the end of the word. He gathered his strength with an effort, looking for the last extremities of endurance. "Perhaps. Trevennen has— studied mirrors. The Lake is a mirror. Of sorts." He tried to remember what else he had said about the Lake. He could not clearly remember.

"Well, I shall ask him," said Lelienne. She held out her hand briskly. "Give me the coal."

He could not believe he had heard her accurately, and for a moment only knelt where he was, swaying. Then he was afraid he had waited too long, and reached out quickly, clumsily, setting his teeth against the fresh pain of movement and supporting his burned hand with the other one. He had closed his hand into a fist at some time during the ordeal, and at first could not make his fingers open.

Impatiently his mother touched the back of his hand.

The pain was gone at once. Unbelieving, the Bastard opened his hand. The coal that fell into his mother's palm was cold and dark. His hand was unmarked. There was no charred flesh. There was no injury at all. All that was left was the general weakness of pain endured and the memory of burning.

"You are my son," Lelienne said mildly, to his astonished stare. "Your pain gives me no pleasure. Another time simply obey me at once, and there will be no need for punishment."

The Bastard bowed his head and pushed himself back to kneeling with arms that trembled. He was afraid to speak, lest his mother hear something in his words or his tone that angered her. This was a new extremity of fear, and it shamed him, but even so he could not bring himself to speak.

His mother did not appear to apprehend any of his struggle. "You may go," she said simply, dismissing him.

Only the thinnest remnants of pride prevented the Bastard from falling over himself to get to the door. He stood instead, making it to his feet with difficulty, and brought his eyes up with an immense effort to look her in the face. He did not know what his own face showed. He could see nothing in hers. He did not scramble for the door, but bowed, carefully, and backed away several steps before turning and setting his hand on the latch.

"Neill," she said at that moment, and he could not keep from flinching. But he made himself turn slowly and stand straight to face her. Her eyes were dark, ageless, unreadable.

"You will join me for supper. At dusk. It is time, I think, for this play to be concluded. You will join me, my son."

"Yes," he said huskily. He would have agreed to anything. When she lifted a hand in renewed permission to depart, he moved the latch without turning his back on her and half fell through the door when it opened because he had not really expected it to yield to his hand. He would have fallen then, but Galef caught him.

After a moment this made the Bastard laugh. "You seem to make a habit of this," he said to the guard captain, helplessly, gripping the other man's arms as he tried to get his feet under him. He found, to his horror, his breath catching on a sob.

Galef jerked his head, dismissing another guardsman and several hovering servants, who faded instantly into the woodwork. The captain, though no taller than the Bastard, lifted him in his arms with a muted sound of effort.

"I can walk," the Bastard protested, torn equally between laughter, tears, and outrage.

"Of course you can." Galef moved rapidly. They met no one, by which the Bastard understood that the captain had sent a man ahead to clear the way.

"Galef," the Bastard said through his teeth. "Put me down."

The guard captain hesitated an instant and then stopped, letting the Bastard stand on his own, though with an arm ready to catch him again if his knees gave. For a moment the Bastard thought they might. Then he steadied.

"All right?" the captain asked.

"Yes," agreed the Bastard, and took an experimental step.

Galef stayed close by his side, ready for a stumble or sudden collapse. He said, "Tipeu told me what she did to you."

Tipeu was the old servant. The Bastard said harshly, "She meant to punish what she called impudence, but also to question me under the spur of pain." He flinched from the memory, but the weakness was at last passing off. He added tardily, as his wits caught up with his mouth, "I suppose it might have been worse. At least I had nothing to conceal." He saw suddenly that the captain had been taking him to his own rooms. He turned and made instead for the stairs that would take him out of the Palace entirely.

"Lord Neill!" snapped Galef, and put himself in his way. "If she calls for you?"

"She will not expect me until dusk." And he added piously, "Of course I will be back by then. I must have air, and space. But I would not dare disobey my mother."

Galef looked torn. "Nor would I. I am not to let you go about the City unescorted. . . ."

"Then you shall have to escort me," said the Bastard, and took a step forward, forcing the captain to shift quickly out of the way.

The Bastard's horse was a black mare, intelligent and quick-footed. The Bastard, one eye on the sinking sun, could hardly bring himself to wait for the mare to be saddled. When he at last lifted the reins, the mare instantly caught his mood, and leapt forward with a will.

Galef swung himself up on a big gray gelding and turned it round to follow. He shouted, "Where are we going?"

"Nowhere in particular!" the Bastard shouted back, and sent his mare flying like an arrow down the hill from the Palace, straight for the shores of the Lake. The captain, whatever he surmised from this answer, asked nothing else, but simply followed.

The mages' house was close by the Lake—close enough that the waters of the Lake lapped against the stones of its wall. The house was set off a little way on its own, outside the City proper, because mages need privacy and quiet. The house itself was low and almost plain, but the garden beside it contained herbs and flowers found nowhere else in the Kingdom. Even in this season a smoky, bitter aroma rose from the dried stalks of some herb when the Bastard's cloak brushed it as he strode up the walk, Galef at his back. It might even, the Bastard thought with a kind of distant wry humor, have been aconite.

The captain's eyes were wide, but he kept his mouth very carefully shut.

The door opened before they reached it.

"Come in," Marcos said quietly. "You may speak freely. She cannot hear you here."

"Your doing?"

The mage's smile twisted. "Not mine. Would that it were." Stepping back, Marcos glanced into the warm light within.

"I thought he said he couldn't help you!" Galef, at the Bastard's heels, murmured.

The Bastard glanced back at him. "What he said and what he meant were perhaps not entirely congruent."

The captain laughed, a quick breath. "A lot of that going around, these days."

The room they came into was a large kitchen, with three fireplaces and one iron stove. The heat in this room seemed to have body and presence, like a live thing. A huge wooden table, much scarred by time and cluttered now with papers, bits of rock and ribbon, spools of copper and gold wire, small unidentifiable bones, and the odd cup of cooling tea, took up nearly a third of the space. Pots and skillets and strings of onions hung from the ceiling. In all the clutter, it would have been easy to miss one narrow wooden chair drawn up close to the farthest fireplace, and the tiny figure tucked into it, except that the Bastard knew where to look.

He went forward at once and knelt quickly at her feet. "Russe."

The woman he addressed was so small and fragile she might have been made of twigs and drying leaves rather than flesh and bone. Her hair was white and fine as dandelion silk. Her wizened face yet retained a fundamental elegance of angle and form, so that in a way she was beautiful still. The hand she lifted to touch the Bastard's face was so frail he feared to take it in his, lest it break at his touch.

"Lord Bastard," she said in a voice like wind through the

reeds, so quiet he had to bend close to hear her. "You have met your mother, and she would own you."

"You know what she intends?"

"Yes," whispered the old, old woman. "She will use you and that child she bore to Kapoen to devour the magic and mystery of our Kingdom. All unknowing, she will take it also from the eternal Kingdom that casts ours as its shadow, and from the dark Kingdom that is in turn our shadow. We shall be left with nothing, exposed to the world in a barren, empty land. She is capable of it, I believe: Deserisien's get, she is. I never liked her, but it took me a long time to understand why, and then I thought perhaps it would not matter. I never guessed she had also borne a child to a mage. I suppose Kapoen could not bring himself to tell me what he had done. No wonder he left the City . . . no wonder he put the great forest between himself and any memory of Lelienne. . . ."

"What shall we do?" Neill asked her, not at the moment willing to be distracted by these ruminations about the past.

"You must prevent her. You must find your father. If anyone can bend the power of the Kingdom toward this woman's removal, it is the King. Above all she must not be allowed to strip the rule from him and settle it on you."

"Yes. How shall I find him? She means to act soon. Tonight." He leaned forward urgently. "There is no time left, Russe! If we are to prevent her, it must be now."

Marcos came a step forward. "We think there may be a way," he began.

"But it would be a shame to interfere when Lelienne is so

close," said another voice drily. Trevennen shaped himself out of a fall of light in the warm kitchen. "You left so precipitously, Lord Neill. I did wonder where you might be off to. I suspect Lelienne would also be interested to know where you went." He glanced around curiously. "And that you have all lied to her from the very beginning."

Galef laid a hand on his sword, but then, as the mage gave him a warning glance, stood still.

Marcos said sharply, "Trevennen, you fool. Do you belong to that woman so completely you will spy for her? Even now? Do you not know what she intends?"

The older mage studied the younger, head tilted a little to one side. "It's very interesting, what she did to you. I expect that soon I, too, will be able to do that."

"Well, not today," whispered Russe.

Trevennen turned his head to meet her eyes. "You needn't think—" he began, but got no further. Layers of wood closed over his face. His body lengthened and twisted, reaching upward; his arms stretched out and divided; leaves burst out of his fingers. A great tree filled the kitchen where he had stood, rooting itself into the earth right through the tiled floor, its branches passing through the ceiling to brush the sky.

Russe leaned her face against one thin hand and said in a voice husky with weariness, "Marcos."

"Yes," said the young mage. He crossed the room to embrace the frail woman gently, then straightened to look at the Bastard, who drew his attention from the tree growing through the kitchen and looked back wordlessly.

"There's not much time," Marcos said quietly. "Trevennen is really extraordinarily gifted with light and movement and fire, but he never understood the slow lives and circular memories of trees. But he will free himself eventually. And Lelienne may know already—if not precisely what happened to him, that something has. Or who has made it happen."

"Russe surely cannot fight her?" The Bastard was appalled at the very thought of his mother coming into this warm and homey room, setting herself against the frail mage she would find here.

"Assuredly not for long," Marcos answered crisply. "And we must be at Tiger Bridge by dusk. When will she miss you, can you guess?"

"Certainly by dusk."

"Then there's no time to stand about here," said the mage. "Pity we can't all move through light as easily as Trevennen." He led the way out of the warm kitchen into the chillier light of the late winter afternoon.

Tiger Bridge was half a mile, perhaps, from the mages' house, but the shoreline was a treacherous place to ride: invisible muddy sinkholes lay sometimes in places where the sand looked straight and level. They had therefore to turn back into the City and take the road that lay just within the wall, folding into the City from time to time where one building or another interfered with its passage, until it came at last to the carved Bridge. This was a ride of at least a mile. The Bastard cast one glance after another over his shoulder at the sinking sun and knew they would

come to the Bridge certainly no earlier than dusk, if they beat the
sun at all.

He had taken Marcos up behind him on his mare. Galef
stayed at his side, silent and grim. None of them were inclined
toward speech. Marcos at least might know whether Lelienne
might hear them if they spoke; the Bastard had forgotten to ask
him before they left the house, and it was now too late to ask
safely.

Shadows lengthened across the streets. Traffic thinned, and
some of the passersby recognized the Bastard's ash-pale hair or
his black mare and made way where they could. And how long,
the Bastard wondered, if they whispered his name, would it take
those whispers to creep back to his mother?

They came to the Bridge just as the sun touched the western
edge of the Lake, sliding down from their horses under the surprised eyes of the odd late traveler. Marcos gripped the Bastard
by the arm and shoved him around to face the sun. "It's up to
you to open the way," he said urgently. "At dusk, when the
Bridge might lead to either City . . . we must find your father,
and you must open the way to go to him."

"How?" the Bastard demanded. He seized Marcos by both
arms and stared into the mage's face, fighting dawning terror. "I
trusted you to think of something useful, and all you thought of
is to find my father in the other City?"

Marcos returned the Bastard's grip. "My friend, if she did not
steal him away and yet he went, where else do you suppose he
might be? And of course you can open the way." He shook the

Bastard gently. "Why do you think she wanted a King-got son at all? You are the key that will make this Bridge run to two destinations, Neill. Think of the Bridge. Think of the way the lilies change at dusk, becoming so real you can smell them . . . think of the tigers: did you never hear them walking behind you through the streets?"

"Can she hear us?" Galef asked suddenly, uneasily. He held the reins of both horses in one hand. The other hand, from long habit, rested on the hilt of his sword, though he had never yet found it useful to draw a sword against either Lelienne or any mage.

"Probably," said Marcos. "So it would be good if we were quick."

"*Cracking ice,*" said the Bastard, and turned away from them both to set his hands on the heavy worn railing of the Bridge. The sun, huge as it sank below the Lake, was in his eyes. The wind died. Below the Bridge, the Lake gradually stilled.

"Hurry," Marcos said tensely.

"Be quiet," snapped the Bastard, his eyes on the water. Colors fell out of the air and welled out of the Lake to meet at the boundary between air and water: crimson and dusky blue and a purple that rapidly shaded away toward black. The air became utterly still. Shadows tangled across the carved Bridge, making sight uncertain, until the Bridge above the water and the Bridge reflected in the water seemed precisely alike.

A voice cried out, seeming to the Bastard somehow both very near at hand and at the same time almost too distant to hear. But he could not spare it attention. He was studying the

Bridge in the Lake. In the Lake, another Lord Bastard looked back at him, face hollowed by weariness and strain, eyes dark as though made of the night itself, pale hair falling down his back like moonlight. The reflection seemed truer to him than any face he had ever seen in any simple mirror, and he reached out his hand as though to touch its hand.

With an almost audible vibration of light and shadow, the world reordered itself. The Bastard still stood on Tiger Bridge, reaching down toward his reflection, which held its hand up as though to reach out of the water to him. But although everything was the same, everything was also, in some indefinable way, different. Around him, the scent of lilies wafted sweetly into the air. He straightened slowly, lifting his gaze: before him the Lake spread itself out to the horizon, as though it alone encompassed all the world.

Somewhere close at hand, unmistakably, a tiger coughed. The Bastard moved to look at the stone plinths that guarded the Bridge, and found them empty now of the tigers they had held by day. Though he stood still, listening for tigers in the dark, there was no other sound. He was entirely alone in the night.

CHAPTER 12

T

he King led Timou and his son through the Palace at a breathless pace, seeming certain of both his way and his intentions, which was more than Timou could say for herself. He swept them up, and farther up, until Timou was dizzy with height, and finally up to the highest gallery of the tallest tower of all. The gallery ran all around the tower, its slim marble balustrade seeming a fragile protection against the fall that lay beyond. The air this high seemed pure as glass, so still a sudden cry might shatter it. Below them the City spread itself out, flushed ruddy gold in the last sun.

The King stood with his broad hands spread wide on the rail, staring outward and down. His voice, when he spoke, was surprisingly gentle, although still gravelly. "You can see all the way to the edge of the great forest from this place. If the air is especially clear. It is like a shadow at the edge of sight."

His son came forward to join him at the balustrade. He had carried his sword with him, out of habit, Timou thought, and now, having mislaid the sheath somewhere behind the mirror, set it aside on the stone floor of the gallery. "And she wants to rule all this."

"Rule it?" said the King. "No. How could she rule it? She is not part of it. She never was."

"Then—"

"She wants to possess it," said the King curtly. "She cannot use you for that, boy. You are nothing of hers. But she can use Neill, especially if you and I are out of the way." His powerful gaze fell on Timou as he turned his head suddenly. "And she can use you, girl. Her son for the right to rule. Her mage-born daughter for the magic. How can Kapoen have been so stupid?" He waved away Timou's answer before she could try to make it. "Yes, I know. The same way I was stupid, I suppose. Neither of us knew her for what she was."

"You seem to know her now," Timou offered cautiously.

The King pinned her in place with his heavy stare. "Yes. Now. One of Deserisien's get, is she?"

"Yes. But . . . how do you know her now, if you did not know her before?"

"Because I am paying attention now," he said harshly, and turned back to the silent City, spread out below. "I have read history, even that which goes beyond this Kingdom."

"I thought I had," whispered Timou. But her father had hidden the book that held whatever story might have guided her. She found she was shaking, and did not even know if it was with grief or with anger.

"Come here. Look at this."

Collecting herself with an effort, Timou came guardedly to the balustrade and gazed over.

"Can you feel it beating in you? Like your heart? Like it contains all your life? All your breath?"

Timou could not.

"I feel it like that," said Cassiel, staring in surprised wonder over the City.

"Of course you do, boy. Do you feel her hand over it? A grip like winter itself? I recognized it. But I did not know what it was, until I saw this girl's face. So like Lelienne. Your eyes are different," added the King to Timou abruptly.

"So I have been told."

"You don't have her eyes. Or Kapoen's. His, as I recall, were dark. Yours are like the Lake itself. Like light through the water. He is dead, you say?"

"Behind the mirror," said Timou. "With a silver knife in his heart and a river of blood running out of it." She made her tone inexpressive, but the King looked at her sharply, and unexpectedly gentled his rough voice.

"I knew Kapoen. I am sorry for his death. He was a fine man, and a good mage, if too cracking serious for his own good. I am sure he acted as wisely as he knew how. But"—the King lifted his voice abruptly in a roar, making Timou flinch—"he was a fool to lie down with that woman! Although," he added, suddenly gentle again, "no more a fool than I. I suppose she set his head spinning like a weathercock. As she did to me. Fools, both of us. Well. That is water under the Bridge, and now here we are."

On the far side of the Lake, the sun was setting. Light ran across the water in jeweled colors: garnet and lapis and amethyst. Cerulean shadows followed the blazing sunset. The moon was already visible in the fair sky, nearly full, promising a pale lustrous light to come.

"What shall we do?" asked Timou at last, rather timidly. She was not used to being timid, but this forceful King made her feel so. The way he spoke of her father shocked her. It had never occurred to her that anyone might speak so carelessly of Kapoen, or so unceremoniously judge his actions foolish and dangerous. Or judge him at all.

As though the King's judgment freed hers, she understood at last—it was a strange understanding to have about her father—that Kapoen had been ashamed. Ashamed to tell her the truth about his own foolishness. And so he had not told her the truth about her mother, or the great sorcerer Deserisien, who had been Lelienne's master, or the dark sorcery that was half Timou's birthright. He had told her nothing at all, leaving her to walk blind into the trap Lelienne had left for her. Timou wanted to weep. She steadied her breathing with an effort and tried to pay attention to the King.

"Do?" the King was saying. "We do what we can, and what we must." He looked at his son sharply. "Right, boy?"

"Yes, sir," Cassiel agreed instantly.

"All right, then," growled the King. "Then I think it's time—don't you agree?—to throw that woman out of our Kingdom. Now that I know what I'm about. Come here." He laid one powerful hand on his son's arm and stretched the other out over the silent City. "Feel that?" he said. "That is our heart, and none of hers." Father and son stared out at the Kingdom. All Timou saw was an expanse of nameless buildings that moonlight turned to cream and silvery dusk, and beyond that the endless smooth dark mirror of the Lake. She thought she might feel a gathering pressure, like the violent stillness that rides before the storm, but she was not certain even of that.

Sweat stood out on the King's face, as from some powerful effort. Cassiel gripped the balustrade with both hands. He made a low sound, swaying. The King shouted suddenly, wordlessly, and swung around to catch his son as Cassiel's legs suddenly buckled underneath him.

Timou pressed her hands over her mouth and stared at them both, not daring to move, because she did not know either what they had tried to do or whether they had succeeded or failed.

"Storms and *ice*," snarled the King in a voice that rose to a shout on the last word.

"She's far too powerful for shouting to help," stated a crisp, half-familiar voice, and Timou spun, eyes widening. "The other—if you care to try again to throw her out, it's possible I might be able to help with that—"

Lord Neill stood in the doorway of the tower. Light fell across him and flung his shadow down the gallery. His stark features might have been carved from stone, his pale hair spun from moonlight. His breathing was quick, his shirt torn, and his black eyes brilliant. He looked like he had been running or drinking or brawling, or perhaps all three. Timou thought that she had never in her life looked anything like him.

"*You!*" roared the King, and lunged to his feet, his fist already moving.

Unlike Cassiel, his elder son stepped economically to one side. The blow whistled past his head, making the King stagger, and Lord Neill caught his wrist as the swing went past and pinned his father efficiently against the wall of the tower. He was not nearly so large a man as the King and certainly could not match his power, but at that moment he seemed to have a wild strength all his own.

"I've been looking for you," he said to his father with a precise inclination of his head, as though involved in a formal encounter in the court. "And you," he said to his half brother, who was sitting now with his back against the marble balustrade, eyes wide and vulnerable. "Though *you're* a surprise," he added to Timou. "Do you know you're my sister?"

"So I have been told," she allowed, fascinated. Then she gathered her wits and added, far more sharply, dread running through her bones, "Oh, no. Oh. Lord Neill. You are her son. And I . . . You should never have come here."

"What?" said Lord Neill blankly. "I assure you, I had very little choice, and was very glad at the time to be able to come here. It seemed very important to us all that my father be found."

"He can't fight her," said Timou. "Don't you know that?"

"Russe said—"

"Thunder and ice, girl, I can fight anyone I need to fight. Let go of me," commanded the King, staring belligerently into his elder son's face. Their eyes were exactly at a level.

"Will you try again to hit me?" his son inquired.

"Cracking ice! I might."

Lord Neill released him, stepping back guardedly.

His father moved with slow deliberation, straightening his clothing, fussing with his sleeves. He said, not quite looking at his elder son, "Well. Are you all right, then?"

Timou thought, astonished through her fear, *Why, he is embarrassed.*

What Lord Neill thought, she could not tell. He said sharply, "Better, now that I am here and have found you. Do you even know what it was you let into this Kingdom and into your bed thirty-odd years ago?"

"I do now," said the King, tone dour.

"You do not," said his ashen-haired son grimly. "You can't. You have been safe here in the Lake, searching your deeper Kingdom for Cassiel, leaving *Ellis,* I might add, to think *I* had done away with you both."

The King gave a crack of harsh laughter. "She thought what?"

"Oh, it was a popular opinion, for a little while. That didn't occur to you?" His son came a step closer, voice lowering in volume, but gaining in intensity. "Along with what else? Here you have been while those you left behind in *your* Kingdom have been at the mercy of a woman who, believe me, hasn't any. Did you never look her in the *eyes* when you bedded her?"

This time, when the King's fist moved, Neill did not step aside. But the King checked, and hooked both his hands deliberately in his belt instead of completing the blow, though he was breathing hard. His voice, when he spoke, was almost mild. "So I was here. You were there with her. So, you tell me about her, then."

Lord Neill took a breath. He glanced at Timou. When he spoke, it was gently. "She makes her children only to devour them, and through them, all the Kingdom."

Timou said, "Yes, I know. It's what I was trying to say. It's why you shouldn't have come here—"

"I told you—"

"Yes, I know." Timou shut her eyes. "I shouldn't have come here either. But for both of us to be here together is worse. Because we are her children. She will follow us, and through us she will devour the Kingdom. She will take its magic and its power and leave behind a land with neither—" Her voice caught.

Cassiel was still sitting with his back against the balustrade, half hidden in its shadow. He said, voice uncertain, "Can she do that?"

"Oh, yes. If she can indeed follow us," said Neill, and moved suddenly to stand over him. "Cassiel. Are you all right?" He offered Cassiel a hand, and, at his younger brother's nod, drew him up and into an embrace. Neill was the taller, but, Timou saw with faint surprise, by very little.

"I'm sorry," Cassiel said, muffled against Neill's shirt, and Timou knew he meant for every doubt of his brother he had entertained, as well as for getting himself trapped behind a mirror in the first place.

Neill shook him a little. "When you climb too high on the roofs of the Palace and tempt the young men to follow you so that someone falls off and breaks his arm, that's your own fault. When you steal Esel's stallion and let it loose in the kitchens so that the cooks have hysterics, that's your own fault. But this was not some boy's prank. You may put the blame for this one where it belongs. With Lelienne." He looked deliberately, an arm still across his younger brother's shoulders, at their father.

"And with me," the King said heavily. "Do you think I do not know that? Well, boy, you found me. Here I am. I've already tried to clean her out of the Kingdom. Now you're here, I'll try again. We'll all try."

"It won't work," said Timou.

The King looked at her, eyes narrowed. "No? Well, what do you suggest, then, girl?"

Thinking about it, she said, "We should have gone to the great forest. We could go now, all of us— No. Cassiel and I. Cassiel needs to stay in the Kingdom. It isn't whole without him, and I think my mother would have trouble finding him in the great forest. But you should stay here, Your Majesty, and Lord Neill should go somewhere else—somewhere very far away, as fast as he can. He should . . . I think he should really leave the Kingdom. All the Kingdoms, this one and the ordinary one and any others that may lie layered with them. If he would." She looked apologetically at her white-haired half brother, trying to gauge his reaction. He didn't show any she could recognize. "I know it's a terrible thing to ask—"

Lord Neill said merely, "Do you think this would keep us all safe?"

Timou did not know. She gave a little helpless shake of her head. "It might make it hard for her to find you."

"I have met her. And I think," Lord Neill said precisely, "that she will find me in the end, if she wishes. Wherever I may go. And you as well."

"Then perhaps you should come to the forest as well," Timou said, trying to think. "We might hide there, better than here." She wondered what the forest would be like, here in this eternal aspect of the Kingdom.

But the King shook his head at this suggestion. "This is the heart of my strength, right here. And, yes, with Cassiel here the Kingdom is whole, and strong. I think we had better stay right here."

"Oh, no," Timou said, amazed that he didn't understand what a terrible, dangerous idea this was. "We mustn't stay here. Staying here is the worst thing we could do—"

"Why?" asked the King in a tone that suggested that he wasn't offended, that he really wanted to know what she thought.

"You are the strength of the Kingdom, Your Majesty, but you are not its heart. Oh," Timou cried in sudden impatience and fear, "if only I had seen the pattern she was making, before she trapped me behind her mirror. I should have seen it—the forest tried to tell me—" She stopped suddenly.

"The *forest* tried to tell . . ." Neill's voice, rising in surprise, stopped abruptly as Timou's had.

Timou made a faint sound, fascinated despite herself now that she knew whom she was looking at. She thought, *She does look like me. Except for her eyes. Even when I know it is her, it is like looking into a mirror. . . .*

The King grated, "Cracking ice, boy, she did follow you here."

"Both of us," said Timou, faintly. "She followed both of us."

"I assure you," Neill breathed, "that was not my intent at all." He had gone chalk-white. He had put a hand on the balustrade for support, and yet he had also shoved his younger brother back behind him. Cassiel was looking from Timou to her mother, as though searching for differences between them was the most important task in the world.

"How touching," observed Lelienne. "A family reunion." She stood in the doorway of the tower, smiling faintly. Her tone was amused. She looked as though she had just poured herself out of the moonlight. She wore a plain white gown. A single strand of black and white pearls dressed her hair. She came out onto the gallery, moving as though she could not imagine anyone or anything in this place offering her the slightest threat.

"It's very interesting," Lelienne commented sedately, gazing over the balustrade. "A Kingdom within a Kingdom . . . layers of truth and magic. Trevennen did not tell me about this." Her eyes, like fragments of the night, went to the King. "Neither did you, Drustan."

The King had not moved. He answered without blinking, "It isn't what I'd consider pillow talk, love."

"I think it would have made lovely pillow talk. You know, Drustan, if you continue with whatever it is that you are trying to do, I will crush your son's heart. Your younger son's, of course. I can do it."

"She can," said Neill sharply, warning.

Timou had not been aware that the King was trying to do anything, but she nevertheless was aware when he stopped trying to do it: it was like a loosening of the air all around them. He lowered his eyes, like a fencer lowering his blade. Then he lifted them again. They were hard as the heartwood of an oak. "You will kill him anyway, so that the Kingship will come to your son."

Lelienne smiled. "Yes," she said, "but when? Now, or in a little while? What are a few seconds worth to you, Drustan?"

Behind Neill, Cassiel caught his breath suddenly, his eyes
widening. His brother, face blank, looking neither at his father
nor at his mother, caught Cassiel as his legs gave.

The King, his face twisting, came forward at Lelienne like a
bull charging. She stood still, smiling, and he crashed suddenly
to a dead halt, as though he had run full tilt into a wall made of
air and moonlight. The shock drove him to his knees, bellowing
with rage.

Neill caught up his brother's strange sword and threw it,
with precise aim, at his mother. Lelienne did not even twitch her
hand or glance at it, but it shattered in the air and rained like
shards of glass to the stones of the gallery. There, it re-formed
under the pressure of the moonlight and lay glimmering and still
on the stones, utterly useless against her.

Timou became moonlight, and fled into the air. Her mother,
forgetting both the King and Cassiel, turned immediately to follow that flight, her head tilting back as though she could track
one gleaming fall of light through all the shadows. She could. She
peeled Timou ruthlessly out of the light and forced her back into
her own shape. Timou, finding herself again on the tower's
gallery, melted instantly into stone and hid herself in unending
time and silence, where even her mother seemed to have difficulty finding her.

"Stop it," said Lelienne, and turned all of Cassiel's bones to fire.
He convulsed, the shock of agony too great even to permit

him to scream. The sound he made instead was thin and bodiless, worse than a scream.

Neill shook his brother as if he could shake the fire out of
him, shouting incoherently. The King cried out, as though giving
voice himself to all of his son's agony.

"Come *here*," said Lelienne, and tapped her foot impatiently.
Timou pulled herself out of the stone, shaking.

"Don't do that again," her mother said, and, against the
balustrade a dozen feet away, Cassiel got a hand under him and
tried, dazedly, to stand. He was perfectly unhurt, but the memory of pain was stark in his face. He looked, in that moment, a
good deal like his elder brother.

"Why my son?" asked the King huskily. "Why Cassiel? What
has the boy ever done to offend you?"

"Nothing," said Lelienne. "Except exist, a slight complication
that will in the end prove, I expect, to be of no consequence. But
you will all yield to me in order to defend him. So he is that
much use to me. I thought he might be." She fixed Timou in her
regard, frowning thoughtfully. "Even you, strangely enough.
Would you defend any chance-met stranger as eagerly? My own
son, perhaps?"

Neill, standing by his brother, did not move. But his face
went still.

"Whom would *you* defend?" Timou asked her. She had
folded her hands tightly together to hide their shaking. She could
hear when she spoke how disturbingly like her mother's her
own voice was. "Anyone? No one? You bear children in order to
consume them. Because only your own are worth the trouble. I

had been told that about you. What are you? Not a mage. I never understood what your kind were. Are."

"Hardly mages," said her mother. Her eyebrows had lifted. "But you, of course, are. Kapoen did well by you, my daughter. You have all the gifts I had hoped for; all the ability to see into the essence of things, and men. That will be a useful skill for me."

Timou swallowed.

"I thought Kapoen might simply kill you," added Lelienne conversationally. "That would have forced me to start again, and even Trevennen knew better by that time . . . but he couldn't simply cut your throat, could he? Not Kapoen. He tangled you in the strange magic of this Kingdom instead, until all the threads I followed to find you ended in a snarl I could not track through. Did he love you?"

Timou closed her eyes, flinching from the pain of a thousand memories. "Yes," she breathed, her voice shaking.

"He should have known better. He should have known that eventually you would ask the right questions and look into the right mirror. But he was a fool." Lelienne ran her hands over her flawless hair, ending with a pleased pat at the strand of pearls.

"And your son was already in the right place," rumbled the King. He was watching her closely, forceful eyes narrowed.

"I knew you would keep him close by you. Why not? Even when you got a true heir, I knew it would not be in you to cut the throat of any son I'd borne you. Even one for whom you never particularly cared." Lelienne studied him. "I don't understand that," she added unnecessarily.

"I can see that," said the King drily. "So. What now, love?"

"Now?" said Lelienne. She glanced around, gesturing lightly to take in all the view. "I am so glad my children led me to this place. There is a fascinating depth of power to the City here. I don't believe I would have managed to absorb the magic of this Kingdom if I had not found this City. Now, of course, it should present no difficulty. I am correct in believing that this is in fact your Kingdom? Not merely the other?"

"Both," said the King. "And a good thing, too." He knelt and laid his hands flat on the stones of the gallery. Lelienne watched him, amused and interested, not at all concerned. She might have believed it was to her that the King knelt; Timou knew it was not. The King, his face intent, rose. Beneath his hands, out of the stones, out of the dark, he drew tigers. They flowed forward like water, muscles rippling under their tawny pelts, eyes green as the water of the Lake in the winter.

"Yes," breathed Neill.

"I hardly think so," said Lelienne, and turned the tigers to stone. They only shook themselves back out of rigidity and yawned at her, showing great teeth as long as a man's thumb.

Lelienne backed up a step, speaking rapidly: her words, heavy and tangible, swept the tigers off the gallery. They did not fall, but only frayed into dusk and then pulled themselves back out of the night. One coughed, low and threatening. They both leapt, but Lelienne was not there: she re-formed herself out of air after they had passed. There was a narrow silver knife in her hand. She did not speak.

Timou caught her breath. From his place by the balustrade, Neill moved suddenly, and then stopped, uncertain. The tigers separated and stalked Lelienne, one from either side. The King himself did not look worried. He was, after all, twenty feet away, and twice her size. And the tigers were readying to spring.

None of them moved in time, or decisively enough—not even the tigers. Lelienne did not step forward and stab the King. Nor did she throw her little silver knife. But suddenly it was no longer in her hand. It stood in the King's chest. In the pale light, the blood that welled slowly up around the blade looked black.

Even then the King did not seem afraid. He raised one hand to touch the knife's hilt. He took a single step forward, firmly, as though he were too large a man to be even inconvenienced by a little knife like that one. His expression, angry, was only just beginning to show surprise. He took another step. When he crashed to his knees, it was all at once, with no warning whatever, and Timou thought she could feel the tower shake. Or the entire Kingdom, perhaps.

The tigers were gone, like smoke; shadows called from the night by the will of the King, they dissolved back into the night once the King had been struck down.

Of them all, it was Neill who was suddenly at his father's side, supporting him, one hand going, appalled, to touch the welling blood.

"Cassiel," whispered the King. Neill's head went back slightly as though he had been struck, although his expression did not change. And then, in one last moment of lucid, unexpected kindness, the King moved his hand to touch his elder son's arm and said, "Neill."

He died. His body faded slowly into the dimness, dissipating into the night. Then, like the tigers, it was gone, leaving his ash-haired son kneeling on the gallery with his arms empty and a stunned expression in his black eyes.

"That's one," Lelienne said briskly. "Now, let's see if the rest of this works properly." The silver knife was back in her hand. She was looking at Cassiel. He did not even see her. He probably did not hear her. His attention was all for his brother, and for the place where their father had so briefly lain. He looked stricken.

Timou slid into light, glimmering down the edge of the silver knife in her mother's hand. When Lelienne, startled, glanced down at the knife, Timou leapt as a flash of silver light at her mother's eyes.

Timou had never tried to kill anyone before. It had never occurred to her that she might ever want to. She was amazed at the way the knowledge of how to do it came to her. She thought of her father, of the King, of Neill's blank expression and Cassiel's pain, and turned her mother's eyes to ice, filled her throat with ice so that she could neither speak nor breathe, sent ice striking inward toward her heart.

Lelienne dropped the knife, which shredded into light and air rather than falling to the gallery floor. She seemed surprised at last.

Timou closed her attention, like cold blades of ice, around her mother's heart.

Then the ice was gone. Timou stood shivering in the cold air, her own form momentarily unfamiliar. Lelienne coughed, spat blood, and shook herself all over, like a dog shaking off water

after a swim. But what she shook away was discomfiture. She examined Timou curiously. "That was startling," she commented.

Timou was not trying to be startling. She was trying to be
effective. She slid once more away from her body, into shadow.
She found there a different form to wear, one that seemed somehow familiar to her heart. As her mother sought her, she formed
herself out of the shadows and stalked forward on massive velvet feet.

Lelienne looked surprised again, this time at the white tiger
that leapt at her out of stone and shadow. It had a head broad as
a man's chest, feet round and wide as platters; stripes black as
night ran across its face and down its sides. Its ivory claws struck
for Lelienne's throat and face. At the last instant, Lelienne threw
up a hand, calling out strange words that, heavy and powerful,
flung the tiger away and pinned it against the tower. She held the
tiger there as she pulled Timou out of it; Timou found herself at
last again in her own body, blinking dazed eyes that should have
been slit-pupiled and able to see in the dark. For a moment she
was unable to understand why she did not have a striped white
pelt and daggered feet.

"That is enough," said Lelienne, sounding more impatient
than angry. "I see you are indeed a child of this Kingdom; good.
But that is enough."

Stone closed itself around Timou's heart: she could not
move. She could barely breathe. It felt to her that she had become stone, but it was not true stone that she might understand,
to shape herself back out of it. It was *not* stone. But it was like
that. She breathed; she moved. But she was trapped. She could

no more change her shape than she could understand her mother's heart.

Lelienne sighed, stretched, and relaxed, dismissing the possibility of further struggle from her daughter. "Better," she said. "Yes. I should not like to have to harm you—"

Lord Neill, face set, stood up from the stones where he had been kneeling when his father's body disappeared. He did not approach Lelienne; he did not even look at her. He did not look at any of them. Instead he took two steps sideways, placed one hand on the marble railing, and vaulted over the balustrade before any of them—certainly before Timou—had any idea what he meant to do. He fell without a sound.

Cassiel, leaping forward, was the one who cried out.

Lelienne sprang to the railing with a sharp wordless cry of her own and reached out into the air. She cried out again, uttering words that had physical weight and power: they rolled through the air like thunder and fell after Neill like hunting hawks.

And they caught him, long before he was broken by the tiles and stones of the City below. Timou was too shocked to understand at first that she should mourn his failure: her first thought was that he had meant to shape himself into air and so escape, and her realization that he had meant to die, and in dying confound all their mother's intentions, was slow in coming. She understood only after the words Lelienne had sent after Neill carried him in their talons back to her feet and flung him down on the stones where she stood. Timou, too stunned to move, saw his face as he gathered himself slowly to try to stand. Then she understood.

Lelienne had never been puzzled. She was not amused at all. She struck her son across the face and pulled silver chains out of the air. With these she bound him by one wrist to the stones of the tower, and Timou also. The silver was cold. Timou looked into her brother's bleak face, then shut her eyes.

Neill touched her hair with one hand and leaned close, placing his free arm around her shoulders. Timou, even knowing that he could not protect her, still found this oddly comforting.

Cassiel had been left free. It was perfectly clear that Lelienne did not mind if *he* threw himself down from this high place. Indeed, she already had the little silver knife back in her hand. The Prince saw this, too. He stood with his head up, facing Lelienne. His breath came rapidly, but he did not otherwise seem frightened. Anger snapped in his eyes. His sword lay on the gallery floor not far from his feet, but pride kept him from so much as glancing at it: the sword had been tried before, and Lelienne clearly would not mind if it was tried again. It was obvious he did not know what else to try.

CHAPTER 13

The Hunter's castle . . . was not like any ordinary castle or tower. When the Hunter moved, drawing Jonas with him, the dark castle seemed to move also, rearranging itself to suit his intentions or wishes. The great hall faded around them while a smaller chamber folded itself out of the shadows. They were now, Jonas understood after a moment of confusion, much higher in the tower: the room in which they stood was square, no more than a dozen feet across, and furnished with tall narrow windows on all four sides. Nothing was visible outside any window but darkness, and yet the sense of great height was so strong that Jonas closed his eyes against a wave of vertigo.

The Hunter's face was masked by the confusion of shadows that crowned him, although his eyes stared down with predatory intent. Wordlessly, simply with a curt gesture, he sent Jonas toward one of the tall windows.

Looking obediently out the window, Jonas could see nothing. But gradually he became aware that someone was standing at his side—not the Hunter; someone else. The first shock of recognition, simply that someone was there, sent Jonas stepping sharply

away so that he came up hard against the Hunter's massive presence and froze in place, flinching.

Look again, said the Hunter.

Cautiously Jonas took a step back toward the indicated window. The man standing there was visible as a shadow among
shadows; a presence more suggested than defined by the air and
the darkness. The figure stood straight and quiet, his hands on
the windowsill, gazing out. He seemed somehow familiar. . . .
Jonas knew him suddenly. "Kapoen," he said, and after the first
startled moment was not surprised.

Timou's father turned his head. "Jonas," he said. "Come here,
if you would." His voice was quiet, but not bodiless like the
voice of the Hunter. He did not, on careful study, seem quite
real. Compared to the Hunter, he still seemed very familiar, very
welcome: a friend in the dark. Jonas, who had always respected
and liked the mage, nevertheless stood still.

"Come," Kapoen said patiently.

Go to him, demanded the Hunter, far less patient.

Jonas thought of what else the Hunter demanded, and dread
ran through him suddenly, like water. He asked the mage, "Why?
What will you do? You know . . . you know what he wants
from me—"

"You must give him everything, but freely," the mage said
gently. There was sympathy in his eyes, in his shadowed face; it
frightened Jonas almost beyond thought. "I can take nothing
from you, whether offered freely or otherwise. All I can do is
help you see out of this darkness. Which you must do. Please,
Jonas. Come here to the window."

The Hunter only waited.

"I don't— I can't— I don't know how you can ask this of me!" Jonas cried suddenly, frightened and furious. "It's easy enough for a mage, I suppose! You have—you have plans or spells or something! Do you think I don't know? You're helping him—you have been—that was you, in the dark, when all I wanted was to lie still! Wasn't that you?"

Kapoen met Jonas's eyes, his shadowy face grave. "Yes. That was I."

"Why?" cried Jonas. "Why?"

"Because if you had given up and lain still on the ice, Jonas, you would have died, and the dark Hunter needs a living man." Kapoen spoke matter-of-factly, even with sympathy, but there was no apology in his face or his voice.

"But why me?"

"Why not you?" Kapoen did not move, but his voice unexpectedly gained depth. "Whom else should the Hunter have chosen? Was it not you who walked out of despair into this Kingdom, four years past? What price were you willing, then, to pay for four years of peace? For a tranquil life, and friends, and the possibility of love? What price are you willing to pay for them now?"

Jonas, struck suddenly wordless, could only stare at him.

"Come here," said Kapoen, and held out one shadowy hand.

Jonas slowly moved to stand at the window, beside the mage. Kapoen moved behind him, reaching around to lay his hands over Jonas's on the window's broad sill. His touch was insubstantial, like the touch of shadows. Jonas kept his eyes on their paired hands: his own solid and real, the mage's overlying his like mist.

"Now," said Kapoen. "Look out."

For a long moment Jonas could not bring himself to move. Then he lifted his head.

At first he saw nothing but darkness. Then light broke through, poured down like liquid, silvery and pure. Moonlight, Jonas recognized eventually, and for a moment that was all he could see: light pouring down through the dark.

Light, light, light . . . light on white stone. On a balcony, dizzyingly high in the air. On Timou, who stood, clad all in white, white hair dressed with pearls, standing with an assured poise that somehow looked . . . odd. Out of place. Unlike her usual natural grace. Her attention was on a young man with dark hair, elegant features, wide dark eyes. . . . Timou held a silver knife in her hand. . . . She was *not Timou*. He knew that suddenly.

"There," breathed Kapoen at his back, and lifted a hand to point.

There was Timou, hard against the side of whatever tower it was she had found herself on, as terrible in its way, Jonas thought, as the Hunter's tower. Silver chains bound her to the stones. She had been weeping. She was weeping still: tears ran down her face. The moonlight turned her tears to pearls, to diamonds. . . .

There was a man with her, bound as she was, with the same white hair and the same face, though harsher and stronger. That face was set now with fear or anger or despair. The man's eyes, unlike Timou's, were black. They held no hope. He had his arm protectively around Timou's shoulders, not like a lover, but perhaps like a friend. The bleak expression in his eyes said clearly that he had no expectation that he could actually protect her. Even so, she had tucked herself close to his side. Jealousy ran suddenly through Jonas like fire.

"What is this?" he asked Kapoen in a fierce whisper.

"Almost too late," breathed the mage. "Almost too late."

"Too late for what? Too late how?" Jonas found himself shaking. On the other side of the window, the woman who was not Timou spoke. Her voice did not enter the Hunter's tower: they could not hear her. The young man she faced heard her. He turned away, went across the balcony to Timou . . . no, to the white-haired man. He stood with his back turned to the woman. He had taken the older man's hand in both of his, and they stood together, speaking quietly. . . .

"She will kill the boy first," said Kapoen softly. His deep voice was heavy with grief. "Then her way will be clear to finish what she began so long ago. She will devour the Kingdom through the children she has made. The children we helped her make."

"*That* is Timou's mother?"

"Yes," said the mage, and bowed his head. Turning, incredulous, to look at the mage, Jonas found that Kapoen, too, was weeping. His tears were made of darkness, and fell into darkness without sound.

The Hunter stood in the center of the tower room, not even

glancing out the window. He did not speak or move. His round yellow eyes watched Jonas steadily, without passion.

Jonas faced him. "What do you want of me?" he asked, knowing what the answer would be.

That is not my Kingdom, said the Hunter. *There I am blind: I need your eyes. There I am voiceless: I need your tongue. There I am bodiless: I need your hands.*

"And my heart," whispered Jonas.

So that I will care to act, said the Hunter. *Do you understand?*

"No," whispered Jonas. "I think I do not understand anything. Yes. I know what you want. All right. All right. Take it, then. Take everything."

Yes, said the Hunter. *Everything.* He reached out.

Even having made his decision, Jonas could not help but flinch away. He tried to draw back against Kapoen, but the mage was no longer there. He was alone. He felt that he had always been alone, that companionship and friendship were illusions he had dreamed once, long ago. He leaned against the stone, turning his face into its cold surface, and wondered whether Timou's father had ever been there, or whether the Hunter had made him out of shadows, a phantasm to break his prey to his will . . . perhaps nothing he had seen through that window had been real. Perhaps it had all been made of shadows. . . .

The Hunter laid his hand on Jonas's shoulder and drew him wordlessly into a cold embrace. And then everything was made of shadows.

CHAPTER 14

A fter Lelienne had bound both her children to the tower, there did not seem very much that either of them might do. Timou leaned wearily against her half brother and thought about the Kingdom, and how one might go about devouring it, and what it might mean to devour a Kingdom. And a little, perhaps, about her father, and the dead King, and Prince Cassiel.

Though Neill held her firmly, he himself had attention only for Cassiel. Timou could not divine what he was thinking.

"Well," Lelienne said briskly, "I believe we shall proceed." She glanced up at the moon, and searchingly into the distant reaches of space. Whatever she saw seemed to satisfy her. The silver knife shifted: light ran flashing down its blade and over her hand.

"Wait," said Cassiel, and when she lifted one graceful eyebrow, he said fiercely, "What difference does it make now? You have everything. You can spare one moment more." He stood straight, head up, oak-dark eyes on hers. He was afraid, Timou could see, but really he was angry. Perhaps his fear had been worn out of him over the course of this past hour, leaving mostly anger. Timou could understand that. Although she felt cold with fear herself, fear that had worn out anger. . . .

He did not wait for Lelienne's permission, but simply turned his back on her—he did not lack courage—and crossed the gallery to his brother.

Neill, still holding Timou, lifted his other hand as far as he could, and Cassiel took it in both of his.

Neill said quietly, "I am sorry now I was ever born." He wore his face like a mask: reserved, cool. An expression he might have worn on all those occasions his father had dismissed him in favor of his younger brother. His tone gave away nothing until the very end, and then began to break; he cut the last word off short.

"I'm sorry *she* was," Cassiel rejoined. "Except I cannot regret that you exist. Neill. You— I—"

"I know."

Cassiel searched his face. "Do you? I hope so. Our father—"

"I know," Neill repeated gently.

Lelienne's mouth twisted a little. She moved her hand, the knife glinting suddenly. Timou flinched, trying to look away, unable to take her eyes off its silver sheen.

But the knife did not disappear from Lelienne's hand. Instead the woman made a faint sound of surprise, turning her head to take in a shadow that moved suddenly in one of the windows that pierced the tower.

Cassiel, facing the wrong way to see the open gallery or Lelienne, heard the sound but not the surprise. He stiffened, gripped his brother's hand hard, and shut his eyes. Then, when pain did not come, he opened his eyes again, startled, looked at Neill's face, and followed the direction of his brother's gaze to the tower window.

The form there moved, shifted a hand on the sill, and then bent suddenly, ducking through the window and onto the gallery.

"Jonas?" Timou said uncertainly, taken utterly aback.

Cassiel's eyes had widened. He stared at the man . . . seeing, Timou thought, something other than what she saw herself. Neill's hand closed hard on his brother's.

"*Who* is this?" inquired Lelienne coldly. "I had thought we were done with interruptions?"

"No," said Jonas.

He was, Timou realized after a second, speaking not to Lelienne, but to her, answering her. His eyes were on her face.

His voice was strange. It was distant, as though carried from a thousand miles away. His face, too, was strange: Passionless. Remote. As though no emotion had ever touched his heart, nor ever would. He stood still. Too still. No man could stand so still, as though he were not breathing, as though his heart were not even beating. . . . He came a step away from the tower, into the moonlight. He turned his face to the light, lifted a hand to it, as though he found the light puzzling, as though he expected it to pool in his hand and flow through his fingers like water.

The moonlight pulled his shadow out before him, clean-edged and blacker than any shadow could have been during the day. It was not, Timou realized, a normal shadow. It stretched out and out, far too tall for the man who stood there; it moved, turning its head, although Jonas stood still. Long branching shadows crowned it, moving as it moved. It was blind, being a shadow, but it looked through his eyes. Jonas should have had brown eyes, but he had instead the eyes, Timou saw, that belonged to his shadow: yellow and round as the eyes of an owl.

First the shadow and then the man turned finally to her mother. He said softly, in that strange voice, "Lelienne. Is that your name?"

"I am not from this Kingdom. My name will give you no power over me," the woman stated. She looked curious and annoyed, but not worried, though terror sang down Timou's spine and made the delicate hairs on the back of her neck stand up.

"Do you think not?" asked Jonas. Or the shadow that spoke through his mouth. "Lelienne. Lelienne . . ." His voice, lowering, trailed off like the end of night.

"Who are you?"

"You do not know me. And yet you would possess me. Does that seem wise to you? You have power, but are you wise? I think not. You would possess this Kingdom. All the Kingdoms, as they lie layered one beyond the next . . . and yet you do not know them. You have not even glimpsed what you would take into your hand."

"I know who you are," Cassiel said unexpectedly from beside Neill and Timou.

Jonas, followed after a breath by his shadow, turned his head to examine the Prince. "Yes," he said. "I know you. Give me your name."

"Cassiel," the Prince said steadily.

"Yes," Jonas said again distantly. "The King above the Lake is dead; long live the King."

"If you would help us," Cassiel said to him, his tone now a little uneven, "I would pay . . . any price you might ask of me. I believe . . . I believe it is my right to offer, is it not—as the King?" His brother moved in slight, instant protest, and then was still again as Cassiel gripped his arm above his bound wrist.

The shadow moved, Jonas himself moving a heartbeat more slowly. The shadow stretched, lengthened, reaching out toward the Prince as Jonas lifted his hand. Cassiel neither moved nor looked away, though his eyes widened. But the dark hand of the shadow passed him, fell instead on the silver chains that bound Timou and Neill to the tower. The chains dissolved into shadow, into mist, into cold. Timou rubbed her wrist, shivering violently.

"I ask no price of you," Jonas said to Cassiel. "All my price has been paid." Those disturbing yellow eyes shifted from the Prince to look into hers. "Timou," he said. "I know your name. I hear it in my heart. Jonas knows you. Do you know me?"

"Yes," Timou breathed. She let her gaze fall on his shadow, on the branching crown that confused the eye around its head, and swallowed. "Oh, yes, Lord. Yes, I know you."

"Well, I do not," said her mother impatiently. She was uneasy, Timou thought, and trying to hide her unease behind a tone of sharp confidence. "Who is this? Is there any reason I should not kill him immediately where he stands?"

"I don't . . . I don't think you can," whispered Timou. She

backed away, drawing both Neill and Cassiel with her. She was aware she was trembling, but could not stop. Nor could she take her eyes from Jonas. From his shadow.

"Oh, I expect it won't be so difficult," Lelienne said briskly, and sent the knife from her hand to Jonas's heart. It stood in his chest.

Blood showed through his shirt, through his jacket. . . . He touched the knife, which faded into the dark and was gone. The blood ran slowly down his chest, but this he did not seem to notice. He bent, and straightened. In his hand was Cassiel's sword: the sword that had gone with the Prince behind the mirror, and then found its way in his hand to this strange reflected City, where it had been changed into a thing of light and darkness. Jonas held it as Cassiel had, as though he did not have to think about it, as though it were part of his body. "Yes," he said softly. "This, too, I know. It is not my usual weapon. But Jonas understands it. It will do." He took a step toward Lelienne.

In the distance something cried, high and piercing, far up in the sky. It might have been geese. Timou knew it was not geese. Despite the clear sky thunder crashed, so loud and sudden that they all jumped.

Lelienne, her eyes narrowed, moved her hand.

Stone closed around Jonas, over his face, over his eyes. Then his shadow moved, and the stone cracked and fell away. He took another step.

She cried out in that heavy, rolling language; her words leaned forward, trying to crush Jonas. He moved the sword, drawing a line that lay between them, from his feet to Lelienne's, and the words parted and rolled harmlessly to either side while he stepped forward between them.

"Run," he said to Lelienne, his voice strange and dark, the voice of nothing mortal. "Run. If you outrun my storm, I cannot touch you. You will not outrun my storm."

Lelienne stood still for one more instant, staring at him. She took a step back. "What *are* you?" she asked in amazement.

"Run," said Jonas softly. He took another step, and again Lelienne backed away.

The storm hounds came then, before the driving edge of the rain. They were lean, long, terrible: each one as tall at the shoulder as a man. Their eyes were fierce as flame, and Lelienne fled suddenly before them, away through the sky, a whisper through the wind. But the storm hounds had her scent and followed, baying behind her with the wild voices of hunting eagles. The first drops of rain fell, cold and viciously hard, like razors of ice.

The white horse of the Hunter fell through the sky like lightning, thunder shaking from its hooves, its dark eyes wild, and Jonas put his hand to its shoulder and vaulted onto its back, his shadow towering above him. The sword in his hand blazed, terrible and brilliant, and the mare flung up its head and leapt away into the storm. The thunder of its going shook stones from the tower. In front of him, running before the storm, the hounds cried; behind him thunder crashed, the sky tore open, and the rain came down in a blinding icy deluge.

He never looked back.

CHAPTER 15

The City seemed unsurprised to have lost its King: perhaps it had felt his death, echoing from the other Kingdom. Or perhaps the understanding that the King had died had spread outward from the Queen. Because Ellis knew. She welcomed her son, returned at last to her side, with love and relief. But she did not ask after his father. She moved quietly through the days following the storm, never shouting or throwing plates, as though the driving rain of that night had permanently quenched her temper. And she greeted the return of the King's elder son with such careful restraint that he understood, to his surprise, that she was ashamed.

"You know, I do not blame you for anything," he told her when, a few days after their return, he made a moment of privacy with the Queen.

Ellis bent her head. They were in her rooms, as they had been once before not so long ago. She had thrown a water pitcher at him on that occasion. This time she did not seem inclined to throw anything. She looked elegant, weary, and, for the first time Neill could remember, as though she might one day be old. "You protected me," she said. "You protected us all. We—I— gave you little enough cause. Thank you."

Neill listened to what she did not say. He said gently, "I would have saved him if I could. I tried. You were wrong, you know. I never hated him. I took any small excuse he ever gave me to love him."

"He gave you so little. I never minded. I encouraged him in that. I wanted everything for my son. I never cared that there was so little left for you. You should blame me."

"He gave me enough," Neill said steadily.

"I am glad," said the Queen, obviously with some difficulty, "that you were there for him, Neill. For both of them. Cassiel told me. . . . I will be grateful forever that you were there."

"If I hadn't been," Neill said drily, "the whole problem would never have arisen."

"One cannot hold against the child the terrible acts of the parent." The Queen studied his face. "Or the stupidities. Or the unkindnesses."

"I hold nothing against you, Ellis. Far less against Cassiel." He met her eyes, and added gently, "Everyone loves Cassiel. He is easy to love. Why should I be excepted?"

"It will make me glad," said the Queen softly, "to know you will stand beside my son when he takes the throne. To know he will be able to depend on your courage and your loyalty."

"You may be sure of it." He looked at her thoughtfully: her wide, guileless violet eyes, her calm face. Those eyes met his for a moment, and then dropped. A faint flush rose under her fair skin. He said, without heat, "Will you believe me if I tell you I do not want it? That I will indeed be content to stand quietly beside the throne?"

Her violet eyes lifted again. "I will believe anything you tell me," said the Queen. "I have learned that, at least."

"I am glad to hear it. I do generally tell you the truth." He rose to his feet and took her hand in his, raised it to his lips as he offered a slight bow. "I'm grateful for your regard. Truly," he added as her eyes searched his face for any trace of mockery.

The Queen rose gracefully and accompanied him to the outer door of her apartment: a signal courtesy. "I shall see you tonight, then."

"Yes," he said, "tonight," and took his leave.

"You've been to see my mother," Cassiel said to him later; it was not quite a question. Waving away hovering attendants, he took his brother by the arm and turned toward the balcony of his room. The air was cold and clear. The view from that balcony, though excellent, did not match the one from the highest Palace tower. Neill did not miss it. He had no special desire to set foot on that high gallery ever again.

"She was more than civil," he said. "She was trying very hard to be kind."

Cassiel studied him. "She doesn't trust you. Even now?"

"She does, in fact, I think. Her doubts of me now are merely habit, and she is, I believe, trying not to listen to them."

The Prince turned and leaned his arms on the balcony railing. "In time she will learn to trust you with her heart. I wish she would begin to throw things again."

Neill smiled. "Then we would both know she was recovered."

An attendant appeared tentatively at the door of the balcony and said, "Your Highness . . ."

"Later," commanded the Prince. He said to Neill as the man vanished again, "They pretend to believe we will not be ready for the coronation tonight, but of course we will be." His tone was light, but grief moved suddenly in his eyes.

"He would be proud of you," Neill said gently.

"I don't know why. I did very little."

Neill tilted his head. "You were kind as well as brave. I remember a certain offer, made at the end, that was very like a King. You will be a fine King. Of course he would be proud."

Cassiel, faintly embarrassed, made a noncommittal sound. He turned suddenly, as though gathering courage from the cold air. He said, eyes searching his brother's face, "Neill, do you mind?"

After the briefest pause, Neill said lightly, "So you doubt me as well. You need not."

Despite the lightness, his brother heard the hurt in that pause. He said swiftly, taking Neill's arm again in a grip so hard it almost bruised, "No. Not your heart, nor your patience, nor your resolve, nor your courage, nor your ability to stand next to me for the next fifty years, if you must, and never show the slightest trace of regret. Even if regret is what you feel. You say I will be a fine King. But I know you could be a great King, and you are the elder. . . ."

"But you are the only son of the Queen," said Neill softly. "And the heart of the Kingdom. My heritage is not . . . not so comfortable. I could be clever and ruthless and powerful, and those are all good qualities in a King. But you will shine like the sun in the sky and bring joy to all the Kingdom. Besides," he said, and smiled suddenly, "I do not want it. If I learned anything in my brief week of rule, it was that. I want you to have it, and I wish you all possible joy of it."

Cassiel gave him a searching look. "Do you mean that?"

"Certainly," Neill said, and took care that this time there was no trace of hesitation.

"All right," said Cassiel softly, and drew him forward into an abrupt, fierce embrace. "I love you," he said, with simple sincerity. "I trust you. Always. Never doubt it, brother."

Neill swallowed a sudden, surprising lump in his throat and returned his brother's embrace, not trying to speak.

Cassiel pushed him back again, smiling, eyes sparkling with sudden mischief. "And since I love you, I have sent your servants suitable clothing for you to wear tonight."

"Oh . . . ," said Neill, recovering all his accustomed self-possession as he made a rapid leap of imagination. "No, Cassiel—"

"Your tastes are far too plain. You know that."

"Cassiel—"

His younger brother only laughed. "You should see what I sent to Timou. Well, you will, of course, tonight."

Neill smiled reluctantly. "Not white, I hope?"

"Thunder and ice, no," Cassiel said cheerfully. "She needs to look like herself, not like your mother." He said this with a lightness that suggested he had already forgotten that night of terror and despair at the heights of the Palace, though Neill knew he had not. But his tone made it clear he meant to dismiss any importance Lelienne had ever had for either of them. "But all that white hair! And that skin! Those eyes! I asked Jesse's advice—Jesse has an eye for women's fashions that might surprise you."

Neill studied him with a sudden faint concern. "Cassiel, you're not— You don't see Timou's face in the falling rain, surely?"

"What?" his brother said, surprised, and then laughed. "Neill, she's your sister, and you're my brother. It would hardly be right. No. But I can appreciate beauty when I see it. She will be exquisite." He rubbed his hands together in anticipation.

Neill said warningly, "If mine is too exquisite, I won't wear it."

"You will. To please me." Cassiel turned back toward the door, making a slight face. "And I will wear all the regalia my attendants insist upon, so you've no cause to complain."

Neill did complain, at length, when he saw the clothing his brother had sent to his rooms. But he did it with a lightness to his tone that set the servants to smiling behind their hands.

His brother had sent him a shirt like midnight, with the puffed sleeves slashed up to the elbow to show the silvery blue lining. The leggings were black, traced with intricate silver-blue embroidery that ran in a narrow line down from his right hip to swirl around his calf. The embroidery continued down his right boot, picked out in silk and sapphire. The other boot was plain. The boots had, Neill judged, undoubtedly been a special order. Someone had probably stayed up for several nights in a row to finish them in time.

Cassiel had sent ribbons for his hair: midnight-blue and

silvery blue and, the one concession to mourning, a single ribbon of lavender. There was a silver hair clasp, set with tiny sapphires.

"The ladies of the court will fall at your feet," said an elderly servant, braiding the ribbons into Neill's hair.

"Wonderful," Neill said drily.

"If you do not look at them, my lord, you will break their hearts." The servant, who was the man who had watched Neill take a coal out of the fire at his mother's command, came around in front of him and opened a little rosewood box to show him a ring. It was made of strands of braided silver, set with sapphires and pearls. It had belonged to the King, who had worn it on special occasions. "Prince Cassiel sent it," the servant said gently. "It will break *his* heart if you do not wear it."

After a moment Neill extended his hand.

The servant slid the ring onto his thumb—the King had worn it on the third finger of his right hand, but Neill's hands were not so heavy. Then the servant bowed his head and touched his lips to the hand he held. Startled, Neill did not move.

"All the court should kiss your hands," said the servant softly. "Some of them know it. All of *us* know it."

Too much touched to speak, Neill laid his hand on the man's shoulder. All the servants bowed, one after another, very carefully and seriously, and retired quietly afterward, to leave Neill standing by himself in the privacy of his room. He found, to his considerable surprise, that for once he did not feel that he stood alone in the heart of the court.

☙☙☙

The coronation occurred at dusk, the correct and proper time to recognize all moments of change. And what could be more momentous a change than the recognition of a new King after the death of the old?

Garlands and ribbons dressed the great hall, which had been flung open to all the Kingdom for the evening; in practice this meant that the hall thronged with courtiers, while people from the City and beyond filled the streets outside the Palace.

Tables along the sides of the hall held platters of thin-sliced beef, soft white rolls, tiny pastries filled with thick cream, cakes garnished with nets of caramelized sugar, and pyramids of glistening red berries that seemed to glow with their own contained light. The same fare, Neill knew, was being offered all through the courtyards and gardens surrounding the Palace, and it was a very good thing the evening sky was cloudless.

No one wore overt mourning on this evening: nothing brought worse luck to the coronation of a new King than extravagant mourning for the old. Courtiers wore bright jewel tones. Even the widowed Queen had put aside her black and lavender; she wore instead a gown in a pure deep blue, embroidered with traceries of creamy thread and white pearls. A strand of pearls and amethysts dressed her hair. She moved through the gathered courtiers with a slightly abstracted air that suggested her attention was elsewhere: thinking of her absent husband, Neill guessed, or of her son, waiting to be crowned in his place. Or most likely both.

Timou, when she entered, wore a confection of silvery

colors—blue and green and rose—that poured like water down her slight form. Pearls and softly colored opals swept down the left side of the gown and were stitched onto her left slipper in a stylistic gesture Neill recognized; pearls and more opals dressed her hair, which had been gathered up to show off her slender neck. The gown and the upswept hair made her seem older than she was; the delicate colors and her air of unstudied grace made her seem like herself and less like her mother.

The court had been wary of Timou, seeing her mother's face stamped so clearly in hers, and never mind that she plainly held the favor of their Prince. Now, however, Jesse and some of the other young men drifted toward the girl, as automatically as clouds follow the wind. Neill came down among them like a tiger among the sheep and sent the lot of them scattering away again in all directions with ruthless dispatch.

Timou watched him with a lifted brow and a wry look in her pale eyes. "Do I need protection?"

"They do," Neill assured her gravely. "They will cast themselves at your feet and beg you to tread over them. You are lovely." She was. The faint air of sadness she had carried with her back into the ordinary Kingdom from the City in the Lake only added to her beauty.

"She is," agreed a familiar voice.

Neill turned to find Marcos standing attentively and hopefully at his elbow.

"She is wasted on a brother," Marcos continued earnestly, and smiled at Timou. "You should adorn my arm, not Neill's. I brought you a bribe." With an expression of wistful optimism, he offered her a plate of cream-filled pastries. "This is the best kind, you know."

"Marcos," the girl murmured with the slightest inclination of her head and a smile that told Neill the mage was familiar and welcome company. "Thank you." She accepted a pastry and asked in a perfectly conversational tone, "Is Trevennen still a tree?"

"I thought he would find his way out of that spell in hours," Marcos confided with a pleased expression. "Days, at the most. He must have underestimated Russe very badly. So must I. I had no idea she could so thoroughly persuade a tree that it really is a tree. She has set the spell so deep by now that he may stand in our house for the next thousand years. We may have to rearrange the kitchen around him. It's inconvenient," he said solemnly, to a faint sound Neill made. "One has to make breakfast ducking under branches. And he sheds leaves into the porridge."

The girl smiled—a smile with a hard edge to it. The idea of Trevennen being turned into a tree for a thousand years clearly pleased her. It certainly pleased Neill. He inquired, "But Russe could undo the spell if she wished? Cassiel may not be content to leave Trevennen standing for a thousand years, even as a tree."

"Of course, if he wishes," agreed Marcos. "At his pleasure. There does not appear to be any need to hurry."

"It is a beautiful spell," Timou said to Neill quite earnestly. She shaped a circle in the air. "It goes around and around, and every layer says, *This is a tree.* It's very convincing. My . . . my father showed me how to listen to the voices of the trees, but he never showed me how to change myself into one."

"Russe spent many seasons as a tree standing at the edge of

the great forest when she was young," Marcos told her. He eyed
the girl speculatively. "She could teach you to do that, I am sure.
If that is something you would like to learn."

"Oh, yes. Yes. Eventually. But—"

"You are going home, of course," Neill finished for her. "You
are more than welcome to stay, if you wish." A glance at Marcos
caused the mage to second this with an emphatic nod. "But I can
understand if you want distance. Or time."

The girl shook her head. Light from lanterns and candles slid
through her eyes, now pale blue, now almost green, now faintly
lavender. There was in fact a kind of distance, an unbreakable
calm, to her gaze that the crowds in this hall could not touch.
She said softly, "I could love this City. I love it already. I would
like to stay here in this Palace. Or go into the City and stay with
the mages and learn from Russe. And from you," she added to
Marcos. "But, yes, I must go home. I promised everyone I would
come back."

"Make us the same promise," suggested Neill. He touched
her wrist lightly. "You will break a hundred hearts when you go.
And," he said softly, "I should be sorry to lose a sister so soon
after gaining one."

She bowed her head a little. "I told those I left behind that I
would go to the City to find my father. I think in truth I came here
to find my mother. But what I found was not what I had hoped to
find." Lifting her head, she met his eyes. "But I found a brother
here I had not even known to look for. That makes me glad."

Neill tried to produce a smile. After a moment he succeeded.
"You must surely return to us."

"I will try," she answered, pale eyes meeting dark. He understood at that moment that she did not know whether she would be able to return, and guessed by that where she meant to go.

He said slowly, "I see, of course, that you must try." He did not mean *try to come back,* and she knew that; she glanced down, recognizing, perhaps, that he had understood more than she had intended. He said, "I could come with you, you know. You need not go alone."

Marcos said plaintively, "What are you two talking about?"

Timou did not even seem to hear the mage. She said quietly, "No, really. I think I do need to go alone. You see . . . you must see . . . it was I whom Jonas followed into the dark." The calm in her pale eyes had become serious.

"An obligation you assuredly need not meet alone," Neill said gently. "It's one we all share."

Delicate color rose into the girl's face. "Oh, well . . . obligation would do for any of us, I am sure. But for me . . . it's not merely obligation."

"Ah," Neill murmured. "I had not known."

"Nor I. Until . . . well." Timou bowed her head a little.

Neill said after a moment, "I would still be honored to accompany you, Timou."

"To where?" Marcos inquired, eyebrows rising. He glanced from one of them to the other, uneasy at their serious tones.

Timou said, still to Neill, "I do not think your brother would thank you for making that offer . . . though I do."

"You underestimate him. He would go with you himself. . . . In fact, I think it is better if he does not know where you intend to go. Much better. Much." Neill's skin prickled all the way down his spine to think of his young brother riding blithely along the road this girl meant to take.

"Where *does* she intend to go?" said Marcos again, and then at last, with sudden, dawning comprehension, "Oh . . ."

"Yes," said Timou, still speaking only to Neill. She understood him perfectly. "That would not do. So I will go by myself."

"And leave me wondering. That is unkind. I will come with you."

"No," the girl said patiently. At that moment, Neill reflected, she sounded very like a mage. "I will come back. In the spring, when the apples bloom. If I do not, then you will know I could not. All right?"

Neill hesitated.

"You certainly cannot ride off and lose yourself in the forest, Neill," Marcos observed in a tone he made carefully neutral. "Or . . . wherever. Your brother would be extremely upset if . . . something happened to you. And he will need your help, you know, especially during the next year or so. He never paid enough attention to the nails and hammers of holding the rule. Not like you."

This was undeniable. The pause lengthened. Before Neill could speak again, horns sang out, flinging a staccato flurry of notes across the hall. The court moved instantly, shifting expectantly into the ordained patterns of rank and precedence, and the moment was lost. Guardsmen took their appointed stations along both sides of the hall, swords drawn and held upright in salute. Galef stood at the foot of the dais, standing so that he could keep both the throne and anyone approaching it under his eye. He held his sword in both hands, its tip grounded against the stone of the floor, his face professionally blank.

Reserving all questions and remonstrations for a later moment, Neill moved toward the front of the hall, drawing Timou with him.

The horns called again, scattering mellow notes like drops of gold into the air, and Cassiel came in while the court called out in acclamation. He wore russet and dark green and gold; gold showed at his wrists and wound in narrow ribbons through the oak-dark braid of his hair. Traceries of gold and copper wound around the tops of his boots and across his broad belt. Buoyed up by the applause of the crowd, Prince Cassiel looked young and full of life, as though he had never been touched by grief or fear. He crossed the hall with a bounce in his step, leapt up onto the low dais that held the throne, and swung around to view the assembly, lifting his hands with a merry, conspiratorial gesture to still their acclaim.

Neill left his sister with a hasty touch on her hand and a word of reassurance and strode forward. Assuming the solemn mien appropriate to the moment, he went first to the Queen, where she stood in her place on the first step of the dais, just to the left of the throne. She held a velvet cushion in both hands, with the King's circlet of golden leaves resting upon it. Neill met her eyes, inclining his head in sober salute. He was rewarded, as he lifted the circlet, by seeing her stiff smile become for an instant warm.

He bore the circlet to Cassiel. Then, as the nearest heir, he stepped up onto the dais and knelt before his brother, offering him the circlet of the King. Cassiel touched his hands first, looking seriously into his eyes, and then, smiling, took the circlet and placed it carefully on his own head. The horns sang for the third time, and the court cried out three times in acclamation. Beyond the hall, out in the City, Neill could hear that cry picked up and thrown onward by a thousand voices.

"Thank you," Cassiel said—the words more seen and felt than heard, because the cry of acclaim was still echoing through the hall. He offered his hand to his brother. Neill bent his head to touch his lips to the back of Cassiel's hand, first among the court to offer the kiss of fealty. Cassiel drew him to his feet and embraced him, but when Neill would have withdrawn to his accustomed place among the court, his brother prevented him. With a smiling gesture, Cassiel directed him instead to a place at the right hand of the throne: a place of signal honor that he, though never Neill, had often taken when their father occupied this throne.

Neill, eyes suddenly burning, took the few steps necessary and turned, standing beside the throne, to face the assembly. The court was quiet again; he wondered how many of them still suspected him, despite everything, of having deliberately struck down his father, or of having conspired with his foreign mother to do so. Fewer now, perhaps, after this extremely public gesture of trust and favor from his brother.

Following Neill, it was Timou, clearly briefed on her role, who walked forward with concentrated poise. Schooled—probably by the Queen—in appropriate behavior, Timou carefully mounted

the three steps of the dais and sank down before the throne with
a rustle of stiff skirts and an extremely endearing air of concen-
tration. Cassiel gave her his hand, which she kissed; he raised her
at once and came a step forward, turning her to stand with him,
facing the court.

"Here is Timou, daughter of the mage Kapoen," he said
swiftly and clearly. His smile was pleased and slightly wicked, as
it was when he planned mischief. "She is the sister of my
brother, and so she is my sister, welcome in my family and my
court." Ignoring the burst of whispers down the hall, he drew
her close, bent swiftly to kiss her brow in welcome and her
cheek in affection. Rather than allowing her to retreat back into
the hall, Cassiel then sent her with a gesture to stand next to
Neill beside the throne.

"Smile," Neill said to her in a low voice that would not carry.
"Did he warn you he was going to do that?"

"No," the girl whispered back, smiling obediently but not
very freely.

"Now you will have to return," he murmured, "or Cassiel
will move all the court out to the villages until he finds you. He
would do it, you know. He would probably enjoy it."

"I know he would," she whispered, but then they both had
to be still again, facing soberly and correctly forward, waiting
with strict patience for the whole of the court to file, one by one,
before the throne to pledge their fealty to their new young King.

After the coronation, there was the procession through the
City, with moonlight and round parchment-covered lamps to

light the way, and the people of the City shouting Cassiel's name and throwing grain before the hooves of his horse. The new King rode an oak-colored stallion, its black mane braided with strands of gold. The Queen rode at his back, her full skirts sweeping down across the shoulder of her bright chestnut horse, sapphires and pearls braided into its creamy mane. A black mare that matched Neill's had been found for Timou, and they rode behind the Queen. Neill was astonished, as they rode through the streets, to hear his name among those cried by the people of the City; a few even shouted the girl's name. The procession wound through all the wider streets of the City so that everyone who dwelled there could see and cheer for the new King, and everyone wanted to see him; the streets were thronged on both sides, and children ran along the rooftops, throwing down handfuls of grain and bright bits of ribbon.

After the procession it was back at last to the Palace, where dozens of musicians had taken up their stations so that the sunlight of the new morning seemed to strike music out of the very air. There was dancing, for anyone still with the energy, and more food had been laid out on the tables: complicated braided loaves, rounds of soft cheese, pastries filled with fruit and sticky with honey. Neill found his brother and a dozen women of the court waiting to sweep him into the dancing, and did not make it back to his own rooms and his own bed until late in the afternoon.

When he woke early the next morning, Timou had already gone.

"There's no need to be disappointed about it. She said she intends to come back in the spring," Cassiel told him cheerfully at a breakfast he invited Neill to share, and that he himself attacked with the energy of the young.

Neill made himself smile and agree. He said, after a moment, "If I may have your leave, I would like to go after her and be sure she comes safely to her home. She took no attendants, I am sure."

"She wouldn't have any. How did you know?" Cassiel was blithely unconcerned. "I'll send a messenger if you like. You, however, I want by my side! Even if you swear to stay on the road and never look aside, crossing that forest is a chancy business. I know you could handle anything you found there," he added earnestly, with a quick look at his brother's face, "but you are my heir now, until I get another. We can't have you turned for a year and a day into a jeweled sword that speaks in tongues, or whatever. Really, Neill. I am sorry. . . ."

"I know," Neill agreed reluctantly. "You're right. All right. . . ." And because this was true, he allowed himself, in the end, to be resigned to the idea of a simple messenger.

But if the messenger did not find Timou safe in her village, or if she did not reappear in the City in the spring, he resolved silently, he would take any road necessary to find her.

imou, riding the black mare Cassiel had insisted she take, crossed Tiger Bridge at sunrise—a gray sort of sunrise, with snow just beginning to fall from a heavy sky. She found the road unrolling before her with unexpected cooperation. It brought her into the nearest town before noon. She was not tempted to halt for the day, although she paused at the inn to eat fresh bread and sharp cheese and to rest the mare.

She found the town smaller and plainer than she had recalled, and was wryly amused to find her expectations so easily altered by so brief an experience of the City. There was a new undercurrent in the town, however: a happiness that seemed to fall through the air along with the snow. Everyone knew that a great danger had been averted, that their own Prince had returned and been crowned. This was certainly reason for happiness and relief, but it seemed sad almost beyond bearing to Timou that the death of the old King cast so little shadow across the mood. Sadness seemed to have become a permanent companion for her since the City in the Lake. Timou rode with her head bowed under the weight of it. She did not know clearly whether the sadness she felt was for the dead King; or for her father, lost to deception and betrayal; or for the mother she had hoped to find but who had never truly existed; or for Jonas, taken into the dark; or even for herself.

From the town, she found it only half a day's ride to travel all the way to the village by the near edge of the forest, so she came to it by dusk of that same day. The surprise of this shook her out of her dark mood, and she wondered that she had come so far and not even known how short the road had made itself for her.

Before her, on the other side of the village, the great forest stretched out, featureless in the deepening twilight. Snow lay lightly on the land and the village, but the forest itself was deep and black: no snow clung to the branches of its great trees. It was too dark for Timou to see whether the trees had lost their leaves at all or still dwelt in an endless summer—too dark for her to go at once into the forest.

At the inn, she gave the mare's reins to a stable boy and went inside. She found as she entered a hesitation in the talk. Timou wondered what the people of the village saw in her face that made them stop in the midst of their conversations to look at her.

The inn was crowded, and very cheerful—fast as she had come, it was clear that news from the City had run before her. The innkeeper came forward after a moment to indicate a table— a private table, vacated rapidly and without argument by several young men at the innkeeper's gesture; he did not suggest this time that she might share a table with others, and Timou was grateful. She wanted to be surrounded by the sounds of life, but was by no means certain she would be able to participate; since leaving the City she had felt set aside, distant, detached, as though life itself were something she observed but did not actually share.

"Beef roast, chicken pie, mutton stew," offered the innkeeper, pulling a chair out from the table for her.

"Yes," said Timou, not really hearing him, and he hesitated briefly and then went away again. When the hot food came, she ate it without knowing what it was.

Her sleep that night was restless, troubled by dreams of a woman who turned into a white falcon, tore apart her own nestlings, and flashed away through a lightning-struck sky, crying in a voice like the voice of a woman. She dreamed of a silver knife thrust into a great tree, blood running down fissures in its bark. She dreamed of a crystalline sword falling without a sound through the air high above the City, scattering light from its blade as it tumbled through the fine cold air.

Waking before dawn, she washed and dressed quietly, easing through the still-sleeping inn. She did not even think of the mare in the inn's stable, but walked through the village in the pearly predawn light and on along the road that led into the great forest.

The sun, rising behind her, turned all the forest to fire and gold: autumn had caught up to the forest, but not winter. The snow stopped where the trees began. All their leaves were gold and flame-orange, and some had fallen, so that the forest was roofed and floored with gold and fire. The early light poured through the leaves and turned to gold; the very air tasted of gold.

Timou walked between the sentinel trees that flanked the road and, turning immediately to the side, stepped off the path and walked in among the trees.

She was lost immediately. Trees closed in behind her, crowding between her and the path; if she turned back to find it, she knew, it would not be there. She went straight on, walking slowly at first and then more quickly. The trees became larger as she walked, older, more strange and contorted in their shapes; they remembered a thousand years and spoke of them in muted whispers she could not quite understand. She glimpsed a ruined tower in the distance, and thought she might be able to make out a dragon coiled among the scattered stones at its foot; she heard voices far away, and somewhere a scattering of harp notes. She was not interested in any of these things, and only went on through the golden light.

"In such a hurry," said a voice she recognized, and she stopped and turned, without surprise, toward the speaker. The black serpent was coiled on a flat stone nestled among the roots of the trees. Light, warmed by its fall through flaming leaves, pooled in its slit-pupiled eyes until they swam with fire.

"I know you now," Timou told it.

"I thought you would."

"You are the soul of the Kingdom. You encircle the Kingdom. All the Kingdoms, as they lie layered one across another, different but always the same. You even existed in my mother's maze of light. To you, every place is the same place. Every shape you take is really the same." Timou paused, waiting for the serpent's response.

"That maze was not Lelienne's," it said. It seemed amused—not, at least, offended. "Though perhaps she believed she possessed it."

Timou gave a little nod. "And you are this forest. Aren't you? You lie between the beginning and the end of every journey, and wait for every traveler. You are yourself the maze in which the traveler finds herself lost. That is why you know the way through all the mazes. Isn't that right?"

"Yes," said the serpent, and waited.

"How many Kingdoms are there?" Timou asked curiously.

"Oh," said the serpent in its sweet smoky voice, "more than you have yet seen."

"I want," said Timou, "to see one more." She was trembling with nervousness and determination.

"I could take you there, but you may find it less easy to return," warned the serpent.

"I know."

"And still you ask me for this?"

"Yes. I have to," Timou explained, not very coherently.

"Give me your name."

Timou gave her name to the forest.

The serpent changed before her eyes: it became huge, nebulous, as though it were made of smoke and shadow. Spines fell like the mane of a horse down its long neck, shining with a darkness of their own; spines frilled out around its flat head, rattling drily as it shifted position. Wings opened behind it, vast as the sky. Its eyes were made of darkness that looked into hers and knew her name; its breath was frost.

Around them the trees straightened and lengthened, their tops lost to sight in the dimness. The air chilled. Shadows reached out from each tree and then spread, outward and up-ward, engulfing the world. The rough ground smoothed out un-derfoot to make a surface as smooth as glass or ice. There was no light, and yet Timou could somehow see into the distance through the endless ranks of featureless pillars.

Timou said shakily, "This is still the forest? The Kingdom?"

"It is a forest. An aspect of the Kingdom," answered the ser-pent. Its voice was a whisper of frost through the dark, and yet somehow it was the same voice.

Timou shivered, hearing it. She longed for the golden warmth of the forest she had left behind. "Is there no light here? No light anywhere?"

"There is only one point of light in all this Kingdom."

Timou, trying incredulously to peer into the distance, could not imagine how even one spark of light could exist in this place. It seemed made entirely of the purest darkness. "If you had brought . . . my mother to this place, if she had seen you like this, she would have fled the Kingdom . . . all the Kingdoms . . . for whatever land she came from."

"No," said the serpent, cold as midwinter. "If that woman had seen this Kingdom, she would have desired its power, and, look-ing into its darkness, she might have come to understand it. Then the Hunter would have been forced to battle her here."

"Couldn't he have?"

"The dark is most powerful when it breaks into the light. As the light is most powerful when it strikes through the dark."

"Oh." Timou considered this. "You could not simply have bitten her head off yourself, I suppose."

The immense serpent tilted its head, wings moving like a mist overhead, spines rattling together with a sound like wind through dry twigs. "No."

Timou shook her head. "I don't understand anything."

"There are some things you understand," answered the serpent, and poured itself suddenly through the cold darkness, marking a path for Timou through the endless pillars that had replaced the familiar trees. "Your way lies there."

Timou could see it when she tried: a plain of ice, and a black tower set far out upon its infinite expanse. "Yes," she breathed. "Thank you."

"You may thank me," said the serpent, "if you think you have reason to be grateful." It melted like mist into the darkness.

It seemed a very long way across the ice, and yet it also seemed to Timou that she drew near to the tower with startling rapidity. She looked at it until she saw its jagged image behind her eyelids when she blinked. When she looked away, down at the ice, she found that faint uninterpretable images moved in the glassy surface under her feet. Engrossed, she paused to study them—then guessed that hours might have passed and tore her gaze away again, to find the black tower rearing suddenly close before her. It was made of ice, or black stone, or perhaps carved from the darkness itself; darkness poured from its tall narrow windows and from its open door. The open door was like an invitation: Timou did not know whether she should be glad or frightened to see it. She was both.

Walking slowly forward, Timou entered the tower.

She found herself in a small square chamber. A window pierced each wall, although the windows and the walls and the air within the tower and the views without each window were all made of varying shades and textures of darkness. It was hard to tell where one shape ended and the next began. Jonas stood in the chamber, gazing out one of the windows, with his back to her and his hands resting on the windowsill: him, Timou could see more clearly. Or at least perceive, according to whatever rules of perception governed in this dark Kingdom.

The Hunter's shadow stood behind Jonas, taller than he— taller than the chamber seemed sensibly to allow, so tall it should have been impossible to see its face. And yet, when the shadow turned its head to look at her, Timou could see its face, flat and strangely featureless. Narrow branching patterns of darkness twisted across the ceiling, or the sky—it was hard to tell.

Jonas himself turned a heartbeat after the shadow. His face was empty of expression. His eyes were the yellow eyes of the Hunter.

"Lord Hunter," Timou greeted him. Her voice shook, and her hands closed slowly into fists, but she did not back hastily out of the tower, which is what she wanted to do.

"I know you. You once gave me your name," said Jonas in the Hunter's passionless voice. "You may do so again."

Timou shut her eyes and gave her name to the dark.

"Yes," said the Hunter through Jonas's mouth. "Why are you here, daughter of Lelienne?"

"To ask you—" It seemed the height of impudence, now that

she was here; and yet why else had the Hunter continued, here in his own Kingdom, to wear the body of a mortal man like a cloak? "To ask you a question, and a favor, Lord."

"What is the question?"

Timou hesitated, now that the moment was at hand, and asked almost reluctantly, "Lord, will you tell me, please, what happened to my mother?"

Jonas smiled, a predatory smile utterly unlike any expression she had ever seen on his mortal face. "She did not outrun the storm," he said—the Hunter said. "My hounds pulled her down. She is now here, a shade among others in my Kingdom, no more nor less to me than any other."

"Oh," Timou breathed. "Good. Thank you."

"And the favor?" Jonas, or the Hunter, pronounced the word with a slight ironic tone. His yellow eyes did not hold irony. They held nothing Timou could understand.

"If you would, Lord Hunter . . . would you please let me take the—the man within whose shadow you stand—back into . . . into the Kingdom of the living?"

"What I once have taken, I do not return."

"No," Timou answered. "But you might open your hand a little."

"Yes," the Hunter said restlessly. "I might do that."

"Please, Lord."

The shadow lifted a hand to touch its chest; Jonas echoed the gesture. "The sorceress's knife is still here. If I withdraw from this man, he will die and become a shade here in my Kingdom. I have," added the Hunter inexorably, "no power to heal."

This was unexpected. Timou had thought persuading the Hunter to release his prey would be the difficult part. And yet— "Let him go," she whispered, "and I will try."

At once the shadow tore itself free from the man and took a step away. It gained solidity; darkness seemed to coalesce within it. Far above, the Hunter opened round yellow eyes.

Jonas sank to the floor without a sound; the silver knife stood in his chest. His hands went to it, but he could not touch it; his hands passed through the hilt as though it were made of mist. His eyes were open: human now, but blind with pain and shock.

Timou went forward hastily and knelt beside him. He saw her then, and tried to speak, but could not; she put her hand over his mouth to spare him the effort.

She moved to touch the silver knife; for her, it was real and solid. It was cold as ice. She drew it out of the wound and held it in her hands: her mother's knife, made with ill intent to do murder. She put her mind into the weapon, shaped it with her mind; found spells of death and undoing woven into the silver, running down its edges, set into its point. She understood these spells: they were her mother's spells, they shaped themselves to her blood and trembled in time to the beating of her heart. Understanding them, she took them apart.

Then, working as quickly as she could, she wove into the knife spells of life and healing. She sent the warmth of summer sliding down its edges; the sweet breeze that comes across a new-plowed field she set into it; the taste of honey on warm bread; the laugh of a friend; the smile in her father's eyes. The smile in the eyes of a lover. Then she drove the knife, warm and full of summer and life, into the heart of the man she supported.

Jonas cried out, his eyes widening, stunned. His hands went to his chest, and again he could not touch the knife. But this knife melted into his body and was taken up by his blood; it dissolved and was gone like the memory of summer, leaving healing behind it where it had struck. His hands moved, incredulously, across unbroken skin.

You are mine, said the Hunter. *I do not release you.*

Jonas flinched at the bodiless voice, breath coming in a sharp gasp of shock or pain or terror; his eyes when he looked up were wide, blind with memory or with the dark. No longer contained within the shadow of a man, the Hunter seemed now far more terrible. Timou looked up and up at the shadowed face with its pitiless eyes and its crown of twisting shadows, and found that, as the hare before the hounds, she could not move.

Then Jonas got to his feet, slowly, as though his own body was strange to him, as though he had to move each bone and muscle separately. But he went to the Hunter of his own volition and sank down to one knee. "Lord. I don't ask to be released."

The Hunter moved a hand, touched the man on the face; Jonas did not flinch now, but looked fearlessly—astonishing Timou—into the Hunter's yellow eyes. *Always my Kingdom will lie a step before your foot*, said the Hunter. *Always you will see the shadow of my door lying in every shadow.*

"After having once seen through your dark, Lord, I fear no shadow."

Then, if you are able to find the way out of my Kingdom, I will open my hand.

"For both of us, Lord?" Jonas asked.

Yes.

"Then we will find the way," Jonas said. He put his hand, for a moment, over the Hunter's hand, where it still rested on his face. Both their hands fell away together, like a hand and its shadow, and Jonas stood up.

He looked at Timou, seeming uncertain—of her, she thought incredulously. He thought he had frightened her, or appalled her—she did not know what he feared. Nor did she know what he saw in her face, but his expression eased suddenly. He said, as though he could not quite believe this, "You came here, into the dark? For me?"

"You came here for me," Timou answered. She held out her hands.

Jonas took them in his. His hands were much larger than hers; they made hers seem fragile. Timou had not remembered the broad strength of his hands. She liked them; she liked the way hers fit so neatly in his. Jonas moved his thumbs gently across her palms and looked into her face. He was not smiling; his expression was very serious.

Timou said, "I went to the City to find my father. And to find my mother. But what I found . . ."

"I know," said Jonas.

Timou was silent. She did not know how to tell Jonas that finding her father's body among the hard pure planes of light behind the mirror had shattered her; she did not know how to tell

him what it had felt like to realize how much her father had always hidden from her. She could not explain how it had felt to
find her mother, and then realize what she had found. Yet it
seemed very important to her that he should understand all this.

"I know," Jonas said again gently, looking into her eyes.

Timou closed her eyes for a moment. "My mother . . ."

"You didn't lose her, you know. She was never there. Not the
mother you should have had."

"Yes," Timou whispered.

"I wish I could have been with you. But it was a journey you
had to make alone. Mine was like that, too," Jonas said. He
glanced to the side, where the Hunter stood silently watching
them out of unreadable yellow eyes, and Timou felt the tremor
that went through his body. But he said steadily, "There is a way
out. A way back to the Kingdom of the living. This time, I hope,
the journey will be one we can make together."

"Yes," Timou agreed fervently.

"The way is here." He sounded certain. "Through a window.
This window." He drew Timou with him to the one at which
he had been standing when she entered the tower. It looked out
onto nothing but darkness. "I was watching you from here when
you . . . The windows look out into other Kingdoms, but I cannot see them now. Can you?"

"No." Timou could not imagine seeing anything from the
windows of this tower but darkness.

"If we cast ourselves out into the dark, we will find, I think,
only the dark. The Hunter can see out." His voice lowered.
"Your father helped me see out, the first time."

"My—"

"He was here." Jonas touched the sill, looked around as though expecting to see her father right there, close by his side. "Is here."

"He is?" To her dismay, Timou felt her eyes fill with sudden tears; she blinked hard, but she could not blink the tears away. She rubbed her sleeve over her eyes.

"Timou." Jonas took her hands in his once more. "Timou. Don't cry."

"I didn't know—when I took out the knife—I didn't know it was to send him *here*—"

"Timou. It isn't the same, when you belong here. It isn't like this." Jonas glanced again at the silent Hunter, who stared impassively back, patient as the dark itself.

"It isn't like this," Jonas repeated, turning back to Timou. "When this is your Kingdom, you see it with different eyes. I have seen it like that, Timou!" His eyes on hers were blind with memory, trying to see past her and past the dark to remembered visions. "It is as though every bit of darkness has been transmuted. . . ."

"To light?"

"No—to beauty." His grip tightened on her hands; his eyes on hers tried to share this vision with her. "I am not afraid to have this darkness lie before every step I take, because once I saw into darkness and it was glorious. Grieve for your father because you lost him, it's right we should grieve for those we lose, but don't grieve for him because he's here, Timou!"

Timou found that she believed him. She wept, covering her

face with her hands, leaning into his shoulder. Jonas held her, stroking her hair softly, waiting for the tears to pass. She fought them, feeling always at her back the ruthless patience of the Hunter.

Kapoen cannot help you this time, the Hunter commented at last as Timou straightened painfully. He was speaking, it became clear, not to her but to Jonas. *When he was freed to come here, he came to me and I set him to help you. I needed you. You needed the shade of the mage. But he cannot help you this time. The way is here. You must find it.*

"How, Lord?"

You must find it.

Jonas went to the window, running his hands across the sill, and gazed out into the dark. "Is this a way we can take, Lord? Without light, we cannot see."

Timou thought she might make a light, or summon light . . . even the memory of light. But she knew that the darkness of this Kingdom would smother any light she might make or call. . . . She said aloud, "One point of light."

Jonas shook his head, startled, looking now at her rather than at the motionless Hunter. "There is no light in this Kingdom."

"Yes, there is," she breathed. "One point of light in all this Kingdom. And I know where it is. I am carrying it myself." In the pocket of her traveling dress she found the mirror that, so long ago, it seemed, she had filled with the light of the setting sun. It glowed in her palm, scattering glints of bright warmth into the dark, which drew back from it.

The Hunter moved away, turning his eyes from the delicate

glow contained within the mirror. But though he had lifted an arm to shield his face, he did not seem offended. He only waited, expressionless and patient.

Timou gave the mirror to Jonas, and Jonas cast it through the window. Light spread out from it as it fell, far more light than such a small thing should have been able to contain: light fell across an infinite expanse of still water that cast it back like a mirror into the blue of the sky.

Jonas caught her hand, or she caught his, and they leapt together through the window, wide now as any door, and fell through light that grew warm and golden and ran against the shore like water . . . and then they came down together onto a wide expanse of sand beside the Lake. The air was still and warm; the summer sun stood above and poured down light as thick and warm as honey. Behind them, the City rose silent and still, golden, filled with truth and time.

Jonas staggered, his eyes blank with shock. He would have fallen, but Timou reached out quickly and caught him by the arm. She looked with quick concern for a wound that might have been left by her mother's knife, or by hers. But there was no sign of injury. It was simply the contrast between the Kingdoms that had undone him. She helped him sit and sat down beside him. Heat struck upward from the sand.

Jonas bent forward and spread open hands to that warmth as a man might huddle over a fire against the cold of a winter night. Sense was coming back into his eyes. They were brown: the color of rich dark earth. Had she ever noticed the exact color of his eyes before? Timou thought it would be impossible now to forget the precise shade no matter how many miles or years might separate them.

"I thought I would never be warm again," he said at last. "I learned not to mind cold . . . but I think I forgot that warmth even existed." He straightened and leaned back, looking up with wonder at the creamy gold of the wall, and the towers visible beyond it. "This is the true City, of course. In the true Kingdom." It was not quite a question. "I saw it . . . through *his* eyes."

"They're all true. But this is the one at the center," said Timou. "It anchors the rest, but doesn't rule them. As stillness anchors but does not conquer the storm. That's not quite what my father taught me. Or maybe it's what he meant to teach me, but I didn't understand it. Then. I realized it . . . eventually."

She did not know what Jonas heard in her voice, but he turned to her at once. "I'm sorry for your loss, Timou. Kapoen was not an easy man to know, but I know he was a good man. And he loved you."

"I know." She did; she had recognized the memory of love in the shock she'd felt at its absence within her mother's eyes. This surety had become immeasurably important to her. But— "My father taught me that stillness is the heart of magecraft. And it is. Yet . . . I think he also used magecraft as an excuse to evade ties to life. I thought that kind of evasion, too, was the heart of magecraft."

A faint smile had come into Jonas's eyes. "No?"

"Stillness can lie at the center of your heart, even if your heart is filled by the storm. I don't . . . I don't know whether my father knew that. Or remembered it."

"Perhaps he was afraid for you, if you learned it. Perhaps he hoped to shelter you from the peril of the storm."

Timou bowed her head. "If he did, that was a mistake. Not . . . not the only one he made. And used you to redeem. I'm sorry for that."

"He had a right," Jonas said quietly. "Anyway, we must all redeem one another's mistakes."

"Yes. I learned that, too."

Jonas gave her a little nod and got to his feet, brushing sand off his clothing. He turned to look back at the timeless City. "It's beautiful, I don't deny it," he said. "But . . . I admit, I would rather have familiar lands about me, and my own home waiting for me when the sun goes down." He gave Timou a sidelong glance, offering her a hand up. "Is that something you might manage, do you suppose?"

Timou found herself starting to smile. "From this City," she said, "I think we might find that home is only a step away. Let me show you the paths of light." And she took his hand and let Jonas lift her to her feet. Then she drew him with her through the bright mirror of the Lake: paths and planes of light tilted around them. Timou did not follow the light, but took them through it, and past it, faster and faster. They were running, running . . . through light and out of light, into snow, into a fine pure winter's day. And then before them was the village, and friends crying out in surprise and running to meet them.

About the Author

Rachel Neumeier got the initial idea for *The City in the Lake* from a painting she bought several years ago called *Temple of the Reality*, by Anatoliy Leushin. She started writing fiction to relax when she was a graduate student; her only previous publications appear in journals such as the *American Journal of Botany*. Rachel now lives in rural Missouri with a large garden, small orchard, and gradually increasing number of Cavalier King Charles Spaniels.